The Cat Caliban Mysteries by D. B. Borton . . .

One for the Money

After thirty-eight years of marriage, Cat's starting a new life—buying her own apartment house and working for her P.I. license. She'll be using her investigative skills sooner than she thinks . . . when she finds her upstairs apartment comes furnished—with a corpse!

Two Points for Murder

When a high school basketball hero is gunned down, Cat knows there's more to the murder than meets the eye—and she's determined to blow the whistle on the killer . . .

Three Is a Crowd

Cat missed the protest movement of the '60s . . . she was too busy with a husband, house, and kids. But now she's learning more about those wild years—as she investigates the death of a protester at a peace rally . . .

Four Elements of Murder

Cat looks into the death of an environmental activist—and finds herself in a mess of murder and deceit . . .

FOUR ELEMENTS OF MURDER

D. B. BORTON

BERKLEY PRIME CRIME, NEW YORK

This is a work of fiction. The events and characters portrayed are imaginary. Their resemblance, if any, to real-life counterparts is entirely coincidental.

FOUR ELEMENTS OF MURDER

A Berkley Prime Crime Book/published by arrangement with the author

PRINTING HISTORY
Berkley Prime Crime edition/May 1995

ISBN: 0-425-14722-3

Berkley Prime Crime Books are published by The Berkley Publishing Group, 200 Madison Avenue, New York, NY 10016. The name BERKLEY PRIME CRIME and the BERKLEY PRIME CRIME design are trademarks belonging to Berkley Publishing Corporation.

PRINTED IN THE UNITED STATES OF AMERICA

10 9 8 7 6 5 4 3 2 1

To Linda Greene,
an eloquent spokesperson,

and in memory of Barley,
who lost the battle, but inspires us to win the war

Acknowledgments

My appreciation goes first and foremost to Linda Greene, who provided me with vast quantities of information. A helpful printed source was Marc Lappé's *Chemical Deception*.

Grey Cavanaugh was my dialect consultant. Joe Combs of the Tennessee Valley Authority Public Safety office graciously answered my questions about his job.

My scientific consultants were Tom Dillman, Amy Tovar, and Rich Bradley.

Charlotte Bell of the Association of Certified Fraud Examiners advised me on corporate matters. Also helpful was testimony by Alan Block of the University of Delaware before a Senate subcommittee in 1984.

Mike Shaffer shared information about computer hacking and supported me through a major computer transition. Austin Winther prevented me from doing the Wrong Thing. Eric Raymond's *The New Hacker's Dictionary* was extremely valuable to me, and any mistakes or anachronisms are my fault, not his.

As usual, John Kornbluh donated his editorial services. Sue Clark and Melinda Metz gave me valuable advice.

And Beany and Cleo interposed themselves between me and the keyboard to remind me continually what Mother Nature intended.

Tennessee

One

July is a wicked month for gardeners. That miraculous encounter of fire, air, and organic elements that entertains us on the Fourth isn't a bad metaphor for what's going on down below, except that the more earthly spectacle isn't half so entertaining. In fact, it's downright heartrending, if not backbreaking.

I should know. After sixty years, what my back wants is a padded deck chair on a Caribbean cruise ship, not a goddam guerrilla war with grubs and dandelions.

I remember the groundbreaking ceremony. It had been a cloudless April day, birds twittering in the trees and a gentle breeze stirring the scent of hyacinths and bananas. I had remarked to Kevin that I thought the suntan lotion was a bit premature, but the promise of summer was definitely in the air, and the gang at the old Catatonia Arms Apartments was ready for it.

Everybody was there, participating in our little pastoral experiment out behind the parking lot. Alice Rosenberg had traded her lawyer's costume for a pair of jeans, and was helping her roomie, Melanie Carter, pace off a garden-sized rectangle and mark it with stick and string. Kevin O'Neill, who, like me, was a graduate of the eyeball, spit, and promise school of home maintenance and horticulture, was fending off boredom by recording the whole process on video. So far, though, I suspected that he'd devoted more footage to Winnie the beagle puppy, who, in her excitement, had already started digging in the middle of our plot. Kevin also had been zooming a lot, to catch Sidney in the act of attacking the string.

In fact, Sidney laid feline waste to the first side of the

rectangle as soon as Mel and Al started working on the second, and might have put a crimp in the camaraderie if Moses Fogg hadn't swept him up and distracted him by letting him untie shoelaces. After a career in the juvenile section of the Cincinnati Police Department, Moses knew a lot about delinquency prevention. Moses seemed determined to keep his agricultural opinions to himself, even though I suspected that on gardening, as on everything else, he had opinions. Off to the side, my black tabby Sadie and my gray tiger Sophie sat placidly, tails tucked in and eyes wide open, watching the whole scene as if it were some unusually interesting zoo exhibit. Me, I was leaning on a shovel almost as tall as I was, dreaming of a summer in the great outdoors.

I should have taken a hint from what happened at the momentous ceremonial instant of the actual groundbreaking itself: nothing. As the owner of the Catatonia Arms, it fell to me, Cat Caliban, real estate entrepreneur and private investigator-in-training, to do the honors. So, camera whirring, I grinned like a television pitchman, swung my shovel, planted my Adidas, and pushed. I damn near broke my jaw as I leaned in, expecting the shovel to give. Nothing. It sank not a beetle's breadth.

The camera still running, I gritted my teeth, shifted all my weight to the shovel, and pushed again.

"Goddam!" I expostulated. "You guys give me a trick shovel or something?"

"Come on, Mrs. C.! Put some muscle into it!" the cameraman said.

"Come on, Cat! You can do it!" Al encouraged me.

"I told y'all we should've given her the pitchfork," Moses muttered. I could see Sidney struggling to break free so he could get a closer look.

Winnie circled my ankles, barking furiously at the

shovel. I'd take all the help I could get, sound waves included.

I planted a foot on either side of the handle, wobbled precariously, and gave a little hop. I am not a featherweight, and figured with the help of gravity I was bringing considerable weight to bear on the damn shovel, but it didn't budge. Or rather, unable to move vertically, it rocked forward and crashed to the ground with me on top. Out of the corner of my eye, I could see Kevin zooming in to catch the first colorful eruption of bruises amid the varicose veins.

"I know people my age who have died this way," I pointed out as Al rushed in to pick me up. "One broken hip and they put you in the hospital to catch pneumonia, and then you're a goner."

"I told you we should've borrowed Deedee's rototiller," Kevin contributed. "This is the eighties, after all, not the nineteenth century."

"And pollute the atmosphere for the sake of our backyard garden? Contribute to global warming? No way!" Mel insisted.

"I think you need to move the plot," I said, examining my hands for blisters. Five minutes into the gardening season and already I felt sore all over. "This part must be solid rock."

"Maybe she should do the groundbreaking over where Winnie was digging," Al volunteered.

"That's cheating," Mel sulked.

"Hey, listen, I was never one for ceremony, anyway," I said. "Kevin's already got Winnie's groundbreaking on tape. What do we need another one for?"

"Cat's right," Moses, my geriatric ally, said. "Winnie broke ground, so let's get started and get this thing dug." He pushed up his bifocals, took a swipe at his moustache, and reached for a pitchfork.

I watched them covertly while they took their positions and turned to their work. I listened with satisfaction to their grunts, and watched the realization dawn on their faces as the first trickles of sweat started down their noses.

"Damn!" Moses was the first to speak. "This ain't nothing but clay!"

"Mine's rock," Kevin said with conviction.

"How did Winnie break through this stuff?" Al asked. We all turned to gaze at the puppy, a small dervish merrily throwing up clods the size of meteors, as if demonstrating how digging ought to be done.

Four hours later, Mel and Kevin were loading Deedee's rototiller back onto her pickup, Moses and I were sacked out in the shade, drinking beer and contemplating a rendezvous with Ben-Gay, and Al was trying to interest us in the layout of the garden.

"Look here, Al," Moses told her, "me an' Cat don't care where you put it, long's we don't have to bend over too far to pick it when it's done."

"Here, here," I echoed faintly, waving my beer can.

To tell you the truth, I was gratified by Moses' attitude. As an ex-cop, he was in better shape than I was. Okay, that's not saying much; anybody could be in better shape than I was. Kevin, for all his complaining, was in better shape than anyone there, except for Mel the martial arts queen. He spent his nights behind a bar, but he made up for them at the gym and on the tennis court. Then there was Winnie, who had turned more earth than anybody and looked ready to go another ten rounds. What do they put in that Puppy Chow, anyway?

By the end of the afternoon, we had neat little rows planted, meticulously labeled with little white plastic markers.

That was April. Now, in July, you couldn't find a white plastic marker if your life depended on it. Not that it mattered all that much, since the animals had rearranged everything when we weren't looking, making it appear to have been planted by a punch-drunk prizefighter in his final round. Then a wet June had turned the Catatonia communal garden into a jungle. The catnip cozied up to the corn. Moses' potatoes sprawled all over Kevin's endive and radicchio. Mel's cucumber had a stranglehold on my zinnias. Al's zucchini plant threatened to crush everything in its path, which looked to be damn near everything. As soon as it hit the parking lot, I was going to call 911.

The first of the tomatoes were reddening, but nobody could figure out how to get to them without trampling something else. And everywhere you looked you saw exotic, strapping plants that you knew we hadn't planted: weeds. Not to mention the grass, which was fighting to make a comeback that would make Richard Nixon's look like a Friday afternoon stock market flutter.

The cats thought we had planted this wonderland for their amusement. They were the only ones who could enter at one end and come out the other unscathed, bean blossoms dangling from their ears. It provided them with endless opportunities for launching surprise attacks on each other, and for hiding from applications of the hated flea repellent oil. We had tried to train Winnie to go in, pick a tomato or cucumber, and carry it out unbruised. But then we discovered that she was terrified of the zucchini and eggplants, which were bigger than she was, so we didn't push it.

Then there were the bugs. In June, the first onslaught had hit the rose garden we'd planted on the side of the building. The buds were thick with aphids and a host of spindly legged sapsuckers.

"I'd better get some bug spray," I'd remarked to Mel.

"*Bug spray?*" she'd gasped, as if I'd uttered the foulest of profanities. Actually, I uttered profanities all the time, and she'd never reacted with this kind of horror and disgust. "You don't want to use bug spray."

"I don't?" I'd use a goddam flame thrower, I had thought, but it might hurt the plants.

"Well, you don't want to contribute to global pesticide contamination, do you?"

"Well," I had said. "No. I guess not. But I don't want to lose all the roses, either. Otherwise, what's the point in planting 'em?"

"What we want is a natural pest control. I think the time has come for some mail order."

She'd let me use insecticidal soap until her mystery package arrived. Then, following the directions carefully, we released several hundred ladybugs into the roses.

I had to admit, they'd done a fine job of decimating the aphid population. But about a week ago they'd decamped in search of greener rose gardens, and been replaced by a horde of Japanese beetles, who were even now chewing their way down the plants, and ignoring the Japanese beetle traps Al and Mel had set out. Last night I'd seen Kevin walking around with one of the green and white plastic trap bags, picking beetles off the leaves and pitching them into the bag. I'd overheard Mel muttering about milky spore, and worried that that was a new disease we were getting to go along with the black spot.

"Who do we call now?" I asked her. "Beetle Busters? Or can we order up some of those mutant giant ants created by nuclear fallout, like we saw on *Sci-Fi Theater* last night?"

Mel had explained to me the whole concept of organic gardening, all about nature and balance and natural enemies—stuff like that. So L figured that for every King Kong, there had to be a Godzilla, right? If every aphid had its ladybug, then every Japanese beetle had its—what? Or more importantly, where? If the Japanese could send us their beetles, why couldn't they send us a Mothra to eat them? Import quotas?

Now, it was July 10th, and hotter than a fry cook's grease. Gardening of any kind between mid-morning and sunset meant certain sunstroke, and probable skin cancer. And, as if that weren't enough, it meant mosquitoes— mosquitoes that had hatched out of the June rains and appeared as if by spontaneous generation.

I slapped at one now, and killed it. Hand to hand combat was one of the few options left me by the head gardener.

"Cousin Cat, you got a phone call."

Did I mention that I'd somehow inherited a teenager, who had also appeared as if by spontaneous generation and seemed, like the Japanese beetles, ineradicable? I turned toward the house with a sigh.

"It's Louella Simmons," my adolescent secretary informed me. "Her uncle died."

Well, I thought grimly, I was in the mood for death.

Two

In fact, I thought, as I made my way to the phone, I had a few relatives to nominate, beginning with the parents of the aforementioned teenager.

As usual, my first mistake had been answering the damn door.

"Surprise!"

My jaw dropped in astonishment. Standing in the entry hall were Buddy and Raynell Sweet, my Texas cousins, and three junior Sweets.

Raynell had never been one to let a pregnant pause go unaborted. She beamed at me.

"Catherine! You should just see the look on your face! I told Buddy, she'll be just as surprised—didn't I, Buddy? And Buddy, he thought maybe we wouldn't find your place, didn't you, darlin'? But here we are, and I would just give anything if you could see the look on your face!" Her own face was a joint production with Elizabeth Arden, and her platinum-blonde hair made her taller than I was. Last time I'd seen her, at my husband Fred's funeral, she'd been redheaded and shorter.

Buddy had one of those reddish-brown leathery Texas faces, creased like an old catcher's mitt, under his cowboy hat. He smiled at me over his wife's head, half apologetically, half proudly, as if to say, Ain't she a caution?

We exchanged the obligatory family hugs, and Raynell exclaimed over my "precious" little old apartment. Everything in it was "cute." Well, there was no denying that they could have fit two of my apartments into the goddam recreational vehicle they had parked out front, which was probably creating one of those urban sinkholes even as we spoke.

Two of the three junior Sweets made a fuss over Sidney. The third, a gangly teenager with glasses and an expression of perpetual irritation, sat off by himself. That was okay; if Raynell had been *my* mother, I would have worn the same expression.

We spent an hour drinking Cokes and swapping gossip. Or rather, Raynell provided gossip; it wasn't an even exchange. She told me everything there was to know about my family, some of whom I wanted to hear about, most of whom I didn't. Eventually, she broached the subject she'd been working up to.

It seemed they had been on the road for a week already, making the grand tour in their new RV. Now they were on their way to the College Football Hall of Fame in Kings Mills, the Air Force Museum in Dayton, and the Pro Football Hall of Fame in Canton. It seemed that Delbert was not too fond of museums and even less fond of camping. I turned to study him, and recognized the signs: clenched fists digging into the upholstery, clenched jaw, eyes avoiding his parents and me. Delbert was at the end of his rope.

"So, we were wondering, now that you're all by yourself and all—" Raynell accompanied this statement with her most sympathetic expression. *Poor little old you.* I choked down a burst of laughter and decided that maybe it was just as well that we were having one of our quieter days at the Catatonia Arms. "Well," she continued, "we thought maybe Delbert could stay here for a few days. He'd be comp'ny for you, and he could hep out, too."

Delbert sank lower in my upholstered chair than I would have thought possible.

"Y'all could have a real good time together, I just know

you would. And then we'd swing by and pick him up on our way to Opryland."

I was stunned. Generally speaking, I'm not the kind of little old lady that people like to leave their kids with. I don't bake cookies. I don't clean any more than I have to. And I drink and cuss a lot. My own offspring only leave my grandchildren with me because it doesn't cost them anything. I've done everything I can to discourage this practice by getting burglarized and shot at, which tends to foster my children's impression of Northside, my neighborhood, as a scaled-down Beirut.

"I don't know, Raynell," I said. "I've got work to do."

"Oh, why, I know you do, darlin'. That's why I said he'd be a big hep to you in your—uh, bidness."

I wondered what Delbert knew about surveillance techniques.

"And if you didn't want him to bother you, why, he'd just go off by himself. He's real quiet."

That I could believe.

"Okay," I said. "Just for a few days." Call me Saint Catherine.

As soon as they left, Delbert turned to me and said, "You got a computer?"

"No," I said, and added, as he was turning away in disgust, "but Al does, upstairs."

I hadn't seen much of him since. His dirty clothes showed up in the laundry, and his dirty dishes showed up in the sink. But even when Delbert was present in the flesh, he wasn't all there, if you know what I mean. Mentally, he was up in Al's apartment when he wasn't there physically, which was most of the time. Al had given him a key. Like most teenagers, he spoke in a code that I couldn't translate half the time. According to Al, Delbert spoke a computer dialect called hackish, which sounded like some kind of designer drug. And, she said, he was in perpetual hack mode, which explained his druglike failure to respond to ordinary stimuli.

As teenagers go, he was an ideal house guest, really. It had taken me about twenty-four hours to get over the notion that I was taking care of him, or that I had to give any more thought to meals than I normally did. McDonald's cheeseburgers, microwave pizza, and Kevin's gourmet casseroles he greeted with equal uninterest. (He never ate, he "fueled up.") Nor did he appear to want my advice about anything. So when the "few days" stretched into a week, it was the principle of the thing I resented more than the actuality. Still, my apartment was small, and there was the damn sofa bed to be dealt with or tripped over every morning. On the other hand, he answered my phone when he happened to be nearby.

I took the receiver from him, and heard Louella's quivery voice on the other end.

"Cat, are you in the middle of anything?"

"Just gardening. Why?" Contemplating the garden in despair burns more calories than you'd think.

"No, I mean—you know. A case."

"No."

"Well, look. My uncle Red just died in a car accident down there in Tennessee. The thing of it is, he was on his way up here to attend those incinerator hearings. Well, I don't know what to make of this, but he was real secretive before he left, said he was in danger and I don't know what-all. Wouldn't let me tell anybody he was coming or anything. Now he's dead and I don't know what to think. I'm his only kin left to speak of, and I got to go down there and take care of everything. Only, I'm kind of scared to go down there by myself."

"Want me to come along?" I owed Louella a lot, after

all; she was more than an old friend, she was my realtor, and had found me the Catatonia Arms.

"Oh, Cat, would you? I'd be so grateful."

We made arrangements to leave the next morning. I worried about Delbert, who probably wouldn't notice I was gone, but still.

I found him upstairs, glued to Al's computer, Sidney sprawled on top.

"Del, we have to talk."

He waved a hand at me and kept typing.

"Del?"

"Control S, Cat. I'm juggling eggs here."

I kind of got the drift, and sat down on the bed to wait.

"Okay." He turned to me.

"You aren't running up Mel and Al's phone bill, are you?" I didn't understand much about computers, but I thought if he was having some kind of a conversation with somebody else, it probably involved Ma Bell. Everything did.

He rolled his eyes at me. "I wouldn't do that, Cousin Cat. Don't worry, I'm phreaking."

"Oh. Okay, I guess. Is that illegal? Wait; don't tell me. I don't want to know. Listen, Delbert, I have to go to Tennessee with Louella tomorrow. Her uncle was killed in a car accident, and we have to see about the funeral and all."

"Okay."

"I think we'd better talk to your parents tonight. Do you know how to contact them?"

"No."

I sighed.

"Do you think they'll call?"

"No."

"I don't like to leave you here alone when I'm supposed to be looking after you."

"I won't be alone," he said. Unlike his mother, he had recognized almost instantly that the Catatonia Arms was no place to hang out if you wanted to be alone.

"I know, but even so."

"Look, why don't you ask Al if it's okay with her? I bet she says yes."

"Well—"

"I *am* fourteen, Cousin Cat. They leave me on my own all the time. I don't know why they insisted I had to go on this vacation in the first place. They know I hate camping, and that bozotic RV is embarrassing. The whole thing is bogus in the extreme. I tried to tell them I'd be miserable, but they had interrupts locked out. What they think I'm gonna do at Opryland I haven't a clue."

"Okay, kid, I'll make a deal with you. If Al says okay, you can stay. But only if you do your own dishes and laundry, and feed the cats."

"Sure, okay. I can do that, if you show me how."

"But if your folks don't call tonight, and then they call while I'm gone, or show up here—"

"It's their own fault, Cat. They dumped me on you."

"Well—I volunteered."

He gave me a look.

"Anyways," he said, turning back to the screen, a computer geek with a Texas accent, "I don't know why you don't let me set you up a computer in your office. You really need one for your work."

"To do what? Send out bills, assuming I ever get licensed?"

He shrugged. "For lots of things. All kinds of things. Anybody who's not online today deserves to lose." He was typing while he talked.

That seemed unnecessarily harsh to me, but it probably didn't mean what I thought it did. "I'm too old," I said. "I wouldn't live long enough to learn how to use it."

He gave me another look before tuning me out altogether.

His parents did not call that night. Neither did my daughter Sharon, who was a hell of a lot more vigilant than Delbert's parents, and a hell of a lot more intrusive. Her lapse excused me from fabricating a senior bus trip to Dollywood so that I wouldn't have to explain to her, for the hundredth time, why I was embarking on a career as a detective. I did laundry and packed, starting with a Mary Roberts Rinehart and a Charlotte MacLeod.

Ten minutes after I got into bed, I changed my mind for the last time that night, got up, and slipped my Wilkinson Diane .25 automatic into my bag. With my luck, I'd get arrested for transporting stolen weapons across state lines.

Three

"So what was your uncle afraid of?"

We were headed south in Louella's blue Ford station wagon. She had an extra gold Century 21 jacket hanging in the back, and I wondered who covered for her at the realty office when she went out of town. Louella was about my size, with frosted gray permed hair that contrasted with my drip-dry straight white cut. She wore red fingernail polish that called attention to the fact that she had fingernails; I didn't have any. She wore those fashionable invisible bifocals, whereas I only had reading glasses, but lately I'd been contemplating a little heart-to-heart with my ophthalmologist—a genial storehouse of such unhelpful phrases as, "Well, you're not as young as you used to be." Louella still talked with a Tennessee accent.

"Lord, Cat, I don't know. He just kept talking about 'them,' you know, like they do. I didn't know who he meant. I didn't take it that seriously, to tell you the truth. He asked me to find out about somebody at the EPA he could trust."

"The Environmental Protection Agency?"

"Yeah. You know, over on Martin Luther King? Well, I didn't know why he wanted it, but I asked around, and I gave him a name and he made an appointment. Gosh, that slipped my mind completely. I wonder if I should call and try to cancel that appointment? I don't even know when it was for."

"I wouldn't worry about it. You've got other things on your mind."

"Well, anyway, he wanted to go up to the church last

night to that meeting they were holding about that incinerator."

"What incinerator?"

"Oh, you know, Cat. It's on the news all the time. They want to build this incinerator to burn garbage, now that the landfill is filling up. But there's this big stink about it."

"I can see why there would be," I said with a straight face.

She went on, oblivious. "Well, Uncle Red—Walter McIntyre's his real name—he wanted to speak at this meeting. I don't know what he wanted to say, except that he thought Cincinnati would be crazy to build one of these things. And I guess he ought to know, because he worked on one a while back. So I guess that's what he wanted to talk about."

"Seems like a long drive just to talk about an incinerator in a city where you don't even live."

"Well, that's what I thought, but he seemed to have something he wanted to get off his chest, and he said there wasn't anybody in Tennessee would listen to him."

"So what did he tell you about being in danger?"

"Oh, he'd just kind of drop it into the conversation, like, 'I'm coming up there to speak my mind and they can just try and stop me.'"

"Well, that doesn't sound serious."

"Well, but then there was the part he said about somebody by the name of Pat Kinneady. He said, 'They got to Pat Kinneady, all right, and now he won't talk to nobody but the Lord. And there's others they've stopped, too. But they ain't gonna stop me.'"

"I see what you mean," I said. "Tell me more about him."

"Well, he was a widower. My Aunt Gerry died, oh, maybe fifteen years back. He lived in a little house outside of Cayter, Tennessee. He was retired, but I don't know where he was working last. I only know that once he worked up at that incinerator place in New Union."

"It doesn't sound dangerous," I admitted.

"I know. Sometimes I thought maybe he was getting kind of senile or something. He didn't even call me from his own telephone; he said it was probably tapped. I mean, we're talking about rural Tennessee, not Chicago or L.A. And I don't think he was in the best of health. So when they told me it was a single-car accident, I thought, well, maybe he had a stroke or something. And maybe he did."

"That's right," I said encouragingly. "Maybe he did."

"But it was that dam that worried me."

"What dam?"

"Oh, didn't I tell you that part? This accident, it happened on the Volunteer Dam. They said he just went over the side."

I looked at her.

"Seems kind of coincidental that he'd have an attack like that just as he was crossing a dam."

Her eyes shifted to mine. "You'd think so, now, wouldn't you?"

We still thought so five hours later, when we reached the dam in question. We'd crossed Kentucky on the interstate, alternating country music on the radio with Louella's tapes; then we turned south, crossed the state again and headed on into Tennessee. We'd been traveling over gently rolling, heavily wooded hills, and according to the map, we were approaching the Volunteer Dam at the Chickawee River. We passed several bait shops and seedy tourist traps selling dam souvenirs. The second time we saw a sign that said "Lock and Powerhouse—Visitors Welcome," we turned in. We parked the car, and mounted the steps to the observation platform. The heat was oppressive, as if some giant were standing over us with a steam iron. We didn't even look down at the lock, and we didn't study the infor-

mational diagram about how the lock worked or sign the
visitors book. The observation platform was crowded, and
nobody was paying much attention to the lock. Cameras
chirped and whirred, and people pointed. We looked off to
the right where they were pointing, our gazes crossing the
blue lake, at the dam itself.

The road we'd been on continued across the top of the
dam, wide open except at the bridge over a break in the
dam where Volunteer Lake became the Chickawee River.
A high railing enclosed the bridge. Sloping down from the
road was an incline covered with rocks—not a steep incline, but a fairly gradual one. The straight line of the dam
was broken at two points, where semicircular abutments
marked turnoffs for observation.

"I don't see anything, Cat, do you?" Louella whispered.

"I see a crowd at the second observation point," I said.
"Let's go have a look."

Two men in uniform were on crowd-control duty there.
We turned in and parked between a Lincoln Continental
with Florida plates and a camper from Georgia. People
were congregated at the far side, peering down, shutters
clacking.

"Would you look at that?" a woman said, shaking her
head. "He just run right over the side."

We saw some skid marks on the roadway, but they were
nothing dramatic. There was some metal and chrome
strewn on the blackened rocky wall below us, but that was
about it. Looking down, I wondered what people were taking pictures of; there was nothing to see. But you know
how people are attracted to disaster.

"They say he ran off the road up here," the woman went
on, "just like he was turning too soon for the drive, and hit
the wall there, and flipped right on into the lake. Is that
right, Officer?"

An officer in green pants and khaki shirt sporting a TVA logo nodded.

"Yes, ma'am." He sounded a little weary, the way anybody would who'd been sent out to deal with the public's morbid curiosity in 93-degree heat.

We stared in silence. Then Louella spoke.

"Maybe we're wrong, Cat. There's not as much to see as I thought there'd be. Now that I'm here, it looks like an easy thing to do, especially if you're driving fast and have a heart attack or something."

"Yeah," I said. "What gets me is that he drove off the side at the worst possible spot. A few yards back, and he wouldn't have had a wall in front of him, just the incline to deal with. A few yards ahead, and he would have driven into the turnoff, with more space to brake or gain control of the car. If he was forced off the road, somebody sure got lucky."

"Unless they didn't intend to kill him," Louella agreed. "Maybe they just meant to shake him up, or put him in the hospital for a while."

We explained to the officer who we were, and he directed us to drive back to the other side of the dam and take the first turn-in for the lock and powerhouse, to find Public Safety. As we headed for the car, I heard cameras whirring behind us, and I suddenly realized they were taking pictures of us. We were goddam celebrities.

Four

The Tennessee Valley Authority Public Safety office was tucked away in a small square building dwarfed by the mammoth towers that overlooked the dam and by the Visitors Center across the parking lot. It looked as if it were made of opaque glass, and the door was made of mirror glass. We sat in plastic chairs while the receptionist paged Officer Boone Danning.

Danning, when he arrived, turned out to be a well-built man in his late forties, with thinning black hair and a well-trimmed moustache. He ushered us to a desk, one hand poised as if to catch Louella if she passed out. He offered us chairs and coffee, in the quiet voice people use around the recently bereaved.

"I just want to hear about the accident," Louella said. She had cried herself out in the car, and wasn't going to give anyone the satisfaction of crying in public anyway.

"I understand, Mrs. Simmons." He was one of those men who have a deeper voice than you expect. "There's not much to tell you, though. Mr. McIntyre appears to have driven off the side of the dam—why, we don't know. It wasn't raining, and the roads weren't wet. Did your uncle have a history of heart disease, stroke, anything like that?"

Louella shook her head. "Not that I know of."

"I guess the autopsy will tell us what he died of," I volunteered.

He shifted his attention to me, seemingly startled, as if a voice had just emerged from Louella's pocketbook.

"Well, yes, that's right, Mrs., uh, Caliban. The coroner will determine the—uh, exact cause of death if he can."

"I assume you saw the body?"

"Well—yes, I, uh, did. See, the Water Patrol sent a diver down, and they couldn't get him out of the car, but they—well, they could see it wouldn't matter. So we waited for a boat with a winch to pull the car up and take it over to the dock. It was the tow-truck driver that finally got him out." He looked from me to Louella nervously, clearly disapproving of my ghoulish interest in the details.

"Was he badly burned?"

"Well, uh, he was burned some, yes, but because of the, uh, water, the fire went out pretty quick, you see. It was just a flash, like, when the car hit the rocks and the tank exploded."

"So you couldn't tell by looking at him what he died of?"

"Well, ma'am, I can't speculate—officially speaking." He turned to Louella. "But I think it's safe to say that if he wasn't dead when he left the road, he died when the car hit the rocks. It would've been quick, ma'am."

"So he didn't drown?" I asked.

"In my opinion, that's very unlikely, ma'am," he said.

"And the autopsy?" Louella was getting into the act. "When will that be done?"

"Well, now, ma'am, I can't say for sure. This being July, I understand they're kind of short-handed at the—uh, that is, the coroner's short-handed right now. I reckon it could be done as early as tomorrow, but then we won't have all the results right away. But if you'd like to go on over to the funeral home and talk to them, why, they'll do whatever needs to be done, in case you ladies need to go back home and come back."

"When exactly did this accident occur? I mean, what time?" I asked.

"We got the call from a passing trucker just after five o'clock, ma'am."

"In the morning?"

"Yes, ma'am."

"Did the trucker see what happened?"

"No, he saw the car hit the water, but he didn't see what happened before that. He heard a noise, and then the crash and explosion."

"Any other witnesses?"

"No, I reckon the road was pretty quiet at that time of day. If anybody saw anything, we haven't heard."

"I suppose you have photographs of the scene. Could we see them?"

"Well now, ma'am, I don't think—" His eyes shifted to Louella. "We don't usually show those to kin."

"That's okay," I said. "I'm not kin, and Louella won't get upset if I take a look."

He looked from me to Louella and back again, shook his head, shrugged, and reached for a file on his desk. He handed me a pile of photographs. I could feel his eyes on my face as I studied them, and I was thankful I'd spent some time lately over at the University of Cincinnati medical library reading illustrated books on forensic medicine.

Compared to some of the corpses I'd seen lately, Red McIntyre looked pretty good; compared to most people still walking around, he looked like hell. The first pictures showed the accident site just after the accident: a blackened rocky wall strewn with debris, and calm blue water below, with the blackened back end of a car sticking up like the Loch Ness monster. There was also a Tennessee Water Patrol boat in the calm blue water, and a diver in a wet-suit hanging on to the side. Then there were some underwater shots of the wreck, including some close-ups through the driver's window. These showed a man, head slumped against the steering wheel that had him pinned to the back of his seat. You could see that the seat belt had kept him from being thrown forward, but since the whole front of the car had been shoved backward, the belt hadn't helped him much.

Next we had a few shots of the salvage operation, including what appeared to be a few artistic studies of the winch. More shots of Red pinned in a dripping car on a crowded dock. Shots of a man with a crowbar, jimmying the door on the driver's side; on the back of his shirt, embroidered in red, was the euphonious epithet, "Owen's Towing." Out of the water and close-up, Red didn't look so good, as I said: eyes open, nasty cuts slashing across his face. There wasn't too much blood, though, because the lake water had washed it off. The last shot showed a bloody hole in his chest where the steering column had penetrated it. Officer Danning was right: if he hadn't been dead when that happened, he sure as hell would have been dead afterward.

"Did you look at the skid marks?"

He frowned. Since when were grieving relatives interested in skid marks? "Yes, but nothing unusual for this kind of accident."

"You get this kind often, where somebody falls off the side of a dam?"

"I meant, for an accident of this general type." I could almost hear the grinding of his teeth as he struggled to conceal his annoyance. *Give me an honest drunk or a juvenile spray-painter any day,* he was thinking, *but God preserve me from morbid old ladies.*

"So how fast was he going when he hit the rail?"

"Well, we can't really calculate that, Mrs. Caliban. We don't really know. The speed limit on that part of the dam is still fifty-five. It drops down to thirty-five on the bridge. I'd say he was traveling closer to fifty-five than thirty-five."

"From the force of the impact, you mean?"

He nodded.

"And I take it you have no reason to believe that any other cars were involved?"

"We don't have any evidence that there was more than one car, ma'am. So without eyewitness accounts, we wouldn't know something like that. Stands to reason that if somebody coming in the opposite direction crossed the center line and forced Mr. McIntyre to swerve to avoid hitting him, and then saw what he'd done, he wouldn't stick around to talk about it."

In the background of some of the photographs I could see the observation deck where we'd stood to survey the scene. Scattered about in the pictures there were also cops in four different uniforms, some people wearing medical scrubs, and the man from Owen's Towing.

"Sure were a lot of cops around," I observed.

Danning nodded. "Tennessee Water Patrol, park rangers from the Volunteer Dam State Park, the Millins County Sheriff's Department, and the Tennessee State Police."

It must have been the hottest ticket in town that day. With all those folks traipsing around, there wouldn't have been much left of the scene of the crime if anybody had arrived and decided to investigate it.

"I guess you need for Mrs. Simmons to identify the body," I said.

"Well, yes, ma'am, we do need that. Not that there's any doubt, I'm afraid, ma'am, but it's a formality."

"Where's the car?" Louella asked.

"We had it towed to a local yard—Owen's Towing, out on Route 48 in Parkersville. You'll want to tell Mr. McIntyre's insurance company that's where it is, or just call them and give them the name of the company and they'll take care of it."

"We'll want to go take a look at it," Louella told him, a little peevishly.

"Well, you certainly can do that if you like, Mrs. Simmons." Apparently he'd decided that his best strategy was to humor us.

"You have his effects?" Louella asked.

"Yes, ma'am, right here," he said, reaching into a drawer and pulling out a zippered plastic bag. Inside were a wallet, a wedding ring, a pocket knife, a pipe, and a half-full pouch of tobacco. "We didn't think you'd want his clothing. It was pretty—well, you know."

"Oh, I want everything, Officer," Louella said.

"Oh. Well. I'll make myself a note to try and find it." He said this as if he had a rummage bin out back.

"Where's his keys?" I asked.

"His keys?" Officer Danning scowled at the Baggie. "They ought to be there."

"They're not," I pointed out.

"Well, they shouldn't be with his clothes or his car, but maybe they are. I'll check. Oh, and Mr. McIntyre's attorney, Mr. Bayberry, called when he heard about the accident and asked me to ask you to call him whenever you felt up to it, Mrs. Simmons. Now, is there anything else I can do for you?"

"Just tell us how to get to the morgue to see Uncle Red." Louella sighed.

He directed us to the Millins County Hospital in Cayter, beyond Parkersville. We decided to go there first and get the worst over with.

I had never been to a morgue before, but I knew from a lifetime of reading mysteries that I was in for an unpleasant experience. It was Moses who'd told me to smear a little Vick's Vapo-Rub on my upper lip, so I'd brought it along and shared it with Louella.

"I just hope we don't pass out, Cat," she confided. "How we gonna solve his murder if we pass out in the morgue?"

As it turned out, they didn't take us into a room full of

corpses, start pulling out drawers, and checking toe tags. They put us in a small room with just chairs, then wheeled in a gurney. The odor that seeped in through the Vapo-Rub was bad enough. A young man in white scrubs pulled back the sheet.

In death, Walter "Red" McIntyre still had the full, graying head of red hair that had given him his nickname in life. Freckles mingled with age spots on his tanned face, and he looked younger than his seventy years. There were a few ugly cuts and bruises on his face, but his expression was peaceful.

"That's him, all right," Louella said, and abruptly left the room.

In the car, she was bawling again.

"God*dam* it, Cat! What kind of a detective am I? If I'da stood there a second longer, I would have passed out, sure. I shoulda checked him for—for bullet holes, and needle marks, and things, and now I missed my chance!"

"First, you're not a detective, you're a realtor. I'm a detective, and if you'd stayed I would've passed out on top of you. Second, I don't think they can hide things like bullet wounds."

"Sure they can, Cat! Didn't you ever read about the Kennedy assassination?"

"Well, but your uncle wasn't the President. He had a car accident. I don't think we could tell by looking at him that it wasn't an accident. And—well, like you say. This is rural Tennessee, after all. This is the eighties. There's a limit to what they can hide."

Which only goes to show how little I knew what I was talking about.

Five

It was getting late in the afternoon by then, so we drove north out of Cayter and checked in at the B & J Motor Court on Route 225. It was small, but well-kept and freshly painted, with a riot of red roses outside the office and not a Japanese beetle in sight.

"Cheer up, Cat," Louella consoled me as I bent down to make a closer inspection. "Maybe the beetles haven't migrated this far south yet this year."

"Yeah, or maybe they're too bloated to fly from feasting on my roses up north. They'll probably take off and then crash in the river like a fleet of zeppelins."

The woman behind the desk introduced herself as Billie Kidd, the owner of the B & J. The room was papered in a tasteful floral pattern, and decorated with Kountry Kitsch—a wreath sporting a bow, a life-size molded concrete goose sporting a bow, little wood cutouts of cows sporting bows. The furniture looked like recycled fifties.

"The 'J' was Jack, my late husband, but I ain't never had the heart to change it. Besides, it would've cost a heap of money to get a new sign."

She was a slender woman, with black hair puffed up and pulled back into a comb, then trailing in a ponytail down the back of her neck. A pencil was stuck behind one ear. High, prominent cheekbones and a chin that pulled her whole jaw line forward made her face seem all planes and angles. I wondered if she had Indian blood.

"Y'all here for business or pleasure?" She puffed on a cigarette while Louella filled out the registration card.

"Louella's uncle died in a car accident up at the Volunteer Dam yesterday," I said. "We're here to see about the funeral arrangements and all."

"Honey, I am so sorry!" She patted Louella's hand. "I heard about that accident. I seen your realator's jacket, and I thought maybe you was up here lookin' at property. Well, if there is anything I can do for y'all, anything at all, why, you just let me know." She had a deep-fried Tennessee accent that went well with sympathy; just the sound of her voice made you feel you'd been cuddled.

"Thanks. For starters, you could tell us how to find a map of the area. We've got Mr. McIntyre's address, but we don't know how to get there."

"Lord, darlin', maps is hard to find around here, unless you want one of the resort area." We'd already discovered this much from our visit to a Tourist Information Center up north. "I tell you what, I got one map of the county, it's my only copy, but I'll let you borry it. I don't know how up-to-date it is. Wait till I get my glasses on, then I'll take a look at that address."

Billie wore half-glasses on a chain around her neck, and now she settled them on her nose, and peered at the piece of paper Louella handed her.

"These roads is hard to find, too, even if you live around here. And they're laid out so crazy. Half of them switches back and then runs in the opposite direction. This one here is real easy, though. You go on into town on 225, and turn left there past the courthouse—that's 617. Sauk Road runs right into that, looks like. It's County Road 1438. Here, I'll mark it for you." She put down her cigarette and pulled the pencil out from behind her ear.

"Thanks. Billie, do you know anything about an incinerator operating around here? Like, a garbage incinerator, something like that?"

She made a face and wrinkled her nose.

"Ever'body knows about that damn incinerator, and if you was here on the wrong day, you'd know it, too."

"But I thought this was a resort area," Louella said. "How could they put something like that so close to a resort area?"

"Lord, honey, *I* don't know. You got to ask them politicians over in Nashville that question."

"Can you show us where it is on the map?" Louella asked.

"Sure, I can, but y'all don't want to go up there, do you?"

"Louella's uncle used to work there," I said, noncommittally.

"He did? Well, then, it's a mercy he only died in a car accident." She was immediately contrite. "I'm sorry, sugar. That was a turrible thing to say. Don't mind me, I speak my mind too much and it gets me in trouble. It's just that—well, I read that your uncle was an elderly man, and there's some folks didn't live too long after workin' up at Chem-Tech or those chemical plants. At least, that's what they say."

I caught her up before she backpedaled too far.

"What do you mean?"

"Well, it stands to reason, don't it? There's all them hazardous chemicals up there—that's what that incinerator's for, to get rid of them chemicals. But what about the people that works there? They got to handle all them chemicals. And you can't tell me the bosses is all worked up about how to protect their workers. Isaiah T. Grubbs only got one worry on his mind, and that's Isaiah T. Grubbs."

"He the owner?" I asked.

"That's him. Listen, don't get me started on that incinerator!"

"No, we're interested," I assured her. "So it's not just an incinerator for burning garbage?"

"No, that's what I'm a-sayin'. They burn these leftover chemicals from the chemical plants around here and the paint factories as far away as Louisville and Birmingham."

"And some people have died from working there?"

"Not so's you'd know from reading any medical records. But you ask anybody around here in Millins County, and if they tell you they don't think that incinerator's killing nobody, they're either lyin' or crazy. We keep them cancer doctors livin' high off the hog. But it ain't just the incinerator. They got a landfill up there, too. Lord knows what kind of crap they're dumpin'. Folks say there's standing water out there lights up in the dark." She made a face. "I don't like to use profanity, I know it ain't right. But that's just what it is—crap."

"Do you know somebody who's died?"

She nodded, and fired up another smoke.

"Personally, I have knowed ten people with cancer in the last five years, and three of 'em's dead. Then there was this man used to service the ice machines here. He was always tellin' me how bad he felt, and he used to complain that he couldn't do things like he used to. 'I know it's them chemicals, Billie,' he'd say. 'I got them chemicals in my blood, and now I can't get rid of 'em. I shoulda never worked for that bastard Grubbs, but hell, what did I know?' Well, he got so his coordination was real bad, and he couldn't hardly walk, and had to quit his job and all, and they put him in a nursing home. I went to see him there, and he didn't hardly remember who I was. He died about six months after I visited him, and his daughter told me at the fun'ral that the doctors never really could figure out what was the matter with him. But *he* knew what was the matter with him. And I bet you can't find a single person in Millins County, and maybe not in Gainard nor Park County, neither, who don't have a story like that. A lot of it's cancer, but there's other things, too."

"Then how can they keep running that incinerator? Don't they have federal inspectors that come in and check to see that they're following some kind of guidelines for keeping the workers safe?" Louella asked.

She rubbed her thumb and first two fingers together.

"You mean, they're paying off the inspectors?" I asked.

"Oh, I don't know who-all's bein' paid. But I tell you what, there's a lot of folks makin' a pile of money out of that incinerator, and they ain't gonna let nothin' stop 'em."

"Hasn't the EPA been involved at all?"

"You mean the Employer Protection Agency? The Environmental Polluters' Aid? We don't think much of them around here. Either they don't do nothin', or they can't do nothin', which amounts to the same thing."

"So show us on the map where Chem-Tech is."

"Well, I'll show you. But if y'all go up there, just hold your breath, and don't get too close, or y'all might glow in the dark too. See here, where the Chickawee River kind of splits, here down below the dam?" She traced the curve with her pencil. We nodded. "Okay. Here's New Union. Now, see this road here, Route 1764? It follows the river. Well, Chem-Tech is right here, on Route 1764." She drew a little star.

"Right on the river, you mean?"

"Not exactly, but kind of across the street-like. They owned this big landfill first, and then they got the incinerators, too. But I mean it, now. Don't y'all get too close, and don't be askin' no questions like you did me. They got guards to keep away visitors."

I didn't like the sound of this.

"Okay," Louella was saying. "It looks like we could find that, Cat. Thanks a lot, Billie."

"That's okay, darlin'. I'm just as sorry as I can be about your uncle. And on top of your cold, too! You just let me know if there's anything I can do for you."

Billie had caught a whiff of our Vapo-Rub.

We didn't need directions to our room, because Billie only had twelve, and they were all strung out in a line, so Number 1 was the first room away from the office.

"I always put ladies up close to the office," Billie had said. "I ain't never had no problems here, but it makes 'em feel more secure."

The window air conditioner was on overdrive, and complaining loudly. We turned it down a few notches so we could hear ourselves talk. The room had that vaguely musty, old motel smell.

"You know, Cat, this Chem-Tech business sounds worse and worse, the more we hear about it," Louella said.

"Yeah," I agreed. "But I don't really understand how they burn chemicals, do you? I always think of chemicals as liquids." I had never thought I'd wish another college major on my daughter Franny, but I was beginning to wish that at some point in her long and checkered academic career she'd taken up chemistry.

"Well, I reckon you can burn some liquids, like gasoline. And there's others that burn, too, like when you pour brandy on top of something and *flambé* it."

"But what's the connection between burning that kind of stuff—hazardous chemicals, I mean, not Cherries Jubilee—and burning garbage in Cincinnati?"

"I don't know, Cat. But there's lots of hazardous chemicals in city garbage, if you think about it. It's not just chicken bones and coffee grounds and grapefruit rinds. There's oven cleaner, and drain opener, and roach spray, and all."

"You have a point," I conceded. "And if this Chem-Tech outfit doesn't care about their workers dying of contamination, it makes you wonder if they'd go a step further and help somebody along if they thought he was going to make trouble for them."

" 'Course, I s'pose it's possible this ice man died of something else," Louella mused. "Rumors can be pretty powerful, once they get started. One person gets sick, and blames it on the incinerator. And then the next person who gets sick blames it on the same cause, whether he's got the same symptoms or not. And then, before you know it, you got a full-blown hysteria, with everybody blaming every ache and pain they got on the same thing."

"That's right," I said. "It's always good to remain skeptical when you're a detective."

We ate dinner at a place called Molly's Log Cabin Kitchen, even though it didn't look much like a log cabin from the outside. Inside, the atmosphere resembled the inside of a smokestack. The waitress didn't take kindly to our request for a seat in the nonsmoking section, and we were too hungry to leave.

Then I made the mistake of asking for a beer.

"This county is dry, Cat," Louella informed me in a low voice.

I gaped at her, horrified. "You brought me down here to solve a case in a *dry* county?"

"Well, I couldn't exactly move it to a wet one, now could I?" she grumbled.

I consoled myself with homemade pie for dessert.

"It's good," I muttered, "but it's no substitute for a beer, especially when it's hot as the blazes outside."

"Well, we can drive over to Nashville if you're desperate, Cat," Louella said. "Unless you want to try some of the local brew."

"Moonshine?" I raised an eyebrow. "Not on your life. I don't do toxic chemicals."

There were still a few hours of daylight left, but we weren't in the mood to start looking through Red's things, so we decided to drive up to New Union instead. We headed up 57 to 1764, playing one of Louella's Patsy Cline tapes.

The green sign that said "Welcome to New Union. Population 1837" was riddled with bullet holes.

On the left side, there were woods and cornfields and some low-lying marshy areas. Then the road swung around, and we saw it: a skyline of stacks and tanks and metallic towers, wavering in the heat and smoke, here and there an open flame.

It took your breath away, which was just as well, because an odor was beginning to creep in through the air-conditioning vents—a smell that reminded me of high-school chemistry labs, as well as some of my own less successful experiments with the chemistry set I'd recently acquired to help with my detection training.

"Would you look at that!" Louella said finally. "There's all kinds of plants out here, Cat. Which one's the incinerator?"

"Beats me," I said. "They're all putting out smoke."

Louella was driving slowly. "I take that back, Cat. There's not all kinds of plants out here. These are all chemical plants."

"Yeah," I said, reading the signs. "Trask Rubber, Tennessee Plastics, BCC Chemicals, U.S. Carbon, Trans-Global Chemicals, et cetera, et cetera."

We crossed a railroad track covered with tank cars. To

my right, a plant yard was crowded with tank trucks. The plants themselves were surrounded by high barbed-wire fences.

We kept driving until we had clearly left the industrial park. Now we were passing houses and fields.

"Let's try again," I said. "There was one place that didn't have a sign out front."

We pulled into the parking lot of a square brick building with three smokestacks. It was dwarfed by its neighbors.

"Can you read that sign on the wall, Cat?"

"It says 'Chem-Tech WDI. Leaders in twenty-first-century waste disposal technology.' "

We parked, and gazed at the smokestacks. The setting sun lit them from the side as they seemed to vibrate in the heat, sending plumes of thick, black smoke into the cloudless sky. Except for the smoke, nothing moved; the whole place appeared deserted, but there were cars parked in the lot around us. A green tank truck with the Chem-Tech logo stood on a loading ramp next to a larger tank.

"Louella, you got your camera?" I asked.

"What you want a picture of that for?"

"I don't know. It might come in handy. I just think we should document everything."

"Want me to pose?" Louella volunteered. "That way, we can tell our friends, 'Here we are on our summer vacation. We saw the most interesting sights!' "

"I think you should stay in the car with the windows rolled up," I muttered. "And if I have a seizure or something, call an ambulance. If anybody shows up with a gun, get ready to floor it."

She shrugged, and I took pictures of the complex: the smokestacks, the barbed-wire fence, the office, the parking lot, the Chem-Tech sign. Despite the heat and the quiet, I felt chilled and exposed, poised to bolt if an armed guard showed up.

"Now," I said, climbing back into the car. "Let's get out of here."

"Crazy," Patsy sang, and we sang along.

Six

I called Delbert from the motel, and reached him at Al's.

"I hope you send him home when you want to go to bed," I said to her.

"Actually," Al replied, "we're thinking of moving the computer down to your apartment. Either that, or we'll move down there ourselves. I mean, if you could see the look on his face when we tell him he has to leave—"

Delbert was his usual uncommunicative self. No, his parents hadn't called. Yes, everything was fine. Yes, he was keeping busy, mostly dogwashing. (No, I didn't ask; I hoped Winnie had enjoyed it if she was the dog in question.) But Al might have some serious work for him down at her office. I should call him if I needed anything. I hung up, congratulating myself on having the kind of teenaged relatives you could entrust with a credit card.

The next morning Louella called the lawyer and made an appointment for eleven o'clock. Then we dropped in at Owen's Towing outside of Parkersville. A burly guy with "Owen" stitched over his pocket was answering the phone as we arrived; that's how I learned that the name of the establishment was something closer to "Own's Tone" than I had previously realized. He handed us the contents of Red McIntyre's glove compartment: an insurance company card (conspicuously on top), a Tennessee map, a couple of gasoline receipts, two auto repair receipts, some hamburger coupons, and a game piece for some game McDonald's had run two years back. No keys.

"Can we see the car?"

He shrugged. "If you want to. It's in real bad shape, and

it's—well, kind of messed up inside." That was his euphemism for bloodstains, I presumed. He called in a long-haired blond kid who was about Delbert's age and build, only healthier-looking. "Take these ladies out to see the McIntyre wreck," Owen told him.

I don't know if you've ever had the opportunity to visit a hard-core towing or wrecking operation, but it's a humbling experience. I'd be willing to bet it would convert the most vehement seat-belt opponent to Mr. Safety First. Luckily, we didn't have to penetrate too far to find Red's 1973 gray Chevy Impala.

"Thar she is," the kid said, nodding soberly at the Chevy. "Took some pretty bad licks before she caught fahr and hit the water."

"Looks to me like he was hit on both sides," I observed.

"Yeah," the kid said.

"How could he get hit like that if he just drove through the railing on one side?" I asked.

The kid shrugged.

I borrowed Louella's camera again and started taking pictures.

"Can we open the trunk up?" Louella asked.

"Sure. We opened it already. Twice. Oncet when it come in, and oncet for that other fella."

"What other fella?" I asked.

He was already fingering the catch on the blackened trunk. He concentrated on that for a minute.

"Don't know who he was. Insurance, I reckon. Had a clipboard and papers. It's purty burnt out." He stepped back to let us see.

"When was this other guy here?"

"Yesterday mornin'." They—whoever "they" were—hadn't lost any time, I thought.

Louella picked up a fragment of damp, badly singed

denim. The whole car smelled like lake water, mildew, and damp ashes.

"Musta had a jacket back there."

"Did you talk to the guy who was here before?" I asked.

He scratched his head. "I showed him the car, an' opened the trunk, like he asked. Didn't do much talkin'."

"Did he give you a card?"

"No, he didn't give me nothin'."

A close inspection of the trunk revealed no more than what we saw when he first opened it: a burned-out, empty trunk. Then we checked the inside of the car. We couldn't get the passenger door open, so I had to slide over the damp, blood-splotched seat on the driver's side to inspect the glove compartment for myself. Nothing. I would have looked under the rubber floor mats, but they'd melted and fused to the carpet; anything Red had hidden under the mats would not be liberated except by a chemical separation process. As far as we could tell, the car was clean. But who had cleaned it was a question worth pondering.

We waited for Owen to get off the phone.

"He said"—I jerked my head in the kid's direction—"there was somebody else looking at the car already. But we haven't called the insurance company, so we're wondering who that might be."

He shook his head, frowning. "There ain't been nobody else here."

"He said yesterday morning."

He looked at the boy.

"You was off on that Ballery job, Daddy."

"Oh, you mean *that* fella. That fella wasn't lookin' for the McIntyre car. He called back later and said he got it mixed up. He come by in the afternoon and looked at another car. Insurance adjuster, he was, got the wrong description. My boy here was on lunch when he come back."

"I see." I did, too.

"You know what surprises me, Cat," said Louella. "If he was going out of town, even if he was only going to be gone overnight, you'd think he'd have some kind of overnight bag—you know, with a toothbrush and a change of underwear. Didn't you find anything like that?" she asked Owen.

"Nothin' like that. Sorry. Maybe it got burnt up."

"Maybe," I said. Maybe not.

"And," I added to Louella back in the privacy of the car, "I'd like to know how come his gas tank exploded in the back if he hit the wall in the front."

By now it was ten o'clock. We had an hour to kill before our appointment at the lawyer's office. I wanted to go to the library and read up on Chem-Tech, but Louella wanted to go shopping in beautiful downtown Cayter. Being in mourning and in need of consolation and all, she won. Not that I objected. Most detectives you read about never have time on their hands when they're on a case. Or if they do, they go for a run or work out at the gym. Me, I'll take shopping any day of the week.

We stood on a street corner in downtown Cayter, and surveyed our options.

"Does it strike you as ominous that what we have here is a heavy concentration of insurance companies and lawyers' offices, with a funeral home and two churches thrown in for good measure?" I asked.

"Cayter sure is a convenient place to die," Louella agreed. "And I reckon if you pay a little extra, the funeral home'll send next door to Ethel's Cut and Curl Salon for a consultant."

I nodded. "Seems kind of an odd time for a makeover, though."

"Cat, let's go in Japhet's Junque—the one with the antiques. That looks interesting."

"Yeah. When somebody dies, you go see the lawyer, then run next door to the insurance office and the auctioneer, and whatever's left after the auction you sell to the antique store. Like you said, Louella: real convenient."

I had to restrain Louella in the antique store, reminding her that she hadn't yet looked over Red's possessions to see what he had. I envisioned us driving home in Louella's station wagon, loaded down like one of those dust bowl families headed West.

I didn't bother to restrain her at Barb's Boutique a few doors down. She had her career to think about, after all. But how anybody could try on clothes in this heat was beyond me. I was already so soaked in sweat that I would've had to peel my clothes off like a Band-Aid if I'd wanted to try something on.

We stashed her bags in the car before we went to meet Foster Bayberry, Esq. Foster Bayberry was a tall, thin young man with sandy hair and moustache and a mournful expression. Whereas Officer Boone Danning's expression of distress was a polite imitation, at least until we started to annoy him, Foster Bayberry's was the real thing, only seemingly permanent. He wore a suit that hung loose on his frame, as if he'd either lost a lot of weight lately or grabbed the first thing off the rack.

"Red and I go way back," he said, which didn't seem possible, given his age. "I used to go fishing sometimes with Red and Freeman Quinn and Hunt Smith. I'm real sorry he's gone."

His office indicated that whatever money was changing hands in Millins County, he wasn't on the receiving end. The coffee table in the waiting room looked like secondhand early American, and the secretary's desk looked like early schoolteacher. A window air conditioner chugged along in the inner office, aided by an antique swiveling fan that rocked back and forth and groaned as if on its last swivel. I kept watching it to see if it would capsize.

"I've got Red's will right here," he continued, after waving us into a couple of unmatched office chairs that smacked of Odd Lots. "He left most everything to you, Mrs. Simmons, as I 'magine you know. He just had a few special bequests. Let's see. Yes, his camera goes to Mr. Smith, and his fishing gear goes to Mr. Quinn. Hadn't fished in a while, though, seemed like. Left his hunting rifle to Mr. Wade Oakley—he lives up in Seattle now. Then he left five hundred dollars to a local group called Healthwatch. That's about it."

"Are there any special instructions about the funeral?" Louella asked.

"No, nothing like that. No instructions of any kind, except something about his clothes. Let's see—here it is. 'To my niece, Louella Simmons, of Hamilton County, Ohio, the remainder,' et cetera, 'including my clothing, which she is to examine and distribute to any of my friends or otherwise distribute or discard as she sees fit.' That's it." He looked up at us sadly, as if apologizing that Red's life had been reduced to this scrap of paper.

"What's Healthwatch?" I asked.

"Oh, it's a local group opposed to the incinerator and all the pollution going on here in Millins County. It's one of those grass-roots, shoestring operations, so I reckon they'll be grateful for Red's bequest."

"Was he a member?" Louella asked.

"I doubt it." Bayberry shook his head mournfully. "He didn't go in much for joining things. He told me once he wasn't a member of anything except the VFW and the OOB, which he said was the Organization of Ornery

Bastards—an organization which he held all the offices in."

"That sounds like Red," Louella agreed.

"Here's a copy of the will for you," he said, and handed it to Louella. "I'll take care of the probate. Now, all you need to do is take that copy down to the bank along with some identification and they'll open up Red's safe deposit box for you. He set it all up that way."

At the bank an efficient woman checked Louella's credentials, then escorted us into a small room that reminded me a little of the room in the county morgue. We had more remains to examine, I thought.

We worked our way down through the contents of the box, starting with the photographs on top—several pictures of a handsome woman Louella identified as her aunt Gerry, a wedding picture of Gerry and Red, and a small album of photographs, birth to young manhood, of Louella's cousin Michael, who had been killed in Korea.

"Do *you* keep any photographs in a safety deposit box?" I asked.

"No, I never thought of it. I guess it makes sense in case of fire, but I don't think most people do."

"Me, neither," I said.

Then there were two little boxes containing Purple Hearts, one of which also held a wedding ring, and another box containing a Medal of Honor.

"One of the Purple Hearts—the one with Aunt Gerry's wedding ring—must be Red's, and the other is Mike's. The Medal of Honor was Mike's, too."

Next we found Mike's birth certificate, and a letter from Mike's commanding officer about his death.

We were both starting to get a little weepy.

"Gosh, Cat," Louella said. "It's like the story of his life in here. And it brings back Gerry and Mike, too. They always were my favorite relatives."

Next was a small pile of pay stubs, dated 1977 and 1978, from Chem-Tech WDI, Inc.

Next was a life insurance policy, taken out just last April, for ten thousand dollars, payable to Freeman Quinn.

The last item in the box, the paper at the bottom of the pile, was another life insurance policy, taken out just last week, for twenty-five thousand dollars, payable to Healthwatch.

Seven

"Holy smokes!" Louella exclaimed. "Cat, would you look at that!"

"Two—count them—*two* life insurance policies taken out in the past four months. And then he's killed in an accident? Louella, either your uncle is psychic, or that accident was no accident."

"Yeah. Thirty-five-thousand-dollars' worth, too. Of course, I guess we should consider the possibility that he'd been having some kind of chest pains or something."

"Did he mention any to you?"

"No. Not chest pains. He said he hadn't been feeling too good, but I don't think it was chest pains."

I started to ask her something else, then changed my mind.

"Here, let's take this stuff and get out of here."

"Yeah. It makes me feel kind of creepy just holding onto it. Doesn't it you?"

"Creepy's not the word, I feel like a goddam moving target. I just wish I knew where the shooting was going to come from."

Out on the sidewalk, we found ourselves scanning the immediate vicinity to see if anybody was watching us. No one was, unless they were looking out of an office window with binoculars.

"Really, though, Cat, I reckon we're being silly," Louella said, with an attempt at a brave smile. "I mean, I'm just the next of kin, why would anybody be after me?"

"That would be easier to answer if we knew for sure why they were after your uncle."

"Well, and anyway, we haven't got anything in the way

of papers that you couldn't get a copy of some other way, right? I mean, the insurance company has copies of the policies."

"Sure, and if the company finds out he's dead, or if anybody finds out he named them in a policy and calls the company to let them know he's dead, then the company'll go looking for their copies."

"Oh. I guess they wouldn't know yet." She thought a bit. "You mean, maybe the beneficiaries don't know they're beneficiaries? Oh, I don't know! It's so confusing."

"And we don't really know what we've got yet. We haven't been through your uncle's house. What's more, we might have something here that's valuable to somebody, only we don't recognize it."

"You know, Cat," she grumbled, slipping on her rhinestone-studded sunglasses, "you are not being a whole hell of a consolation to me in my bereavement."

"God Almighty, Louella, you don't need to be consoled, you need to be protected, for crissake!" I slapped on my mirror sunglasses. "Somebody probably just ran your uncle off the side of a dam when he was on his way to see you. You might be the only person who knew where he was headed—apart from the person who killed him, of course."

She knew all this. Otherwise, she wouldn't have asked me to come along. But like most people when they feel threatened, she was grumpy and turned on the closest target. We got into the car and cranked the windows down.

"Okay. You're right. I guess."

"Just think of me as your bodyguard."

"With that little old excuse for a gun you tote around? You gonna protect me with that?"

"My Diane is a perfectly respectable firearm," I said huffily. "Besides, I have other resources."

"Did Mel ever give you any more self-defense lessons after that one where you bruised your hip?"

"She's taught me a few things."

"Well, look, Cat, you know I have great respect for your mouth. I do. But I'm beginning to think what we need is bulletproof vests."

"A bulletproof vest wouldn't have helped your uncle. Listen, you want me to tell you something that will make you feel better?"

"What?"

"If Red thought you'd be in danger, he would have left his rifle to you."

She thought it over.

"Okay. You could be right. Unless he assumed I was bringing my bodyguard with me."

"I want to know more about this decision to come to Cincinnati. I want to know everything you can remember about what he said and when he said it."

"Okay." She sighed. "But can we go someplace air-conditioned to have this conversation?"

"I'd feel a hell of a lot safer if we had it in the air-conditioned car with the windows rolled up."

So we headed out of town in the general direction of the river, and cruised around. We would go looking for Red's house after lunch. Louella put on a Willie Nelson tape.

"It was maybe three weeks ago I first mentioned about the public meetings on the incinerator when I was talking to Red on the phone."

"Not April?"

"No. I might have mentioned something before about how they were starting to talk about an incinerator in Cincinnati, but not about the meetings."

"When did you first mention anything about an incinerator?"

"I don't know, Cat. How'm I supposed to remember

something like that? I wasn't paying it that much attention at the time, but I knew he might be interested."

"Do you remember what he said when you first mentioned it?"

"Oh, well, he just said that Cincinnati would be crazy to get into all that."

" 'All that'?"

"Well, I guess he just meant building an incinerator, I don't know. I didn't ask him what he meant."

"Do you know of anything that happened this spring that might have induced him to buy a life insurance policy?"

"No." She shook her head. "Like I said, he said he wasn't feeling too good, but that was—oh, maybe some time in March. I don't think I talked to him again until that time three weeks ago when I told him about the meetings."

"And he said he wanted to go up to Cincinnati?"

"Well, not right then, he didn't. He just said I should go, and tell them my uncle lived near one, and it was a 'goddam death trap.' That's what he called it."

"So then what?"

"So then, a few days later, he calls me up again, and asks me if there isn't an EPA office in Cincinnati. I said yes, down across from the university. So he said he wanted to talk to somebody there, and he asked me to get him the name of somebody trustworthy who knew something about hazardous chemicals."

" 'Trustworthy'?"

"That's how he put it. Like I was going to go around asking for names, and then say, 'But can I *trust* this person?' Besides, I wasn't supposed to say why I wanted the name. So I asked around, and I called back to give him the name of someone he could call, and he asked me when the meetings were being held."

"What was the name?"

"Gosh, I don't remember. I got it written down somewhere. So anyway, he calls back then a few days after that, and says he's coming to one of those meetings, and he's going to meet with this man from the EPA while he's here."

"Who gave you this name?"

"Well, I didn't have much luck at first, because I didn't know who to ask. Then I saw in the paper where this Ohio Public Interest Research Group was opposing the incinerator, so I called them, and they called back with a name."

"But you didn't tell them about your uncle?"

"No, Cat, that's what I'm saying. He told me not to tell anybody."

"So he called you the week before he was going to come? Do you remember what day?"

"Let's see. I think it was on Saturday, because I was listening to Garrison Keillor on the radio."

"So some time within a week of his death, somebody found out that he was going to Cincinnati to talk to the EPA and speak out at a public meeting. And during the same time period, he took out a new life insurance policy."

"Yeah." She pulled over to the side of the road. We had run into the river. Our road dead-ended, and we had to decide which way to turn. "But I still guess it could all just be a coincidence."

Yeah, I thought. And I'm the ghost of Rachel Carson.

Eight

Red McIntyre's house was set back from the road and sheltered from it by some tall bushes. He had neighbors on both sides, though not near neighbors the way they'd be in an urban neighborhood, and a shallow creek, or as Louella called it, a crick, running along his property line. It was a pale blue frame house with aluminum siding and a front porch that ran the length of the house, bordered by a white balustrade and supported by narrow white posts.

As we headed up the gravel drive, we got a stereo dog-bark effect from the neighbors' houses.

"Nice to know we'd get some warning if somebody was coming," I observed.

"Who do you think is going to come?" Louella asked nervously.

"Get a grip, Lou," I said. "Anybody who was going to come has probably already been here. After all, somebody has your uncle's keys."

"You think so?" she said, running her hand across the top of the door frame, and bringing down a key.

"Well," I retorted, "even if they don't have the keys, your uncle's security system is a bit lax. A four-year-old could break in if he had somebody to carry his ladder for him."

We stood in the front room and looked around. The dining room was off to our left, and the kitchen behind that. A hallway led out of the front room to the back of the house. The air was fragrant with the sweet, woodsy smell of pipe tobacco.

"Well," Louella said. "None of the cushions are slashed."

"No," I agreed. "And the pictures are still hanging on the walls. Looks downright peaceful."

"Let's open some windows," Louella said.

I headed down the hallway. The first door on the right was a bathroom, decorated, I suggested, by the late Aunt Gerry.

"He used to talk to her all the time," Louella said over my shoulder. "After she died, I mean. I even heard him do it, once or twice. He said he often felt her presence."

"Spooky," I said. My late spouse hadn't listened to me when he was alive, so I damn sure didn't waste my breath on him now that he was dead. If Fred was still hanging around now, I didn't want to know about it. I didn't want to feel the little breeze every time he shook his head.

There were two bedrooms in the back of the house. One was clearly in everyday use. The other contained, in addition to a bed and dresser, an old cabinet Singer, a desk with a Remington manual typewriter, and a box of paperback Westerns, along with the requisite number of those lamps you bought with S&H Green Stamps back in the fifties. Again, nothing appeared to have been disturbed in either room. We opened the windows, and went back to check the dining room and kitchen. In the dining room was an oak table covered with a lace tablecloth topped by a centerpiece of plastic flowers. The kitchen featured painted wood cabinets and countertops, and a refrigerator that looked as old as my youngest daughter. Off the kitchen was a walk-in pantry, and an entrance to the basement. I took a quick look, but it looked like my basement, only neater.

"He sure was *neat*," I said, surveying the kitchen with awe. "The whole house is so damn clean!"

"Yeah," Louella agreed. "I think it was a habit he picked up in the navy."

"I should have sent Jason here for basic training," I said, thinking of my son's various bachelor apartments.

"There's nothing in here that's ready to spoil," I said, checking out the refrigerator. "We might as well hunt for something that can tell us who killed Red, and why."

"Okay, but first I'm going to call that Officer Danning and see if they've done the autopsy yet—just in case they got it done early."

I surveyed the living room while she was in the kitchen phoning. I started with the mail that had been piled on a table just inside the front door. Most of it was pretty mundane—mail-order catalogs, flyers for a post-Fourth of July sale at K-Mart, bills. I was scanning Red's bank statement when Louella returned.

"The autopsy's done, so we can have the funeral whenever. I figure Monday, if we get over to the funeral home yet this afternoon. So I called a place in Cayter, and said we'd be in at four."

"Did he say when the autopsy results would be in?"

"He said two weeks, at least for all the tests, but they think it was the impact that killed him. I called the car insurance company, too. Say, Cat—"

"Yeah?"

"You know how to tell if a telephone's tapped? Red always seemed to think it was, so I was just wondering."

"Don't you unscrew the whoosis, and look inside there?"

"That's how they do it on TV, but if he did it and found one, wouldn't he just take it out?"

"I guess, if he knew how." I followed her into the kitchen.

"He was real good with mechanical things."

I thought about the antique refrigerator.

"I don't see anything to unscrew," I said. "Maybe you have to pop this doojigger off with a screwdriver."

"Maybe we'll break it," she said. "Then we'll be stranded without a phone."

"There's another one in the bedroom. If we break this one, we'll call a repairman, and he can tell us if it's tapped."

I cracked the thing open with a screwdriver we found in a kitchen drawer, but I couldn't tell anything from looking at it.

"Wait," Louella said. "Didn't I see a movie about this? Yeah, it was one of those cop movies, you know. They didn't even have to go inside the house to do it. They just climbed up on this telephone pole and tapped into the line there."

"That must be how it's done, then," I agreed. "Movies never lie about stuff like that. But if you have any ideas about me climbing up a telephone pole to check the line, don't even think about it. I'm afraid of heights, and still recovering from my basketball injury." I went back to Red's bank statement.

"Find anything?" she asked, following me into the living room.

"Yeah. Red was a dues-paying member of the National Rifle Association."

"You know, I never could figure that out. He was just too soft-hearted to shoot anything. He used to have a dog, too; I wonder what happened to him? Not a hunting dog, just a mongrel. Red'd go shooting at the rifle range, but he hadn't shot *at* anything in donkey's years."

"Well, anyway," I said, putting down the mail with a sigh, "I don't see any anonymous letters saying, 'You're next.' I'd like to take a look at his desk."

We each took a drawer.

"Well, I haven't found any evidence that he was paying blackmail or engaging in it," I said twenty minutes later. "You?"

"No, but Cat, look at this. It's a letter from somebody—I can't read the signature and there's no date. I can't make out his handwriting too well, but it's something about Pat Kinneady. Can you make it out?"

I squinted at the blue scrawl on yellow legal paper.

"Dear Red," I read slowly.

"Thanks for letting me know about Pat Kinneady's death. I feel real bad about it. But I told him when he got started that he was making a mistake stirring things up. If you know what is good for you, I told him, you will let sleeping dogs lie. That is my advice to you and Freeman and Hunt too. Unless you want to get out, like I done.

"Seattle is a pretty place, but it rains too damn much. Still, those murdering bastards—you know who I mean— are not here, and neither is their chemicals. I am sorry I missed the funeral but I did not know nor probably could have made the trip anyway. I have not been feeling too good. Old age will do that to you, I reckon. But you'd know more about that than me. (Ha, ha!)

"Think of me the next time you go fishing—or the next time you hit you-know-where at the rifle range. Your old fishing buddy, Wade."

"Where'd you find this, Louella?"

"It was kind of stuck in the back of the drawer. Wow! That sure makes Pat Kinneady's death sound suspicious, doesn't it?"

"Yeah, with your uncle's death running it a close second. You got the envelope this came in?"

She shook her head. "It was just the letter, all by itself. I reckon if we could find Red's address book, though, we could look up this Wade. I kind of remember him. He was younger than me, and real shy."

"We'd better try and contact Freeman and Hunt, too, before they have accidents."

"Gee, I wonder how Pat Kinneady died?"

"Me, too. That's one question I want to ask them."

"I don't remember any Pats. But Freeman and Hunt were Red's pals, and they used to take me fishing when we visited, and sit up late playing cards with my daddy. Hunt's wife had the prettiest antique carved locket, I remember, and she always used to show it to me when I asked. Mrs. Quinn was always baking up a storm, and I remember she was in charge of the food after Aunt Gerry's funeral. Those three—Red and Freeman and Hunt—were a real hoot when they got together. They were so much fun to be around." She sighed.

There wasn't anything else in the desk. Moving to a beat-up beige metal file cabinet in the corner, we found old income tax returns, and old bills and receipts, but that was about it.

As I shut the drawer, something stirred in the little puff of air it generated. I examined the top of the filing cabinet.

"Louella, you see this?"

"What?"

"This ash here. It kind of fell apart when I shut the filing cabinet. And there's some on the carpet there, too."

"Well?"

"Your uncle Red smoked a pipe, didn't he?"

"That's right, Cat! He smoked a pipe, and that's a cigarette ash! Somebody's been in here smoking a cigarette, and they've gone and dropped their ash. Ooh, Red would be madder'n a hornet if he knew somebody was creeping around, messing up his clean house! I mean, it's bad enough they snooped. But they didn't even bother to clean up after themselves. That just burns me up!"

"If we catch them, we'll give them the Slob of the Year award. But first, we'll have to ask them what they found." I sighed. "If they found what they were looking for, that means we won't."

"I reckon. But Cat, Red was being real careful. I bet whatever it was, he had it hidden real good."

Two hours later, I was willing to affirm that whatever it was, it was hidden too well for us to find—assuming there was anything to find in the first place.

"You'd think if he had anything on paper about this Chem-Tech business, he would have taken it with him to show the EPA," I said. "That means it either got burned up in the car, or removed from the car before we arrived. On the other hand, if they found anything at all, why come search his house, unless they thought there was more here to find? In which case, our Marlboro man probably already came and found it and took it away."

"Well, we got to go now to the funeral home, but we haven't even searched the kitchen or the basement."

"Or the light fixtures or the laundry hamper or—"

"Yeah, I still got to go through his clothes, and—"

We looked at each other.

"His clothes!" we both shouted, and raced back to the bedroom.

"You know, Cat, I thought at the time that was awful peculiar, that part in the will about distributing his clothes. I mean, why would you have to tell somebody that in your will?"

"Yeah. I thought maybe Red thought his friends were looking a little threadbare and needed a boost in the wardrobe department." I opened a closet and stared at the neatly hung clothing inside.

"Cat, look at the time! We got to go to the funeral parlor. I could go by myself, but to tell you the truth, I'd like to have company."

"I'll go," I said. "But Louella, we can't just walk away and leave this place wide open for the opposition to waltz in and help themselves."

"What're we gonna do? There's clothes everywhere."

"Look, we don't have time to be neat. We'll just have to pile everything up and take it with us. There's a big suitcase in that closet in the spare room."

"But Cat, what if somebody's, you know, watching the house, and they see us take a suitcase out?"

"Good thinking. We better use paper bags, and that laundry basket from the basement. That way, they can see that all we're taking out is clothes."

Within ten minutes, we'd cleaned out every drawer, closet, and chest we could find, and crammed it all in brown paper bags. At the bottom of one, I stashed Red's little address book, which we'd found in the bedroom under the phone at the last minute.

"Just act natural," I cautioned her as we started lugging bags to the car. In a louder voice, I added, "Boy! The Salvation Army is sure gonna be excited when they see us coming!"

The only audible attention anybody paid us was a volley of barks from both sides.

"I don't know, Cat," Louella's voice emerged from behind her bags. "Some of this stuff is just rags."

"That's okay," I said. "Let them sort it and throw it out. That's what they're there for."

We finished loading the station wagon. In the back next to her gold jacket, Louella hung the suit she was taking to the funeral home.

"You drive," she whispered, "in case they come after us."

We climbed into the front seat and looked at each other.

"I feel like I'm driving a goddam Brink's truck," I muttered.

The barking followed us down the driveway and out into the road.

Nine

If you've seen one funeral home, you've seen them all, give or take a few thousand dollars' worth of coffins. Our PBR (Personal Bereavement Representative) looked a smidgen more cheerful than Foster Bayberry, Esquire. This was probably related to the fact that he looked too damn young to be on intimate terms with death. Much as he tried to suppress it, he still had that slightly smug air of somebody who considered himself invulnerable.

He looked even more cheerful when we admitted that we didn't know who Red's minister was, and hadn't contacted one yet. We didn't tell him that we'd been too busy investigating Red's murder, nor did we offer to root around in fifteen bags of clothing to find Red's little black book. He volunteered to undertake—if I can use that word—the responsibility of engaging a suitable person of the cloth, but Louella didn't want to pay for any services we didn't need, and didn't want a stranger, besides.

"You know how they do, Cat. They'll be calling him Walter the whole time, and folks'll think they've come to the wrong funeral. His friends'll know who to call."

So we made the decisions we needed to make, chose the things we needed to choose, and split, assuring our PBR that he would be hearing from us in the morning.

We drove straight back to the motel, and started to unload bags. Billie came out of the office to watch.

"What in holy heck are you two gals doin' with all them bags o' clothes?"

"These are Uncle Red's," Louella said noncommittally. "Oh, darn, Cat, look here. We went and forgot to leave his suit at the funeral home."

"Any calls?" I asked Billie.

"One," she answered. "It was just some realtor calling to offer her services. She said she was real sorry about your uncle, and if you was wantin' to sell his property, she'd be real pleased to help you out. Now, don't that just beat ever'thing? Here the poor man ain't been buried yet, and there's folks lookin' to make some money off him. Well, I told her, I said, 'Miz Simmons ain't thinkin' 'bout none of that yet, and I'll thank you not to trouble her while she's still a-grievin' and a-worran' about the funeral.' I was real snippy."

"Good for you," I said.

"Y'all want to wash them things?" she asked.

"No, thanks," Louella said.

" 'Cause if you did, I was going to say, there's washers and dryers behind the office." By now, she was carrying bags in, and dumping them on the floor next to the others.

Louella and I exchanged a look.

"Billie," I said, "we need to talk. But I don't want to take you away from the desk."

"Well," she said, "when are y'all goin' to supper? I can come down when Em'ry comes on duty at seven."

"Okay. See you then."

"When *are* we going to supper, Cat?" Louella asked. "I'm kinda hungry already, what with all this toting and hauling and detecting and selecting."

"I don't like to leave this stuff unguarded," I said.

So she volunteered to go out and find us some dinner while I got started on the clothes.

"But Cat, don't you dare find anything till I get back!" she warned me.

Fat chance, I thought, as I surveyed the room. We'd been in such a hurry, we hadn't bothered to sort or label anything. If we had, we could have approached this search methodically. As it was, you could start with a promising-looking pile of shirts and hit underwear two inches down.

Before I got started, I called home, on the off chance that my cousin Delbert was taking a break from the computer and engaging in some normal teenage activity, like eating dinner or watching television. What I got on my answering machine was some kind of electronic music, followed by a voice I vaguely recognized as Delbert's: "Neither Catherine Caliban, of Caliban Investigations, nor her assistant, Del Sweet, can come to the phone right now. Please leave your name and number at the bark, and we'll get right back to you. When you hear the yowl, your time is up." And damned if it wasn't followed by a bark from Winnie, and eventually a yowl from Sidney—I stayed on the line just to make sure.

I called Al's, but I couldn't get through; instead of a busy signal, I was getting some kind of high-pitched screech. So I called Moses, but he wasn't home. He probably had better things to do on a Friday night than sort through fifteen bags of a dead person's clothing.

I hadn't made much progress when Louella returned with a bag of barbecue.

"You got the will, Lou? Read me the part about the legacies again."

"Oh, here it is. It says, 'To Freeman Quinn I leave my fishing gear so he can stop lying about his catch. To Hunt Smith I leave my camera to replace the one he has worn out taking pictures of his grandchildren, with apologies to Freeman and anybody else who has to look at them. To Wade Oakley I leave my hunting rifle and fifty dollars to get his eyes checked.' Heck, maybe we got it wrong, Cat. Maybe what we're looking for is stuffed in the barrel of his hunting rifle or hidden in his tackle box."

"Yeah, or maybe it's a roll of film that's still in the camera."

In fact, we hadn't made much more progress when Billie showed up at seven. She made a space in the middle of a pile of socks, and lit a cigarette.

"Here's the story, Billie," I said. "We think Louella's uncle was murdered."

"Murdered!" she clapped a hand—the one without the cigarette—to her chest and looked appropriately shocked.

"That's right," Louella put in. "And Cat here's a detective and she's gonna find out who murdered him."

"My lands! A detective!" She looked at me. You could tell she was thrilled to bits.

"Actually, *Louella* and I"—I threw Louella a look—"are going to find out who murdered him."

"Well, this beats ever'thing!" Now she was thinking things over. "And you think it has something to do with that incinerator?" She took a long drag off her cigarette, and then looked around at the clothes strewn everywhere. "And you got all his clothes here, and you're goin' through them, lookin' for clues!"

"That's right," I said, "because of something he said in his will. But we have to be really careful, because whoever killed him must've thought he had something or knew something. At least, that's what we think."

"Yeah, and now they might think we have it or know it, whatever it is," Louella chimed in.

"Lord, y'all could be in danger!" Billie exclaimed, glancing at the windows. I had already drawn the curtains.

"That's right," I admitted.

"And somebody already searched Red's house, and left his cigarette ash behind!" Louella added.

"That's terrible!" Billie said, brushing some of her own ash off the night stand.

"Yeah! But Cat's got her gun, in case they come after us!"

Louella was really enjoying performing for an apprecia-

tive audience, but this enthusiastic allusion to my own un-
licensed firearm made me nervous.

"Anyway," I said, "we thought we ought to let you
know, in case you saw anything suspicious."

"Well, I surely am glad y'all told me," Billie said.
"Why, if I'da known, I'da kept that realator on the telephone longer, and wrote her name down! That phone call
might could have been suspicious, but I didn't know
nothin' about it."

"That's okay," I said. "She was probably legit."

"But if you see any gun-toting thugs around, you give
us a holler," Louella said.

"I will." Billie stubbed out her cigarette, and lit another.
She was settling in for the duration. "Now, what was it
you's lookin' for in these clothes?" She parked the cigarette between her lips, frowning in concentration, picked
up a pair of khaki work pants out of the pile nearest her,
and turned a pocket inside out with one deft motion.

"That's the thing: we don't know," Louella confessed.
"The will just says to examine his clothing."

"Could he sew?" Billie asked. "Reason I'm askin',
some men can't thread a needle to save their lives, while
others is real handy with a needle and thread. It would
make a difference in what we was lookin' for." She turned
the pants inside out.

"He was in the navy," Louella said. "I think he could
sew as well as he could cook and clean."

"Well, what makes you think he was murdered?"

So we told her the whole story, beginning to end, with
a few detours along the way. She kept busy the whole
time, turning things inside out and back, running her fingers over the seams, holding things up to the light. I was
beginning to think we should give her the stuff we'd already looked at.

"Well," she said when we'd finished, "like I said, that

Isaiah T. Grubbs don't care whether people in Millins County are dyin' from his chemicals. Don't seem like it'd make him no never mind to kill somebody if they stood in his way. He's got some real mean boys workin' for him, that's for dang sure."

"I wish we were working with the state police," I said. "The TVA officer is nice, but I don't think he's had much experience with homicide."

"Girl, don't you know where you're at? This is Tennessee. Them state patrols has been tight with the industry bosses since God made the mountains, like warts on a warthog's ass. Used to be all the stories you'd hear was from coal-mining country in Eastern Tennessee, where my granddaddy was from. But that was before the chemical plants come to the area. Now, don't you know the state police have their hands full, between the chemical plants and the landfill and the tourists. They don't have time to be investigatin' no murders, and they surely don't have time to go accusin' nobody that's payin' half their earnin's, tax-free, under the table. I don't know whether the federals is any better or not, but they couldn't be no worse."

"How about the Millins County Sheriff's Department?" Louella asked.

"God A-mighty, girl, they're just as bad."

"Aren't there any honest cops around here?" I asked.

"Sure, they's a few. You go find one that don't own him a RV and a cabin cruiser, and you've found you an honest one. But you just can't tell to look at 'em. Them federals might be your best bet."

"So, what you're saying is, even if we figure out who killed Red, and find the evidence, we'll never get anybody to prosecute."

"Now, I didn't say that. Might be you could get some help from that group your uncle left money to—that Healthwatch group. They like to stir things up. I got a friend who does some work for them sometimes. I could ask her who to call."

"Would you?" Louella asked. "That would be real helpful."

An hour later, we were feeling pretty discouraged, and I was contemplating a drive to Nashville to drown my sorrows.

"I thought sure we'd find something!" Louella wailed.

"What about that suit you've got hangin' in the car?" Billie asked. "His buryin' suit, I reckon."

So Billie was the one who finally hit the jackpot.

"I found it! Leastways, I found somethin'," she said. "Hand me them scissors, Louella." She applied the scissors to the light brown polyester knit coat. "I reckoned it had to be somethin' worth savin' for one of his friends. If Red was as careful as y'all was tellin' me, he wouldn't want to take a chance that Louella here might just go and give it away to the Salvation Army. Say, I tell you what, your uncle could sew a mean seam!" She picked and cut, her brow furrowed in concentration. "There!" Triumphantly, she produced a folded sheet of white paper, covered with typing.

She unfolded the page, and smoothed it out on the bed as we gathered around it.

"And would you look at that!" she exclaimed. "He's gone and got it notarized!"

Sure enough, at the bottom of the page, below Red's signature, was a notary seal, and a signature. The page was dated July 5, 1985.

"You read it out loud, Cat," Louella urged.

So I picked it up and read it. It was typed with the uneven strokes of an amateur typist using a manual typewriter.

"I, Walter McIntyre, of Millins County, Tennessee, wish to reveal an incident that happened in October of 1977

*while I was employed at Chem-Tech WDI. Pat Kinneady,
Wade Oakley, Hunt Smith, Freeman Quinn, and myself
was asked to work a special job one night. Pat Kinneady
and myself was directed by Mr. George Packer, who is
Isaiah Grubbs's operations manager, to dig a trench out
back on the edge of the landfill. We dug a trench eight foot
deep by fifty foot wide that run almost from one end of the
property to the other. Wade Oakley and Hunt Smith used
forklifts to move thirty-five-gallon drums from the turn-in
to the edge of the trench, and me and Kinneady pushed
them into the trench with the dozers. These drums contained hazardous chemicals. They contained arsenic, acetone, benzene, and other harmful substances. Freeman
Quinn was involved with the loading and handling of the
drums. We moved maybe 3,000 drums, and then buried
them, even though we could see that some of the drums
was already leaking and even though we knew that the soil
underneath them was clay. Mr. Packer told us not to tell
anyone about what we had done, and we was paid double
time for overtime. This is the truth, as God is my witness."*

We sat in silence for some time.

"I don't reckon y'all know who George Packer is." Billie sighed.

"Who?" I asked.

"He chairs the Millins County Commission."

Ten

"But what does it mean, exactly?" Louella asked. "I mean, according to Billie, these Chem-Tech bastards are always up to something. Why kill somebody over this?"

"Maybe because this adds up to more than their usual shenanigans," I mused. "Three thousand thirty-five-gallon drums is a lot of chemicals. What do you think, Billie?"

"I think," she said carefully, "that if we could prove they was three thousand drums of dangerous chemicals dumped illegally up there, we might could get that place shut down. But I don't know. They got an awful lot of friends in high places."

"The only chemical I recognize is arsenic," I said. "Anybody who reads mysteries knows that stuff can kill you, but that's if you eat it. The villain is always bumping people off with arsenic-laced tea cakes."

"But Cat," Louella pointed out, "don't you remember those cornfields we passed? What if it was leaking out into those? Wouldn't it get into the corn somehow?"

"It might, I guess," I conceded. "I don't really know enough about it. But if it was, you'd think folks would be dropping dead right and left, and they'd all have arsenic in their hair and fingernails."

"And acetone—that's what they put in nail polish remover," Louella said, waving her own fingernails for emphasis.

Billie nodded. She had polished fingernails, too.

"Lord, I hope that ain't one of them carcinogens," she said. "Rate I use that stuff, I'll be dead time I'm fifty."

Louella nodded glumly. It was a new idea for me—the notion that having no fingernails might save my life.

"What do you figure that other stuff is—that benzene business?" I asked. "Got a dictionary, Billie?"

She went off to look for one, and Louella sat and stared at Red's statement.

"You reckon that's the only copy, Cat?"

"It's the original," I said, running my hand over the notary's seal, "but I'd be surprised if it was the only copy. From everything you've told me, Red was pretty careful. Still, I would have expected him to keep a copy in his safe deposit box."

"Yeah, and it's not as if anybody else could've searched that and walked off with anything."

"Here it is," Billie announced from the doorway, talking through her cigarette. "Says it's a flammable liquid, and— listen to this!—it's used in detergents!"

I was aghast. "You mean like I use in the washer?" I squawked. "That kind of detergent?"

Billie shrugged.

"Well, shoot," she said, "these chemicals can't be that toxic the way most people use them, or the government wouldn't have approved them in the first place, would they?"

Billie and I just looked at her.

"Girl, you talkin' about the same gov'ment that approved that DDT bug spray and that—what was it called?—DES that deformed all o' them babies."

I started to say something about tobacco, but caught myself in time.

"Billie," I said, "this Chem-Tech place is right near the river, right? I mean, when we were following Highway 1764, we were following the Chickawee River, right? And there seem to be a lot of little creeks and streams around here that must empty into the river, and marshland, too. So if these drums are buried there, and leaking, they might be leaking into the river."

"Lord, yes! Into the Chickawee River and on up the TVA to the Ohio River and then into the Mississippi."

"But I guess the chemicals get all watered down by then," I speculated.

"Well, you better hope they do, 'cause they's a lot of towns takes their drinking water out of them rivers."

I hadn't thought of that, and now that I had, I felt sicker than ever.

"Okay," I said, with an effort at rekindling our energy. "Now we know what we're up against. And we know how Wade was involved. Louella, did you find Red's little black book?"

She nodded, and held it up. "It was all tangled up in the long johns."

"Well, if there's a number for either Hunt Smith or Freeman Quinn, you'd better call one of them, and tell them you want to meet to talk about the funeral. I don't think we'd better mention anything else on the phone, in case your uncle was right about phones being tapped, or in case it scares them off."

She found Quinn's number and called him.

"He was just as nice," Louella said, hanging up. "He got all choked up on the phone, and said he'd call the minister himself and set up a meeting for tomorrow. He's even going to call Hunt Smith and ask him, too. He said he had some ideas about the funeral."

While Louella and Billie folded clothes, I tried the Catatonia Arms again. Al's phone gave me the same screech as before, but this time I got through to Moses.

"Did I wake you up?"

"No, you didn't wake me up. I was just sittin' here, watching television." But he sounded grumpy, and I knew he'd fallen asleep in his chair, and was embarrassed to get caught at it.

"Have you seen Cousin Delbert any time recently, by any chance?"

"Lemme see. Last time I saw Cousin Delbert, him an' Sid was sitting in front of Al's computer, and he was trying to teach Sid to play 'What's New, Pussycat?' some kinda way on the keyboard. He called it 'dogwashing,' but it wasn't no kind of dogwashing we do at *my* house."

"I know what you mean," I said. "Do you think Mel and Al are getting sick of him?"

"I don't think you need to worry about that, Cat. Al's hired him as a consultant to redesign the computer network in her office. Those two are thick as thieves."

"How's the garden?"

"Well, the Japanese beetles are still attacking the roses, 'case you had any notion that they might disappear if you turned your back. You know where Mel put down straw to mulch under the cucumbers?"

"Uh-huh."

"Well, it's all sprouted now, and you can't hardly find the cucumbers for the straw sprouts."

"What about the ones that were wrapped around the zinnias?"

"I got bad news for you there, Cat. The weight of the cukes pulled the zinnias down, and you can't find them, neither. You know how Mel likes to go on 'bout how weeds are just underplants? I told her I didn't mind underplants, 'long's my overplants could get over them."

"Yeah, but I'm beginning to think Mel's right about chemicals." And I told him some of what was going on in Tennessee—not all of it, because Moses tends to worry, though he'll never admit it.

"Well, you best be careful down there, Cat. You on foreign territory, girl, and it don't sound too hospitable to me."

I hung up, thinking the same thing. Looking back on the conversation twenty-four hours later, I would see how indiscreet I'd been. But that night, I was still naive enough to think that wiretapping was something that only happened to other people's phones.

"Where did you put Red's statement?" I asked Louella.

She held it up. "What do you think I should do with it, Cat?"

"I don't suppose Billie has a copying machine."

"This ain't the Hyatt, so you suppose right," Billie said, only "Hyatt" sounded like *Height*. "Nor no fax machine nor no whirlpool, neither."

"So what we need is a good hiding place." I looked around, at a loss. "Hey, Billie, what about a box of tampons or sanitary pads—you got one of those?"

"I reckon I got a box of Kotex around here."

She went and got it, and we folded up Red's statement longways and stashed it in the middle of the pile of sanitary pads.

"We're safe, as long as they only send men to search us," I said.

"That's where I used to hide my mad money." Billie nodded. "My husband didn't never think to look in there."

She told us to call Emery at the front desk right away if we heard any prowlers during the night, and promised to load up her shotgun. She also told us that staying in Rooms 10 and 12 were two truckers, regular customers, who could crush a semi between them, and we could count on them for reinforcements.

When I went to bed, I considered putting my Diane under the pillow, but I was afraid I'd go to turn over and blow my brains out, so I put it on the nightstand instead.

But what woke us up in the middle of the night wasn't a prowler, as it turned out. It was the telephone.

"Miz Caliban? I'm real sorry to disturb you. This is Em'ry, at the front desk? The police just called to tell Miz Simmons that her uncle's house was burning."

Eleven

"Mmmph" was Louella's response when I tried to pass on the information. She didn't even open her eyes. She had a head full of those plastic hair rollers the color of Pepto-Bismol and those little plastic pins sticking out like antennae. She looked like a cartoon caterpillar.

I decided there wasn't any point in waking her up enough to get a more articulate response out of her. I wasn't going anywhere. This whole thing could be a diversionary tactic to get us out of the room so somebody could search it—somebody who'd seen us leaving Red's house with our bags.

I put in a call to the Cayter police just to confirm that they were the ones who had telephoned. The man on the other end went away for about five minutes, then returned to confirm that there was a house burning "out that way." They thought it was the McIntyre house, and the Millins County Sheriff's Department had probably called.

"It's hard to keep kids out of these abandoned houses," he volunteered.

Bullshit, I thought. We're not talking about the local haunted house, with boarded-up windows and creaky stairs. We're not talking about a crack house, assuming there are such things in rural Tennessee. We're talking about a shipshape twentieth-century frame house left empty for less time than most folks spend on vacation.

I got up, turned on the desk lamp, and contemplated our security system, which was nonexistent. If I'd had a nice, sturdy chair, I could have propped it under the doorknob. What I had was two armchairs on casters. So I turned on the television instead, with the volume cranked down. I climbed back in bed. Louella snored through the whole business.

I slept maybe two hours total, and woke cranky from bad dreams. I heard a noise, and started awake like you do when one of the cats is throwing up. I had the gun in my hand before I realized it was Louella.

"What time is it?" I asked.

"It's pretty late, Cat," she said. She already had her makeup on. "It's past eight."

Now I was really cranky.

"Want me to get you some coffee from the office?" she asked.

"No, Louella, I don't want you to get me some coffee from the office. Coffee would wake me up, and I don't want to be awake. I want to be sound asleep."

"Well, I *tried* to be quiet," she said huffily. "I can't help it if I dropped my pocketbook."

"It sounded like you dropped the Chrysler Building on a junkyard the size of New Jersey."

I sighed, sat up in bed, and rubbed my face to get the circulation going.

"Say, Cat," Louella said. "I had the funniest dream. You were telling me something about Uncle Red's house burning. It was just as real!"

"It *was* real," I grumbled. "Somebody called last night to tell us."

"Who called us?" I had to hand it to Louella. She was learning to ask the right question. Not when, or how, but who.

"The Cayter police thinks it might have been the county sheriff, but they didn't seem to know for sure." I focused in on her, sitting perched on the edge of her neatly made bed. "Louella, why in hell would anybody in their right mind wear a polyester pantsuit when it's ninety degrees out? And why did you make your bed?"

"Well, I don't want Billie to come in and see it messy. Just 'cause we're in a motel is no reason to live like slobs. And I reckoned I'd better dress up some 'cause we're meeting with that minister."

"Are those pantyhose on your feet?" I asked, incredulous. "Do you mean to sit there and tell me you're wearing plastic *under* the plastic pantsuit?"

"They're just knee-highs, Cat," she said, offended.

"I'm wearing shorts," I muttered. "I'd wear a bikini if I thought I could get away with it."

So I went for my Lana Turner look—shorts and a sleeveless top that I tied up under my boobs. Young people think they've got everything going for them, but lots of women my age have plenty to show up front if they can pull it up far enough.

"Okay," I said. "We take the Kotex box with us, along with some of the bags of clothes just for authenticity. We still need some kind of security system." I went into the bathroom and brought out a container of baby powder. I shook some out onto my hands, and then rubbed them together in front of the window.

"You're getting that stuff all over Billie's chairs!" Louella complained.

"That's the idea," I said. "And then we tell Billie to make sure the maid skips this room. That way, if we have any visitors, we'll know."

We stopped in at the office, and told Billie not to let anyone into our room. She gave us a conspiratorial wink, and showed us the shotgun she had stowed under the counter.

"Now, y'all be careful, hear?"

We stopped first at a convenience store, extracted Red's statement from the Kotex box, and made five copies. Three of them we stuck in envelopes addressed to ourselves and to Moses, and dropped them into the first mailbox we spotted. The original we returned to the Kotex box. A fourth we stashed in the bottom of one of the bags of clothes. And a fifth I slipped into the pocket of Louella's gold jacket.

When we arrived at the scene of the fire, it was pretty depressing. Where yesterday a pretty, neat little house had stood, today there was a pile of blackened rubble, sunk into a hole in the ground. A few dark, twisted skeletons were all that remained of Red's furniture. Below what had once been the kitchen area, the charred hulk of Red's venerable refrigerator stood defiant guard, but I suspected that it had finally stopped running. The air was heavy with the smell of wet ashes; beneath that was the pungent odor of kerosene.

"Goddam it, Cat," Louella said, tears starting to her eyes, "it's not enough they killed him. It's not enough they messed up his house. Now they have to go and burn it down. It's like now they want to destroy every trace of him."

"I guess they figured that if they couldn't find what they were looking for, they'd make sure nobody else could, either."

"I reckon I should be grateful that Red kept as much as he did in his safe deposit box," Louella said, stooping to pick up a charred piece of crochet.

"You know, Lou, the fact that they took the trouble to burn this place down means that they don't think we've found anything," I said.

"Well, we'd better do what we can to encourage that line of thinking, unless we want the B & J to burn down, with us in it."

I heard barking and the jingle of dog tags close by, and turned to see a black Labrador bounding toward us. Louella spotted him, too, and stepped behind me, so that

I took the full brunt of his greeting. I could feel Louella's hands on my back as she tried to avoid the line of fire.

"I've heard of hit men before," she gasped, "but hit dogs?"

I was getting a face full of tongue when the dog's elderly owner caught up to him.

"Down, Sissy! Down, girl! Folks don't appreciate it when you do 'em thataway, you silly old monster." He emphasized his point by seizing Sissy's collar and yanking on it. She subsided with a satisfied bark, and stood, happily wagging her tail. "There! That's Daddy's sweet girl."

"My!" I said. "What a big girl you are, Sissy!"

"She's big, but she still thinks she's a puppy." He scratched her ears fondly. "Miz Simmons, I don't know if you remember me. I'm Emmett Cassidy, Red's neighbor."

"Oh, sure, Mr. Cassidy, I remember you," Louella said. "This is my friend, Cat Caliban. How are you and Dottie getting along?"

"Well, to tell you the truth, Miz Simmons, we're pretty upset about what-all's been goin' on around here. First, Red gets killed in that accident, and now this. I told Dot, I said, whyn't you drive up to Clarksville and spend a few days with Gracie and Tom? She don't like to leave me alone, but hell, I got my twenty-two. Ain't nobody gonna burn *us* out if I got anything to say about it.

"But that ain't your problem, Miz Simmons. I come over to tell you we're real sorry about Red, and all this other business here, and if there's anything we can do, why, we'll do it."

"Can you tell us what happened last night, Mr. Cassidy?" I asked.

"Well, like I told the deputy, the dogs woke me up about two o'clock, and I got up and looked out the winder, but I couldn't see nothin', so I went back to bed. Then, it wasn't an hour later when I woke up again on account of the smoke. Dot, she smelled it, too, and it woke her up, and she said, 'Lord, Emmett, the house is on fire!' And I went to see, but then I heard the sirens and looked out the winder again, and I told Dot, 'It ain't us. It's Red's place.' So I telephoned the Fire Department and got dressed and come over to see if I could help, but the place was mostly gone by the time the fire truck showed up. I stayed around a while, talkin' to the deputies and firemen. I told 'em about how the dogs was barkin', but the deputies didn't seem too interested. They said it was likely kids. But we don't have that many kids around here.

"Anyways, the firemen knowed it was an empty house, so they wasn't tryin' to get inside. I'm sorry about all your uncle's things, Louella, but they wasn't much they could do. Well, I went home around four-thirty, and the fire was out, but the ashes was still a-smolderin' and all, so nobody had went into the house. It was still dark then. I didn't hear nothin' about the body till this mornin', when Garner up the road called me."

"The body?" we chorused. We stared at him.

His brow creased. "Oh, Lord, didn't y'all know nothin' about it?"

"We haven't talked to the police yet this morning," I said faintly.

"They was a body inside," he said solemnly. "Some poor soul went and got burned up in your uncle's house last night, and if anybody wants my opinion for free, he didn't go in there by hisself."

Twelve

As it turned out, Emmett Cassidy didn't have much to add to his astonishing announcement. When asked why he thought that the dead man found in Red's house hadn't arrived there by himself, he could only tell us that he "had a feelin' " about it. Not that I discounted Emmett's feelings, I didn't; often, people's feelings and impressions are grounded in evidence they aren't conscious of having received. But for more information he sent us up the road to talk to Garner and Clara Wells, who had spotted the body in the ruins.

Sissy raced us down the driveway, and then arrived at the Wellses' before we did. She was rolling around in the grass with a golden retriever and some kind of German shepherd mix by the time we cut the engine.

Clara Wells was a pretty woman in her fifties, with dramatic white streaks in her dark brown hair. She told us that Garner was running errands, and invited us in. Her apron told us that she was in the middle of something, so we sat in the kitchen and watched her roll out pie dough. All in all, she looked downright placid for a woman who'd discovered a corpse not three hours before. Plus, she looked cool for a woman who was working so hard in the summer heat.

"We heard the commotion last night, of course, so Garner, he got dressed and walked over. He came back in about half an hour, and said there wasn't much he could do, that Red's place looked to be burning to the ground. So first thing this morning, we walked over to see, and took Rosie and Goldie with us." She had the dough in her hands, and was pressing it into a ball with the practiced hands of a brain surgeon.

"Well, as soon as we came close, Rosie took to barking, and then Goldie did, but then they were more whining than barking. I went to see what they were looking at, because I wanted to keep them away from the hot ashes, you know. And I saw something poking up out of the rubble—something black and, I don't know, strange. And I stood there and looked at it and I said to the dogs, 'Why, it's somebody's legs sticking up. There's somebody down in there.' You couldn't see because of the roof falling down and the walls and all and covering everything. But you could see these knees sticking up. I mean, you could tell this person wasn't alive, because it was all bone." She had thrown some flour around on the kitchen table, smoothed it across, and slapped her dough down.

"So I called Garner over, and he took one look and said we'd better go call somebody, and I came home to call, and he stayed till the Sheriff's Department arrived. And I went back, and the Fire Department came out again, too, because they had to cool things down some more before they could get to it—the body, I mean. It's a volunteer fire department out here, you see; that's why they didn't stay there the whole time. It was kind of interesting, really, to watch them work, because they had to be careful not to disturb the body." Having rolled out her circle, she paused in her account to fold the dough over her rolling pin, slip it over the pie plate, and unfold it.

"They took a whole bunch of pictures, and then they lifted it up real carefully, and put it in this black bag like you store coats in, and zipped it up. And I remembered I had my pies to bake for our church supper tonight, so I came on home."

"Could you tell anything about who it might be?" Louella asked, clearly awestruck.

"You couldn't tell much of anything," Clara said, trimming her crust, and then folding the edge under. "It was burned pretty badly. It looked all scrunched up, with those knees sticking up and the arms bent at the elbows and the hands clenched, and the skull grinning up at you."

"A man?" I prompted.

"You couldn't even tell that," she said, pinching the edges of her crust. "It looked kind of small for a man, so I guess it could have been a woman, though I really never thought of that."

"And the sheriff's deputies didn't say who it might be?"

"Not while I was there. I think they found a wedding ring, though, so maybe they can tell from that. I hope to gracious it isn't somebody I know, but then, it's bound to be somebody that somebody knows, isn't it?"

We agreed with that, and silently hoped that it was nobody we knew, either, or nobody that we were hoping to meet. We decided to drop in on the county Sheriff's Department, where, you might say, we were greeted with open arms.

"I've been looking all over town for you two," said a burly gray-haired deputy. He looked at us as if we were a couple of high-school truants who had knocked off a liquor store in Nashville and stolen a car for the sole purpose of wreaking mayhem on Millins County.

"We've been looking for you, too," I said, matching his look and tone of voice. The best defense is a good offense. I helped myself to a wooden chair, and glanced around his office as if I were casing the joint. My attitude made Louella nervous, and she went into her Southern belle routine.

"Deputy, I am Mrs. Simmons, Mr. McIntyre's niece, and this is my good friend, Mrs. Caliban. I'm so pleased to meet you." She seized his hand and shook it. "I have always so enjoyed my visits to Millins County. I just wish I could be here now under brighter circumstances."

The deputy looked a little punch-drunk. He stared at his captured hand in consternation. Good granny, bad granny—take it from me, it works every time on cops.

"We'd be interested in the preliminary results of your arson investigation," I said. "Louella, give the man his hand back and sit down."

"Nobody's said it was arson, Mrs.—uh, Calloway." As soon as Louella's grip loosened, he jerked his hand away, then looked embarrassed. Unfortunately, like most people, embarrassment made him crabbier. "What makes you say it was?"

"Christ! The whole place stinks of kerosene," I said. "You don't have to be a fucking bloodhound to notice the fumes. But, then again, it may just have been the kerosene can where the living room used to be that tipped me off."

He sat heavily in one of those old-fashioned wooden swivel chairs, and it groaned. "The whole house collapsed into the basement, Mrs. Calloway. That's what houses do when they burn: they collapse. For all we know, that can might have been stored in the basement. We don't even know at this point what it had in it."

What is it about me that brings out this patronizing attitude in cops? I swear, this guy attended the same law enforcement academy as my old pal from the Cincinnati PD, Sergeant Fricke.

"For all *you* know it could've been stored in the basement, that's true," I said.

"Now, Cat." Louella cut me off and smiled at Deputy Dawg apologetically. I'd gotten up on the wrong side of the bed, her look said. Mine said there was nothing wrong with the side I'd gotten up on; it was the hour I'd gotten up that had soured my normally sweet disposition.

"Well, he started it," I grumbled.

"As a matter of fact, Mrs. Simmons," the deputy said, pointedly ignoring me, "we do think the fire was set. We have a few—well, groups of teenagers around here that like to get into mischief."

"Jesus H. Christ on a raft!" I exploded. "I thought this area was a retirement center, not Tennessee's answer to South Central Los Angeles. If you're going to make up something, you could at least make it plausible. Why not a chapter of retired Hell's Angels? Or retired cult members? Why not a band of geriatric satanists? *That* I'd believe—maybe. Meanwhile, you dug a body out of the ruins. I'd say your young people in Millins County must have one hell of an initiation ritual."

"We don't have an identification on the body yet, Mrs. Simmons," he said to Louella, again ignoring me. "That was one of the reasons we wanted to contact you, on the off chance that you might know who this individual was. Was there anybody staying at your uncle's house?"

"No."

"Nobody who might have come to town for the funeral and stayed there?"

Louella shook her head.

"We found a wedding ring that we think the deceased was wearing. Inside are the initials BGM and WJO and the date June 10, 1940. Does that mean anything to you?"

I'd written the initials down on the back of a deposit slip, and we both stared at them a minute.

"Gosh, Cat, do you think W—?" Louella began.

"No, Louella." I stepped on her line. "I don't think we know anybody with those initials."

"That's too bad," he said, narrowing his eyes at me. "Can I ask, for the record, where you two ladies were last night between, say, midnight and four A.M.?"

"We were bar-hopping," I said, "in downtown Cayter."

"We were asleep," Louella said, giving me a reproachful look, "at the B & J Motor Court."

"Oh, that's right." I slapped my forehead. "The barhopping was a dream I had."

"Fine," he said, writing.

"Are you trying to tell me that you're not the person who called in the middle of the night to wake us up and inform us of a disaster in progress that we couldn't do anything about?" I asked him.

"No, that wasn't me," he said. The little smile he was trying to hide said he wished it had been. "Might've been one of the boys, though."

Then he and Louella had a friendly chat about salvage and insurance while I caught forty winks in my chair. Louella roused me in time to catch the name he was giving her: Jasper Treat. She was writing it down.

"Shake hands, Cat," she said. And I did.

"Now what was that all about?" she asked as soon as we hit the sidewalk. "Are we not telling the police about Red's letter? That's withholding evidence, Cat."

"Look, don't you remember what Billie said about honest cops? You can't trust that guy."

"I thought he seemed real sincere," she said.

"Sincere my ass," I said. "What was his name? Jasper Treat?"

She nodded.

"Well, listen up, Lou. We don't know ol' Jasper well enough yet to ask him if he owns an RV and a cabin cruiser and a retirement condo in Miami Beach, and until we do, we're not telling him anything we don't have to. Anyway, sooner or later, he's bound to find out about Wade Oakley."

"If that's who 'WO' is."

"Who the hell do you think it was? Wawrence Owivier? Wyan O'Neal?"

"Wayne O'Newton?" she chimed in. "Wayne O'Gretzky? William O'Buckley?"

"Wishful thinking on that last one," I said. "God, it's hot."

"I don't know," she said. "Feels cooler out here than in there." And then added in her best Tennessee drawl, "Girl, you liked to burn my ears off in there!"

Thirteen

According to Billie's map, we weren't that far from Freeman Quinn's house, located on County Road 2022B, but getting there was another story. We'd been traveling for thirty minutes when we arrived at the same intersection we'd visited twice before. We were driving on a narrow, densely wooded road, with houses occasionally sprouting on both sides. Every road, including the one we were on, was apparently numbered. Some roads had regular names as well, like "Tubbs Road," and these sometimes replaced the numbers on street signs. The more enterprising and foresighted residents of some roads had also added their own last names to the street signs in a series of rough boards that made the signs resemble barn ladders.

"I vote we take 'CR2022' and ignore the 'B' for the moment," I said. "Maybe '2022B' runs off of 2022."

"Yeah," Louella said gloomily, turning onto the road in question. "Or maybe it runs off of 2022A or 2022Q."

County Road 2022 was also called Rymer Cemetery Road, and I was beginning to wonder if the numbers didn't correspond to plot numbers when we came upon 2022B—a short street that did indeed circle an old burial ground about half the size of my cousins' recreational vehicle. At the entrance to the circle stood a basketball hoop, with the cemetery behind it.

"Don't you think that's a mite sacrilegious, Cat?" Louella asked me.

"I don't know," I said. "Maybe it's there to entertain the ghosts."

Freeman Quinn's house was built out over an incline that descended into a creek bed. It was surrounded by trees, including a spectacular mimosa draped over the front walk.

"Say what you want to, Cat, but I think it's creepy to live in a house across the street from a cemetery," Louella whispered as we started up the walk.

"Yeah, well I say you'd have quieter neighbors than we've got in Northside."

Freeman Quinn was built like a Cincinnati bus kiosk: big and sturdy. He was a handsome man with a tanned face that he couldn't have gotten from hanging out in his heavily wooded backyard. Freeman looked much younger than Red's seventy years, yet he must have belonged to the same generation, give or take a few years. He was showing a little gray at the temples, and laugh creases around his gray eyes.

He gave Louella a fierce hug that made her start crying again. Then he cried a little, too, and so did I, and so did the young woman across the room, who looked a little like Pippi Longstocking in coveralls, T-shirt, and Birkies. I figured her for some poor relation.

She'd been sitting on the couch in Freeman Quinn's early American living room, all autumn-toned skirted up-holstered chairs and couch and a bronze eagle over the fireplace. A ceiling fan stirred up the tepid air a little, so when I first caught a movement on the couch, I thought the fan was blowing the crocheted coverlet. Then I took a closer look, and discovered a lump the size of a loaf of bread that turned out to be a baby. Its cute little baby butt was sticking up as it wiggled its head and hiccupped.

Freeman Quinn introduced them as Poppy MacDougal and her daughter Ruth.

"*Reverend* MacDougal?" Louella's jaw hit the floor like a runaway elevator in a disaster movie. I couldn't blame her. I mean, if we had asked you on an etiquette quiz, "Which one of these women is dressed appropriately to meet a minister?" how many of you would have picked me over Louella?

We shook hands with Reverend You-Can-Call-Me-Poppy MacDougal.

"So you were Red's minister?" Louella ventured, giving Ruth a wide berth and sitting in an armchair. I sat on the other end of the sofa, putting enough distance between me and the baby so that nobody would mistake me for the grandmotherly type.

"That old reprobate?" Poppy made a face. "Hardly. Red was never a sheep that took much to shepherding. He didn't want to be part of anybody's flock." She had some kind of a Southern accent, though slight, but I couldn't tell whether it was Tennessean or not. "Red and me, we were pals. Freeman introduced us, and somehow, we took to each other. We went fishing a few times. But mostly, I'd just turn up at his house every now and again, or he'd turn up at mine, and we'd drink beer and talk. I'm still pretty mad at him, if you want to know the truth. He always promised he wouldn't up and die on me before I got the chance to show him the error of his ways."

She swiped at the corner of one eye with the palm of her hand. "Not that I'm worried about him. The Lord knows the difference between bad and ornery. But we miss him, me and my husband, Mike—and Ruthie too."

Freeman reached over and patted her knee. "You know Red wouldn't want us to sit around here and mope. Hell, he'd be wanting us to tell stories on him and laugh."

"We kind of got out of the laughing mood, Mr. Quinn," I said. "We went over to see what was left of Red's house this morning."

"Call me Freeman, Cat. Yeah, I know. Hunt heard it on the radio, and called me up with ants in his pants."

"So he told you about Wade Oakley?" Louella asked. Me, I like to think I would have introduced the subject more tactfully, but maybe not; one reason I've got such a big mouth is to accommodate my foot.

"What about Wade?" Freeman spoke sharply.

Belatedly, Louella turned to me. "You tell him, Cat."

"They found a body in the ruins, Freeman," I said. "We think, from the wedding ring, it might have been Wade Oakley."

He was already shaking his head. "Wade's up in Seattle. It must be some kind of mix-up."

"The inscription inside the wedding ring said 'BGM and WJO, June 10, 1940,' " I said gently. "Does that sound like Wade?"

"Yeah," he said slowly. "Bertha Grace Mattson and Wade James Oakley. They got married just before he shipped out. But what the hell was Wade doing down here? And if he was coming down, why didn't he call me and let me know? It don't make no kind of sense."

"We'd like to know that, too," Louella said. "And who killed him and Red."

Freeman looked at her, surprised. As a matter of fact, he was the only person in the room who looked surprised. Even Poppy didn't look surprised. Ruthie looked asleep.

"What makes you think somebody killed him?" Freeman asked. "Is that what the police said?"

"It's TVA Public Safety," I said. "They think he drove off the side of the dam."

"We think somebody sideswiped him," Louella said, "and then he drove off the side of the dam."

"Maybe," Freeman conceded. "Hell, probably. But we'll never prove it."

"Why do you say 'probably'?" I asked. "You think he was murdered? How come?"

To tell you the truth, I didn't like the way the conversation was going. Louella hadn't yet learned the golden rule of homicide investigation: suspect everybody. She wanted to share all our secrets with damn near everybody we met. I could see that I was going to have to take her aside and explain the difference between detective work and a game of Gossip. After all, in my short career as a detective, I'd already met one teary-eyed killer who'd bumped off a friend or two.

Poppy's head was swiveling back and forth like that of a tennis-match extra in *Strangers on a Train*—a little cinematic reminder, by the by, that polite, affectionate people like Hitchcock's killer, Bruno, can be just as deadly as Dirty Harry, and often with less reason.

Meanwhile, Freeman had stood up and started pacing.

"There's a lot going on around here that you don't know about," he said. "And I'm not sure Red would have wanted you to know about it, Lou."

"In that case, we've already violated his wishes," said my motor-mouthed sidekick. "We know a lot."

He stopped at that, startled.

"Like all about the burial of those toxic waste drums at the landfill that you and Red witnessed," she continued. "And if he didn't want me to know, he wouldn't have left instructions in his will to help me find his statement about that."

"Red left a statement?" he asked.

"Maybe we shouldn't hold up Reverend Poppy here to discuss all this," I put in. "Maybe we should be talking about the funeral."

"Hell, I'd have a better time at Red's funeral if I thought I could nail the bastards that killed him!" Freeman exclaimed.

"So would I," Poppy said. So much for turning the other cheek. "Besides, I know all about the Chem-Tech incident. After all, I was Red's spiritual adviser." She said this last with a hint of a smile.

"Did you know," Louella began, "that he was coming to Cincinnati to talk to someone from—?"

"Hey, time out!" I said, signaling as I jumped to my feet. The baby's eyes popped open, and she made a noise almost as loud as mine, and probably almost, from her perspective, as obnoxious.

"Cat's right," Freeman said. "This is getting pretty dang confusing." He heaved a sigh. "Okay. Here's what let's do. Me and Poppy'll tell what we know, and then y'all tell what you know."

"Yeah, we don't even know for sure that it was Wade Oakley's body they found," I said. "Somebody could've planted that ring on whoever it was."

"Well, I have to deal with a stinky baby in the immediate future, or we'll all succumb to air pollution," Poppy put in. "Freeman, why don't you get us a beer or something so we can talk better?"

Ruthie made a dignified exit, winking at us over her mother's shoulder. Freeman took drink orders, and disappeared. I was so happy to be in a little corner of Millins County that wasn't dry I nearly wept with gratitude.

Instead, I said quietly to Louella, "Loose lips sink ships."

"What are you talking about, Cat?" she said, indignantly.

"You don't have to tell everything you know, Lou."

She let a little puff of air slip past her vocal chords. "I'll have you know that *Uncle* Freeman is practically family. He probably changed my diapers when I was Ruthie's age."

"Most homicides are committed by members of the family," I muttered.

"Well, fine," she said, folding her arms. "If you want it to be just me and you, sitting by our lonesomes, when the killers come out of the woods with their gasoline cans and torches, fine. I won't say another word."

She had a point there.

"If you think Mel's beginning self-defense lessons and your little Wilkinson Diane are all we need to take on a ruthless gang of murderers who think nothing of killing off a whole county, much less knocking off a couple of little old gray-haired ladies, fine. My lips are sealed."

"I like to count Billie's shotgun," I said crossly.

"Oh, right. But if you think we can shoot our way out of an ambush with a .25 caliber purse-size handgun, backed up by a shotgun bigger'n the person who's going to use it, fine. If you think our Lucille Ball and Vivian Vance imitations will stop our enemies in their tracks, fine. I will be silent unto death, which I very much suspect is right around the corner."

"Okay, okay!" I sighed. "Point taken. I'm just saying that in general, you know, you could stand to use a little more discretion."

She was freezing me with a glare when Freeman arrived with my first alcoholic beverage in thirty-six hours. Hell, he'd saved my life already.

Fourteen

"Here we are again, fresh as a daisy!" Poppy chirped, patting Ruthie.

There was some kind of commotion coming from the kitchen, composed of barking, scrabbling noises, and some general crashing around. Then a run of staccato clicks, and the Hound of the Baskervilles was upon us. I got a face full of hair and a nose full of a sour, doggy smell. When I disengaged a tongue from my ear and pulled back, I was nose to nose with a canine bigger than Emmett Cassidy's Sissy and harder to describe, a great melting pot of a dog with paws as big as industrial-size ladles and liquid brown eyes the size of rutabagas.

"Why, that's Uncle Red's dog!" Louella cried. "I'd know him anywhere!"

"Really?" I gasped, using both hands to pry a paw off of my windpipe. "How can you be so sure?"

"Yeah, that's old Junior," Freeman conceded from the doorway. "Red made me take him here about a month back. He's been kinda lonesome ever since, so when he heard y'all, he was real excited. I hope you like dogs," he said to me.

I liked dogs—in moderation. What we had here was not a moderate dog.

"Junior! Here, Juney! Here, boy!" Louella called him.

Juney? It sounded like the kindergarten name for a future linebacker-turned-bodyguard.

He jumped down and bounded toward Louella. I felt like the Volunteer Dam had just been lifted off my chest.

"Y'all hungry?" Freeman asked. "I got some lunch

meat I can put out if you want to come on in the dining room."

We sat down at a cherry-wood table, and I noticed that the colors in the braided rug matched the wallpaper and the ruffled curtains pulled back over folding shutters. I also noticed that Junior was tall enough sitting down to be within striking range of the bologna. Every time he licked his chops, I got a shower.

"Are you a widower, Freeman?" I asked.

"Yes, I lost my wife to cancer about five years back. 'Course, now, I can't help but wonder if those damn chemicals got her. But back then, I wasn't thinking about that."

"The cancer rate is really high here in Millins County," Poppy explained. "Three times the national average."

"So we've been told," I said. "Freeman, what can you tell us about this alleged cover-up of Chem-Tech's disposal of hazardous chemicals?"

"Ain't no alleging about it," he said. "We was all there: me, Hunt, Red, Wade, and Pat. George, he told us he had a special job for us to do later on that night. He'd pay us overtime, he said. Well, we didn't think nothing of it. When we seen what it was, we knew why he was doing it at night when there wasn't nobody around to see, but hell, we didn't care, so long's we got paid. We'd all been workin' there a while, you see, and we'd got kind of used to seein' things done that wasn't quite legal or straight. But we kind of figured the gov'ment regulators for a bunch of muddle-headed bureaucrats who earned a living off of making our jobs harder and thinking up new things to worry over. We thought the EPA was full of sissy scientists who was afraid to breathe.

"Even so, I reckon we was impressed with the amount of chemicals we had to bury that night. Three thousand drums is a lot of chemicals to make disappear into thin air. They brung 'em in on the railroad cars, you see, which they had parked off on the siding. Closed cars, they was, so nobody could see what was in 'em. We had to unload them drums off the cars, and move 'em maybe forty yards to where we'd dug a pit with the 'dozer. Even in the flood-lights we could see they was leakin', some of 'em. And even though we was wearin' gloves and all, Wade, he came away with a bad burn on his arm. And when we was finished, George, he took and paid us off so there wouldn't be no record on our time sheets, and told us not to tell anybody what we'd done.

"Well, that was October of 1977. I recollect that it was one of the wettest Octobers on record. Ever' now and then, somebody would be passing comment on the rain, and we'd kind of look at each other, and you could always tell what the other man was thinkin': *I wonder what's happening to the chemicals in them drums.*

"But, like I say, people didn't think so much in those days about toxic chemicals and all. Ever' now and then, why, you'd hear some rumor in the plant about how ever'body who was cleaning trucks was sick, or ever'body who was workin' on incinerator number one on such-and-such a day was sick, but you didn't really think it was dif-ferent from any other job. I can't even tell you now when things started to change. Pat, he said it was Dr. Barks and Dr. Cranch who got the ball rolling, but I just don't re-member."

"Who were they?" I interrupted. I dropped my sandwich and turned around to reach for my purse to dig out a pen and notepad. When I looked at my plate again, my sand-wich was gone. Nobody else seemed to have noticed. I frowned at Junior, who I'd swear looked smug, and made another sandwich.

"Dr. Barks was a veterinarian. That wasn't her real name, it was—let me see—Barksdell. She moved to Cayter in the late seventies. I b'lieve she had a degree from Ohio State. Well, she said she was seein' too many tumors in the cats and dogs of Millins County. Said there wasn't no good reason why the incidence of cancer should be so high here. But she was real suspicious, she said, about all those chemical plants and that incinerator. Animals are close to the ground, she said, and anything that's affectin' them will eventually affect us, only it shows up faster in them because they're smaller and more vulnerable. Unfortunately, she died in a car accident back in 1981."

"A car accident?" Louella echoed.

"Yes. There was rumors she'd been drinkin'. Now Pat, he said he didn't think it was an accident, and I hate to admit it, but I thought Pat was, well, overreacting. But now, I just don't know."

"And the other doctor you mentioned?" I asked.

"Dr. Cranch. He was a pediatrician. Him and Dr. Barks knew each other, and the way I hear it, she got him started thinkin' about cancer rates. Well, he started lookin' into the incidence of leukemia and some other things, and he took to talkin' to people about how maybe Dr. Barks was right."

"Is he still alive?" I asked eagerly.

"He's alive," Freeman admitted, "but you won't get much out of him."

"He's in a nursing home," Poppy explained. "His mental health seems to have declined rather quickly in the early eighties, and he was forced to retire. He was only fifty-seven at the time. That made it easy to dismiss what he was saying. People said, 'That poor man has Alzheimer's. He doesn't know what he's saying.' "

"Is there any way somebody could have induced Alzheimer's?" I asked.

"Nobody really knows the answer to that, Cat," Poppy replied. "I mean, a lot of these chemicals we're talking about can affect the brain. We may be a retirement center here in Millins County, but I'll bet dollars to doughnuts we've got more than our share of Alzheimer's diagnoses. And not everybody that's got it is old, either. So we don't really know whether what we're seeing is Alzheimer's or something else caused by the chemicals. Whether or not anybody could arrange to expose somebody to those chemicals to get them out of the way—well, we don't know that, either."

"Okay, go on," I said to Freeman. By this time, ol' Junior was kind of leaning up against my shoulder, eyeing my sandwich and drooling on my bare arm.

"Well, in the last two years, some local folks started organizin' against the incinerator and the chemical companies. That Healthwatch group was formed, and they called in those Green people."

"Green people?" Louella and I echoed in unison.

"He means Greenpeace," Poppy said. "They sent down somebody to help the local group get started up—you know, give them advice about how to do it."

"Yeah—the whale people," Freeman said. "You know who we mean?" Louella and I nodded.

"Well, dang, I always thought those folks was loonier'n a skunk on moonshine—the way they go out there in those rubber boats and cut tuna nets and interfere with people tryin' to make their livin'. I saw 'em as some kind of radicals, gettin' in the navy's way and all. But after what they done for us around here—well, I reckon you got to be a little crazy to take on the rich and powerful like they do. Not that I paid much attention at first. I didn't much believe the accusations that this Healthwatch group was puttin' out. Thought they was a bunch of whiners. We all did—I mean, me and Red and Pat and Hunt and Wade."

"What changed your mind?" I asked. Junior's head on my shoulder was like having a sandbag parked there.

Whatever gave him the idea that I liked dogs? I hadn't even offered to shake hands.

"It was Pat Kinneady who changed. He'd lost a daughter to breast cancer in 1980. Then last fall, he found out his grandson had leukemia. They lived in New Union, on a road not half a mile from the Chem-Tech landfill. Well, sir, he was so upset he couldn't hardly eat nor sleep for worrying about that boy and turnin' things over in his mind. He went to some meetin's of the Healthwatch group, and he brung me some literature to read. 'Freeman,' he says to me, 'I was blind but now I see. Them bastards is a-poisonin' the whole damn county and beyond, and we was part of it. We probably both of us got cancer growin' in us right this minute from what we handled, and I don't know but what we helped to kill my daughter and make my grandson sick.'

" 'So what are you aimin' to do?' I asked him, seein' as how he was still workin' at Chem-Tech at the time. I had gone to work somewhere else, and then retired. 'Well,' he said, 'it appears like I can do some good by stayin' put, and a-spyin' on the company for those activists. Hell, I'm fixin' to be an activist myself, only undercover-like.' 'Ain't that dangerous?' I asked him. 'Hell, yes!' he said. 'So's livin' in Millins County.' "

"What can you tell me about his death?" I asked.

"Not much," he conceded. "He was livin' by hisself in a house he'd rented. He didn't have a telephone, and I stopped by—it was on a Tuesday in March—to see if he wanted to play poker on Thursday night. I found him a-layin' there, on the kitchen floor. 'Pears he'd been dead maybe twenty-four hours—that's what the coroner said." Here Freeman's voice wavered, and he stopped a minute.

"The place stank of whiskey and vomit. There were two empty Jack Daniels bottles on the counter, and one layin' on its side on the table, spillin' whiskey on the floor."

"How long was this after he'd talked to you about going undercover at Chem-Tech?"

"Oh, I reckon two, three months maybe."

"Did you ever see the autopsy report?"

"Yes, I did. The fam'ly got a copy from the coroner's office, or whatever you call that place, and his daughter Colleen showed it to me."

"What did it say?" Louella asked.

"It said he died from alcohol poisoning. I don't recollect all the scientific words, but they said he drank enough to go into convulsions and die."

"Was he a heavy drinker?" I wanted to know.

"Sometimes," Freeman conceded, "when he was feelin' low. But he was mostly a beer drinker. I never saw him drink whiskey like that. And he wasn't feelin' low at the time, Cat. Hell, he was out for blood, and he was happier'n a bird dog at a turkey shoot. There wasn't nothin' the matter with his spirits."

Freeman leaned forward and planted a forefinger on the table for emphasis. "But what I say, officially, unofficially, or any which way you like, is that Pat Kinneady found out for himself just how dangerous it is to stir things up in Millins County, Tennessee."

Fifteen

"Just what was it Red had in mind, Freeman, when he decided to do something about Pat Kinneady's death?" I asked.

"Well, he wasn't sure at first. It wasn't like he wanted to catch the bastards who killed Pat, exactly. I reckon he would've took that if he could get it, but he didn't figure he would. No, Red wanted what Pat and those Health-watch folks wanted—to close down Chem-Tech and clean up Millins County. He wouldn't say no to a jail term for Isaiah Grubbs, but what he said was, 'We'll cross that bridge when we come to it.'

"Trouble was, you couldn't get nobody interested in our situation down here. That Healthwatch group had already tried. The local papers and television stations wouldn't touch it. The regional EPA office in Atlanta, hell, they'd issued a truckload of citations against Chem-Tech for violatin' this and violatin' that, but they never followed up or canceled any permits or nothing like that. The local law enforcement don't care if Chem-Tech wants to set off an atom bomb over Tennessee. And the state police don't care because the gov'nor is in Isaiah Grubbs's hip pocket. That's how come Red reckoned he had to go outside the state, maybe outside the region."

"You mean, to the national media?" I asked.

"It might've come to that," Freeman agreed. "He wasn't thinkin' of that at first, just talkin' to the Healthwatch folks to see what they'd tried."

"Did he tell them about the buried drums?" Louella asked.

Freeman took a pipe out of his pocket. "Mind if I

smoke?" He unwrapped his tobacco pouch, methodically stuffed his pipe with tobacco, and lit it. It gave off a sweet smell.

"No, he didn't tell the Healthwatch folks about the buried drums. He wanted to, but it wasn't only his secret, you see; it was me and Hunt's and Wade's, too. Well, Wade didn't care—he was way out in Seattle. I was gettin' ornery enough so I didn't care, neither. But Hunt— well, he wasn't ready. Besides, much as Red liked those activist folks, he didn't know 'em well enough to trust 'em yet. And he couldn't be sure there wasn't a comp'ny spy in the group."

He paused for a while and studied the pattern in the curtains. Junior had collapsed next to Ruthie's carrier, and both were sound asleep. The ceiling fan rustled the lunch meat and cheese wrappers.

"It was your story, Louella, that got him going. 'Louella says they want to take and build a garbage incinerator in Cincinnati,' he told me. 'What's that got to do with the price of potatoes?' I said. 'A garbage incinerator don't burn hazardous chemicals.' 'The hell it don't!' he said. 'You know what kind of chemicals goes out in the garbage, Freeman, and you know what some unscrupulous bastards will put in that garbage, and you know just as sure as you're a-settin' there, that crap will be in the smoke and ash, and in the air and ground and in the Ohio River quicker than you can say EPA, and they'll have some bastard like Isaiah T. Grubbs runnin' it on contract, with city cops and hired thugs escortin' trucks in in the dead of night that the city don't know a thing about. I got a mind to go up there to Cincinnati and speak at one of those hearings.'

"A week or two later, he says, 'Freeman, they got an EPA office in Cincinnati, too. I've seen it there—acrost from the university. You reckon I'd find somebody there who might take an interest in them buried drums?' 'I don't know,' I told him. 'Can the Cincinnati office do anything about a problem way down in Western Tennessee?' 'Well,' he said, 'the EPA's fed'ral. They ought to take an interest. And maybe them boys won't be on the gov'nor's payroll.' 'Maybe,' I said, 'or maybe they're just on some other gov'nor's payroll.' "

"So he asked me to find somebody he could talk to?" Louella asked.

"That's right. And whoever it was, at least they was willin' to see him. I know he had an appointment before he left."

"And he was planning to tell them about the drums?"

"He was going to see how it went. If he believed he could trust this EPA fellow, why, he might tell him the story and see what he said. He was going to leave Hunt's name out of it. After all, if you wasn't from around here, you wouldn't have any reason to believe that Hunt was involved. And the EPA ought to have the power to go in there and see if the drums are there or not. You wouldn't need to make a court case out of it; all you'd need was a bulldozer and a fed'ral warrant to use it."

"Freeman, who knew where Red was going and why?" I asked.

"Nobody knew. Just Louella and me, that's all."

"He didn't even tell me, because he probably didn't want me to worry." Poppy smiled ruefully.

"Well, and he was right." Freeman nodded. "Worryin' wouldn't have done a thing for him."

"Didn't the Healthwatch people know?"

Freeman shook his head. "Nobody. He was smart enough to keep it to hisself, especially after what happened to Pat."

"Do you think his phone was tapped?"

He shook his head again. "It might've been, but I doubt

he called Louella from the house. He was careful about things like that."

"That's right, Cat," Louella agreed.

"So maybe he was being followed," I observed.

"That's the only thing that I can figure," Freeman said.

"But they wouldn't know where he was going," Poppy protested. "I mean, isn't it just a little too coincidental that they got him on his way out of town to expose them?"

"I see what you mean, but I suppose coincidences happen," I said. "If they knew he'd been talking to Healthwatch, they must have known it was only a matter of time before he'd tell what he knew."

"But how did they know he hadn't told already?" Louella asked.

I sighed. "Maybe it didn't matter, as long as they could—"

"—get rid of all the witnesses," Freeman finished placidly.

"Yes. Unless they knew he hadn't told already."

"Because they had a—a plant in the Healthwatch group!" Louella said excitedly.

The telephone broke in at this dramatic juncture. Freeman put his pipe in his pocket and ambled into the kitchen to answer it. We looked at each other like conspiring terrorists expecting an ATF raid any minute.

Junior had raised his head when the phone rang. Now he favored us with a troubled gaze, one ear cocked toward the kitchen. He got to his feet and followed Freeman.

"Wrong number," Freeman reported, frowning. He looked a few shades paler than when he left the room. "What was we sayin'?"

In the kitchen, Junior howled.

Sixteen

A few hours later, I was the one who was howling.

Junior, for his part, was drooling on my right shoulder, his head stuck out of my car window and his ears flapping in the breeze.

"I don't know what you think we're going to do with him," I wailed. "We don't exactly have a fenced-in backyard."

"Well, it only seemed right, since Freeman asked me," Louella replied. "After all, Uncle Red went to a lot of trouble to keep him out of danger. It's the least we could do."

"Wrong," I said, wiping an ear out of my eyes. "The least we could do was nothing. Poppy would've taken him. Ruthie could've ridden him around the neighborhood."

"I know. But Uncle Red was kin, so that makes Junior my responsibility."

"But he's not mine!"

"Oh, come on, Cat. You're an animal lover from way back. I've never seen you fuss about helping a poor, defenseless animal."

"I specialize in small animals," I muttered. "This one's not small, and he's definitely not defenseless."

Junior planted a paw chummily on my right shoulder and breathed in my face, enveloping me in a hot cloud of garlic and dog biscuit. He had this dopey expression on his face, like he was falling in love with Tammy Wynette, who was singing on the radio.

"What do you reckon that telephone call was about?"

Louella asked, changing the subject. "You know, the one he took before we commenced to planning the funeral?"

I noticed that the more time Louella spent in Tennessee, the more she sounded like a native.

"It wasn't a very long one," I mused. "From the look on his face, I'd say it was something of a shock. Maybe somebody threatened him."

"I thought that, too. And he didn't tell us 'cause he didn't want to scare us. But then he asked us to take Junior, so it's not as if we didn't know he was in danger."

"That's true. So if it was a threat, why wouldn't he tell us? Because the threat was against somebody else? Poppy, maybe, or you?"

"Good heavens! You don't think they'd murder a minister, would they?"

"Come on, Louella! The guys we're dealing with are not the type to take the Ten Commandments too seriously, so why would they stop at killing a preacher?"

"Gosh! I declare it almost makes me wish we were dealing with the Mafia. At least they're Catholic."

I left that one alone. We dropped off Red's suit at the funeral home and drove back to the motel. Billie greeted us from the office door, waving her cigarette.

"All quiet on the western front! Did y'all get the funeral planned?"

"Yes," I said. "Any calls?"

"Just one, from that Mr. Owen at the towin' place. He says the insurance man is done lookin' at the car, and he wants Louella to sign a release so he can sell it. Lord have mercy! What you got there? A dog?"

"He was my uncle's dog," Louella said. "He gave him away for safekeeping, and now my uncle's friend wants us to keep him, on account of he's worried that Red's murderers will come after him."

"Maybe you've got a place—a garage or something—where we could keep him tied up?" I asked hopefully.

"Sugar, you just take him right on in the room!" Billie said to my dismay. "I always say that pets make the best customers—they ain't never goin' to burn the place down nor bust up my furniture nor steal me blind. Cute little thing, ain't he?" She patted his head. "You sure got a lot of kinds of dog in you! What's your name, precious?"

"It's Junior." Louella beamed at her.

I unlocked the door, and grabbed Louella's arm as she pushed forward. Since she was holding Junior at the other end of a leash, he jerked to a stop.

"What?"

"We need to check our security system."

"But Billie said nobody was here."

"Shit, Louella, guys that do this kind of thing for a living are trained to make Billie think nobody was here!"

"What guys?" she asked skeptically.

"Well, that guy, for one," I said, pointing to the outline of a foot in the trail of powder I'd left on the carpet. "And that guy, for another." I pointed to a second print, this one a powdered impression on the dark carpet in front of the television.

Louella looked shaken. "Maybe it's the same guy," she whispered.

"Not unless his feet come in different sizes." I flattened myself on the ground.

"Cat! What are you doing? You're getting all dirty!"

"I don't know," I admitted. "I just know this is what Sherlock Holmes would have done. But I can't tell anything." I shook my head in chagrin. "Maybe he left a cigarette wrapper in the trash can." I got up and stepped cautiously into the room.

"Yeah, or maybe he changed the channel on the television, and we'll find out whether he's an Atlanta Braves fan."

Louella let go of the leash, and my careful preparations came unraveled like a cable-knit sweater as Junior bounded into the room. He circled the room twice, leaving a trail of powdered paw prints, sniffed at the powder trail by the door, and sneezed, obliterating the first footprint.

"Way to go, Juney," I said. "Louella, I think that dog has been bought off."

"Well, I reckon you'll be singing a different tune in the middle of the night when you get another telephone call, or hear noises outside. You'll be glad enough to have a big dog when that happens." She looked around. "What do you think they did in here?"

"Well, they didn't turn the beds down and drop mints on the pillows. So, they probably searched the room. Maybe they even bugged the place. Or tapped the phone."

Louella put her hands on her hips, and stage-whispered, "Well, if they bugged the place, don't you reckon you oughtn't to go around saying maybe they bugged the place?"

She was right, of course.

I motioned her into the bathroom, flushed the toilet, and sat down on top of it.

"Well, at least we know they searched the place. I left a funeral home brochure sticking out of that stack of papers on the desk, and now it's all tucked into the pile."

"Why, Cat, that's so clever! I would've never thought of a thing like that!" She gave me a look of approval, as if I'd redeemed myself for broadcasting our suspicions a minute ago.

"I didn't. It was in a junior detective manual I bought for one of the grandkids."

"Do you think they were looking for that paper—you know, Red's statement?"

"That, or something like it. We don't know for sure that they know for sure that Red's statement exists. But they must be worried at least that he left something. Let's turn on the TV while we search the place, and see if they left anything behind."

"What are we looking for?"

"Hell, Louella, how should I know? Anything that looks like it could be a microphone—or a bomb. If you run across any sticks of dynamite with an alarm clock taped to them, give me a holler, and don't wait for a commercial."

An hour later, we hadn't found anything. Junior followed us around, sticking his nose in everywhere, but since he hadn't been trained to sniff out small electronic devices, he wasn't much help. And since he carried the scent of Freeman's pipe tobacco around with him, not to mention the garlic, baby powder, et cetera, I couldn't even tell if the intruders had been smokers or users of after-shave.

"Maybe we should ask Billie to move us, just in case," Louella proposed.

I agreed. It took another hour to move next door. I took a bath and dreamed of gin while Louella laid out her clothes in the drawers and arranged her cosmetics on the top of the dresser.

Through the door, I heard her ask, "Cat, don't you want me to take some of these things out of your suitcase and hang them up? They're getting awful mussed." I ignored her. Then she spent an hour in the bathroom, and when she came out it looked like one of those Hollywood casbah rooms, only damper, with things draped and hanging all over the place. I could see it now: I'd get up in the middle of the night to use the bathroom and get slapped across the face with wet pantyhose.

We drove to Nashville for a decent meal and a supply of gin. Back at the motel, Louella spent an hour on the phone, doing business in a hushed voice as if she thought our enemies were going to beat her out of a real estate deal in suburban Cincinnati. She clamped the phone to her ear with her shoulder, and did her nails. I watched one of those old Miss Marples on television—the ones with Margaret Rutherford in tweed—and then started *The Yellow Room.*

When it was my turn, I called home, without much hope of raising Delbert. The receiver smelled like a carcinogen. I got the same funny whine on my phone, and dialed upstairs.

"He's around," Mel said vaguely. "Want me to get him for you?"

"That's okay," I said, "as long as he's doing all right. Has he heard from his folks?"

"I think they called yesterday from some Civil War battlefield. He said they were happy to hear about his job with Al. That's about all he said."

"He didn't happen to mention when they were going to come get him?"

"No."

"Well. How's everything? How are the cats?"

"They're fine. You know, they've been sleeping in the garden during the day while it's been so hot. But yesterday one of the Brussels sprouts fell over on Sidney, and now he won't go near the garden. Oh, and we lost one of the zucchini, so your pepper plants aren't nearly so crowded. Al cut the thing open in an attempt to surgically remove the squash borer, but she couldn't save it. How's the case going?"

"Okay," I said, and added, "Not a good idea to talk about it over the phone."

As I was hanging up, she said, "Delbert has a big surprise for you when you get back."

Now what could that be? I wondered. If he'd adopted a large dog, I would ship him back to his parents UPS, C.O.D.

Seventeen

I figured we couldn't do much investigating on Sunday. We went to services at Poppy's church, and Louella made me wear a skirt, but I drew the line at pantyhose. Junior had somehow gotten into the bathroom in the middle of the night and shredded her pantyhose, so we had to stop at the Piggly-Wiggly to get new ones. Louella didn't buy my version of the situation, which was that God had told Junior to destroy those pantyhose because they were instruments of the devil. I drove while she wiggled into the new pair in the back seat, and by the time we reached the church, she was limp with heat exhaustion. She applied fresh lipstick and smiled bravely.

We shook hands with a lot of people who had known Red. They all told us they were sorry, and what they were bringing to the lunch after the funeral.

"He just loved my Hawaiian salad," one woman sobbed. "He just loved it, and now there won't be nobody to appreciate it the way Red done."

I also met Hunt Smith, a slight, nervous man who kept trying to smooth his thinning brown hair over his bald spot. He looked well-scrubbed, but he had that telltale black line under his fingernails that indicated he worked with machinery. His wife, Alma, was a head taller than he was, thin and straight as a poker, with a dark brown dye job and glasses. Alma was bringing the ham; it was the least she could do.

Since I'd already been told that Hunt didn't want to be involved in any investigations, I didn't ask him anything. Besides, I couldn't think of anything to ask. In a way, everything seemed so clear to me. The hard part would be proving what had happened, and Hunt wasn't going to be any help with that. I wanted to ask if he'd received any threats, but I didn't think he'd tell me. He kept scanning the crowd, as if he was afraid of meeting somebody.

After church, we went back to the motel and changed clothes. Then we went out to see the sights.

"This is a tourist area, Cat," Louella had said. "I want to be a tourist."

My enthusiasm for touring was dimmed by the 90-degree heat, but I didn't want to spend the day cooped up in the room with Junior, no matter how many cable channels we could pull off Billie's satellite dish. That morning I'd rigged up a new security system, a couple of threads that would break if anybody entered through the door or window. With Junior in the room, the powder trail ploy was out of the question.

We spent the afternoon taking advantage of the entertainment that Millins County had to offer. We drove go-carts and bumper cars, and Louella showed a vicious streak I'd never seen before. Every place we went was populated by boys between the ages of nine and thirteen. After the first time she got elbowed out of the way by a ten-year-old determined to beat her to the fastest go-cart on the track, she took to elbowing them back. The second time through the line, she tripped one kid and never looked around, not even when two of his friends fell over him.

"It's us or them, Cat," she said.

They retaliated by buzzing our fenders and trying to run us off the goddam track.

We moved on to the bumper cars, and by then my blood was up.

"Age and beauty first, sonny," I said as I edged out a pre-teen punk and clambered into a bumblebee-yellow car.

Louella landed in a lime-green one.

"I think I injured my hip getting in here, Cat," she confessed. "I hope you don't have to call the rescue squad to get me out."

"I know what you mean." I snapped on my safety belt, and flashed a grandmotherly smile at the juvenile delinquents in the next car over. When the buzzer sounded, I'd slammed them before they even knew what hit.

When the session ended, I helped Louella out of her car, and she limped to the exit, leaning on me heavily.

"Is it half time, Coach?" she murmured.

"That's the spirit, Lou," I said. "A little Gatorade and an ice pack and some fresh lipstick, and you'll be ready to go again."

That was when Louella took a notion to go on a helicopter ride. She'd seen a place on Route 48 where you could fly over the whole area.

"What kind of a detective are you, Cat?" she asked when I met this idea with a noticeable lack of enthusiasm. "Don't you want to get a different perspective on the case?"

"Louella, we are not going to solve this case in the air. Why don't we just go play putt-putt, like normal tourists?"

"I can take it off my taxes," she bubbled, "seeing as I'm a realtor."

"Fine," I said, and added, "It's your funeral. I'll hold your purse."

I sat on a bench and fanned myself, wishing they had a bar. After twenty minutes, Louella stumbled out of the helicopter, shaky, drenched with sweat, and exhilarated.

"You ought to go, Cat. You can see everything just as clear!"

"I can see it from here, and it's even clearer," I said. "Come on. Let's go back to the dam."

"Why? What are we looking for?"

"Witnesses."

We started at Bobby Ray's Bait and Bite, which advertised "Bait and Burgers." Nobody there could add anything to what we knew about the accident. The same was true of the garage next door, where we found two young men putting in overtime on a Ford pickup. And the souvenir shop across the road.

"It was so early in the morning," Louella fretted. "None of these places were open."

I turned off again at the second "Lock and Powerhouse" sign. I was driving because Louella was weak from the excitement of her helicopter ride. I turned off the engine and waited for something that was about to hit me.

"You need to use the restroom?" Louella asked, turning down the sun visor to check her makeup in the mirror on the back.

But now I was out of the car and up the steps to the first landing. There it was, on a little covered stand—a clipboard with loose pages attached. A place for visitors to sign in.

I dug to the bottom of the pile, and found the date I wanted: July 10, 1985. Number 1 on that page was a "Lester Perkins and Family" from Chattanooga, Tennessee. Number 2 was "Charles Jones" from Birmingham, Alabama. Number 3 was a "Brown" from Chicago.

"If I have to go beyond Number One, I'll shoot myself," I vowed.

There were three L. Perkinses listed with Chattanooga Information. The second turned out to be the one I wanted.

"My name is Catherine Caliban, and I'm investigating a car accident that happened on the Volunteer Dam the morning of July 10. I'm looking for a Lester Perkins family from Chattanooga who visited the dam that morning, hoping someone may have witnessed the accident."

"Yes ma'am, that was us," a young female voice said on the other end. "It was just terrible, the way it happened, with the noise and the explosion and all. You could smell it, too, and there was this big old cloud of smoke."

"So you did see the accident?" I couldn't keep the excitement out of my voice.

"No ma'am, not to *see* it, exactly. I mean, it was kinda far off, you know? And we were looking out at the lake, except for Brian—he's my brother. He was looking at the lock. But then we heard the crash, and so we looked over there and saw, like, this giant fireball, and smoke, and then that's all we could see from where we were standing. We were still trying to figure out what had happened when we heard the first sirens."

"Was there anybody else around?"

"No ma'am, just us, if you mean at that lookout place. It was real early, but my daddy, he's got a notion that we shouldn't ought to waste time when we're on vacation, so he always gets us up at *dawn*, practically." Her voice expressed contempt for this attitude, and I sympathized entirely. This was an ongoing source of family-vacation feuds among the Calibans as well. Where is it men go to learn this stuff? Probably the same place they learn to shop at top speed.

"Was there anybody around anyplace else that you could see?"

She thought a minute.

"Well," she said slowly, "there was this truck on the bridge, but I don't guess you mean that."

My heart gave a little bounce.

"Yes, that's exactly what I do mean. Tell me about the truck."

"Well, it was a tank truck. It was coming awful fast, I remember that. We were all kinda surprised, 'cause you know lots of times truck drivers are real helpful, like, with car accidents or if you run out of gas or something. But this one—it was almost like he was running away, like.

Daddy said maybe he was behind schedule. Or else, like Mama said, he just didn't want to get involved. Or maybe, like *I* said, he didn't want to get blamed. Maybe he tried to pass that other car on the dam, and caused the accident that way. Because he must've heard it. You couldn't help but hear it."

"Were there any markings on the truck?"

"You mean like lettering or advertising or something?"

"Yes, anything that might identify it."

A pause. "Yes, ma'am, I believe there was, but I don't recollect what they looked like."

"Do you remember what color? Were they black?"

"I don't believe so. But you can see it on the video. Want me to take a look?"

"Video?" I gasped.

"Yes'm. I warned Mama what would happen if we gave Daddy that video camera for his birthday, but she said we shouldn't deprive him of his fun. So of course, when we went on vacation, he had to carry that thing everywhere, and take pictures of every little thing. I mean *everything*— even things that were standing stock-still. You ever know anybody to shoot videos of things that were standing still?"

Yeah, I thought—every video camera owner I knew.

"So anyway, he had that camera out, and he was filming the lake when the accident happened. You can see it on the film—about five boring minutes of nothing but lake, and then you can hear the sound of the accident, and then there's this jumpy part, and the camera swings around to the dam. First, all you see is the smoke far away, but then the camera moves and you can see the truck coming across the top of the dam."

"Do you think I could get a copy of that video?" I asked.

"Sure, I guess so. The police didn't seem too interested before, though."

"The police?"

"Yes, ma'am, when Daddy called. He wasn't going to, but Mama said maybe they'd be looking for eyewitnesses, and would want to talk to that trucker."

"And he offered them a copy of the video, and they turned him down?"

"Yes'm, that's what he said. We guessed they didn't need any more evidence about the accident."

"Well, I think they made a big mistake, and I'd like to talk to your father about it, and find out who he called and what they said. I definitely want to see a copy of that video."

She sighed, and spoke apologetically. "I ought to warn you—there's a lot of zooming in it."

Eighteen

When Brenda—that turned out to be her name—put her daddy, Lester, on the phone, he confirmed that he had a video shot during and just after the accident. And he confirmed the presence of a tank truck on the bridge going east. He was only too eager to send me the tape by overnight delivery service. He would have sent it before, he said, but the police officer he had talked to had not wanted it.

"He was real polite and all," Lester said, "but he didn't think it would be necessary. He took my number in case they needed it later, though."

"What police officer was this?" I asked. "I mean, from which law enforcement agency?"

"Oh, now, let me see. My wife was the one who told me to call. It wasn't actually the police, I guess; it was the county sheriff."

"Which county?"

"Which county? Well, I suppose it was the county the dam's in. What county would that be?"

"Well, that's a good question, Mr. Perkins. I'm looking at a map that shows two counties bordering on the dam—Millins and Park."

"Oh. Well, what outfit are *you* with, Mrs. Calobar?"

"I'm an independent investigator representing the family of the deceased, Mr. Walter McIntyre."

"Oh. Well, who's investigating the accident for the police?"

"The Tennessee Valley Authority Public Safety office."

"Oh. I never thought of them. Well, we ate supper in Cayter. What county is that?"

"Millins County, Mr. Perkins." The same county in which New Union and Chem-Tech WDI are located, I added to myself.

"That's probably who I called then. Got an office in Cayter?"

"That's right."

"That's who I called, then. And you say the accident wasn't even in their jurisdiction? Why didn't they tell me that?"

"I don't know, Mr. Perkins."

"Say, what kind of an investigator are you? An insurance investigator?"

"A private investigator." After all, he couldn't ask to see my license over the phone.

"You're not from the insurance company or anything, are you? I mean, I wouldn't want to—"

"I'm trying to find out if someone caused the accident to happen, Mr. Perkins. Mr. McIntyre was in possession of some fairly sensitive information."

"Oh. Well, as long as you're not trying to prove he killed himself or anything, so they don't have to pay the insurance. Those insurance companies, they're just like leeches, you know—they suck you dry, and then they disappear and don't want anything more to do with you.

"But, say—you don't think—I mean, by 'causing the accident,' you don't mean to say that man might have been *murdered*, do you?"

"It's a possibility," I said smoothly.

"And my tape might be the evidence you need to prove it wasn't an accident? Because of the tank truck, you mean? Say, that's really something!"

Before we hung up, though, something else occurred to him.

"Listen, Mrs. Calloran, you don't think—I mean, you won't need us to testify or anything, will you? Not that we wouldn't—'cause we would—I mean, if we were needed and all. I'm just thinking about the Cub Scout summer powwow coming up in a few weeks."

I told him I didn't think we'd need his testimony, just the video. What the hell did I know? Somebody might need his testimony, sooner or later, but why dampen his twigs before there was cause?

I also asked him to keep a copy of the tape, and mail two—one to the Catatonia Arms in Cincinnati, and one to the B & J. He was relieved to be told to keep a copy, not only because it had taken on a whole new meaning as a summer vacation chronicle, but also because it contained documentation of the biggest fish he had ever caught.

We sat around the funeral home that night, talking in hushed voices to everybody who showed up. Louella was subdued, on top of being pooped after her day of fun in the sun. She had the coffin open because she thought they'd fixed up Red so that he looked pretty good, and she thought his friends might want to see him one last time. It gave me the willies, if you want to know the truth; he looked dead to me. But I had to put up with a lot of chit-chat about how natural he looked. It had taken a shitload of chemicals, I thought, to make him look that natural.

Little Ruthie MacDougal had the right idea: she burst into tears as soon as that cold floral air hit her in the face, and her wails nearly shattered the windows.

"Cat, I'd like you to meet Mamie and Wynn Grayson," Poppy whispered, as soon as she'd transferred the scream-ing baby and cumbersome diaper bag to her husband and sent them home. "They founded Healthwatch."

"Poppy's giving us too much credit. A lot of people helped found the group."

The speaker looked like a grandmother from Central Casting—white curly hair, glasses, and a beatific expression. She wore a flowered print cotton-blend dress. Her hubby was a similarly ordinary-looking older man wearing a blue polyester suit and tortoise-shell bifocals. He had thinning gray hair and a slight stoop.

Were they for real? Thanks to my daughter Franny, who was sitting-in before she could march, I'd met a lot of activists in my day, old and young. These folks didn't look anything like anybody on Franny's telephone tree. It wasn't just the synthetic fiber, or the fact that neither Mamie's dress nor Wynn's hair was as long as I was accustomed to in political types. It was their sheer ordinariness that made me wonder.

"I'm glad to meet you," I said, shaking hands. "I'd like to talk to you some time about your group and its work."

"We'd like that," Mamie said cordially. "We'd like to talk to you, too."

The way the light caught her glasses, I couldn't tell if she meant more than she was saying.

"What about tomorrow afternoon, after the funeral? Are you busy?"

Mamie nodded. "That would be fine."

Hunt Smith kept blowing his nose loudly and shaking his head, while Alma Smith sat erect in a chair next to Louella, patting Louella's hand and speaking in a low voice. The Cassidys and the Wellses appeared together, sans dogs, Emmett with a toothpick stuck in his teeth like they'd just come from Bob Evans. Foster Bayberry looked as sad as ever, perhaps in part because of the damp stain down the front of his shirt; I thought again how little he resembled the lawyers of my acquaintance.

Freeman Quinn was conspicuously absent, but then, we knew he would be. He'd told us he had no desire to see Red dressed up, made-up, and laid out in a box. Louella had understood.

A herd of gray storm clouds moved in on Monday, the

day of Red's funeral. The air was thick with a damp, heavy heat. Everybody said they hoped the heat would break, but they hoped it wouldn't break over Red's burial.

The church was full, and the service was about to begin, when three men slipped into the back row, and I felt my heart constrict in my chest.

I didn't know who they were, but I knew what they were. Psychopaths are harder to spot; they look like everybody else, except that they're always alone. Bullies, on the other hand, can't help revealing the pleasure they take in their power. And they're never alone. These guys were bullies. As far as I could tell, they weren't carrying, but I kept an eye on them anyway.

There was some singing and praying, and then Poppy gave her speech. It was funny and affectionate, and I could tell Red would have liked it—maybe did like it, if he was hanging around, watching the proceedings. Then it was Louella's turn. She looked nervous, and I gave her arm an encouraging squeeze, but once she got started, she was fine. Then there was another hymn, and when it was over you could hear a distant rumble of thunder in the sudden silence. Hunt stood up and read the Twenty-third Psalm in a quavery voice. You could tell it kind of gave everybody the creeps, because about that time the wind picked up and you could hear it round the corner of the church and scrape the tree branches against the windows. Even the bullies in the back row were getting restless.

Now it was Freeman's turn. He strode to the front of the church, put on his glasses, opened his Bible, and looked out at the assembly. I knew something of what was coming, but I hadn't expected the sound effects—or the rest of it. Freeman was tall, and he looked imposing standing up there. When he opened his mouth, his voice boomed out and filled up that little church, bouncing off the walls and rolling around like the thunder that competed with it outside.

"For the day of the Lord of hosts shall be upon every one that is lifted up, and he shall be brought low.

"For wickedness burneth as the fire: it shall devour the briers and thorns, and shall kindle in the thickets of the forest, and they shall mount up like the lifting of smoke.

"They that see thee shall narrowly look upon thee, and consider thee, saying, Is this the man that made the earth to tremble, that did shake kingdoms; that made the world as a wilderness, and destroyed the cities thereof?

"The earth mourneth and fadeth away, the world languisheth and fadeth away, the haughty people of the earth do languish. The earth also is defiled under the inhabitants thereof; because they have transgressed the laws, changed the ordinance, broken the everlasting covenant."

Freeman raised his eyes and stared at the men in the back row, speaking from memory now.

"For thou hast trusted in thy wickedness: thou hast said, None seeth me. Thy wisdom and thy knowledge, it hath perverted thee; and thou hast said in thine heart, I am, and none else beside me. Therefore shall evil come upon thee; thou shalt not know from whence it riseth: and mischief shall fall upon thee: thou shalt not be able to put it off: and desolation shall come upon thee suddenly which thou shalt not know."

At this point, the room was lit by a flash of lightning, then plunged into darkness. A terrific crack of thunder rattled the windows. There was a collective gasp from the congregation, but nobody moved. Freeman's voice continued, but now it was joined by a second voice which seemed to come from everywhere at once.

"The sinners in Zion are afraid; fearfulness hath surprised the hypocrites. Who among us shall dwell with the

*devouring fire? Who among us shall dwell with everlasting
burnings? He that walketh righteously, and speaketh up-
rightly; he that despiseth the gain of oppressions, that
shaketh his hands from holdings of bribes, that stoppeth
his ears from hearing of blood, and shutteth his eyes from
seeing evil. He shall dwell on high: his place of defense
shall be the munitions of rocks: bread shall be given him;
his waters shall be sure."*

The second voice dropped away, and Freeman con-
cluded.

"This ends the reading from the Book of Isaiah."

A dead silence followed. Then, we heard Freeman's
measured tread as he descended the wooden steps from the
altar and came to stand next to Louella, who gave him a
hug.

The silence was broken by a clear, beautiful voice, singing the first line of "Amazing Grace." The congregation
joined in on the second line, while the ushers passed out
candles, which made flickering pools of light in the dim
room. I turned around. The men in the back row were
gone.

Nineteen

At the graveside, the wind stirred up the overheated air for a change, and the storm broke just as Louella threw in her shovelful of dirt. We ran for the cars again, our Personal Bereavement Representative trotting alongside trying to hang on to this enormous black umbrella that was determined to get the better of him. Just as he got us in the car, the wind tore it out of his hand, and sent it sailing over the headstones. The last I saw of him, he was bounding after it, dodging headstones like a pinball.

The luncheon was at Poppy's—a pleasant little frame house about the same vintage as Red's, but decorated in an eclectic mix of modern and antique. Ruthie was in her element. A matched pair of Lhasa Apsos, made delirious by the arrival of company and the change in the weather, raced around underfoot.

Red's friends and neighbors were determined to give him the best party they could, and Poppy's house now looked like the site of a bake-off that had gotten out of hand. Alma Smith's attempts to bring order to the chaos were being ignored, so there were pies cosied up to plates of fried chicken and ham, and hot vegetables melting molded Jell-O salads next to them. Most of the produce was freshly picked, and I eyed it wistfully, wondering if the bugs had left us anything in our garden back home.

Freeman was the man of the hour, and he'd been cornered by a small crowd of admirers.

"Who was it, Freeman?" they kept asking. "Who was that other voice we heard?"

"Never you mind who it was," he'd say. "The Lord knows."

"What *I* want to know, Freeman," a man said, "was how you got the Lord to throw that lightning bolt at just the right time."

Freeman laughed, and gently pushed through the crowd.

"Stand back and give a man some room," he said. "I got me a date with some Hawaiian salad."

He gave me a conspiratorial wink as he passed.

"What I don't see," said a man near me, "is how Red come to drive his car off the side of that dam. I bet he drove that road a million times."

A woman, probably his wife, frowned at him and shook her head.

Another man looked around for Louella, and spotting her across the room, leaned toward the first speaker and said, "If you ask me, it wasn't no accident. That feller from the dam told the newspaper Red must've fallen asleep at the wheel, but you know Red didn't fall asleep at no wheel of no automobile. I say he had help, and I don't care who hears me say it." He pointed his pipe for emphasis, then sat back in his chair and looked around at his listeners as if challenging them to contradict him.

"If he had help, who do you think helped him, and why?" I asked.

"I ain't sayin' who did it." The man glanced at me. "But I reckon I know who paid the bill, and he's the same bastard who's behind ninety percent of the criminal goin's-on in this county, and don't a one of you wonder who it is I'm talkin' about. And if them thugs has the indecency to show up here after what Freeman give 'em from the pulpit, why, I'll say the same to them."

Some of his listeners looked uncomfortable, while others looked enthralled.

"Now Frank," said the first man's wife disapprovingly, "this ain't the time to be talkin' about such things. Poor Louella's just buried her uncle."

"Well, and if this ain't the time, I'd like to know when is!" Frank rejoined heatedly. "If a man's funeral ain't the time to stand up and say he was murdered, I'd like to know just when we're aimin' to do it, because I, for one, want to be there with my twenty-two when we take and run them bastards out of Millins County!"

"If you think he was murdered," I pursued, "why do you think they did it?" I was feeling like a traitor to my sex, and earned an exasperated look from the wife, but I needed to know the local gossip.

"Why, Wynn here can tell you that, can't you, Wynn? Didn't he join your group and commence talkin' against that incinerator? And didn't he used to work at that very place, for Mr. Isaiah Grubbs? I reckon he give your group an earful, didn't he, Wynn? I reckon he knew a lot about that place that somebody didn't want him spreadin' around."

"He didn't tell us much, Frank," Wynn said soberly. "Nothing to get killed for, anyway. But I reckon he knew more than he was telling."

"There you go. He knew something, and them bastards made damn sure he never told what he knew. I don't know how they done it. They might've fixed up his car somehow, or maybe they just run him off the road, but they got him. And there's others they got before him. You can call me a old coot if you want to, but what I say is that incinerator is the biggest threat to the public health we got here in Millins County, and it ain't just hazardous chemicals I'm talkin' about."

A woman broke in at this point to offer more coffee, and the discussion shifted. I went looking for Freeman. I found him in the kitchen, feeding Ruthie and talking to Poppy's husband, Mike.

"Don't ask," he warned me, a twinkle in his eye, before I could open my mouth. "I ain't a-goin' to tell you."

"What I was going to ask," I said, a little huffily, "was about those three guys sitting in the back row at the church."

He nodded. "Those are the commissioner's boys. They report to George Packer—you know, the operations manager at Chem-Tech. He likes to kid around and call them his 'bodyguards.' But why in hell should a Millins County commissioner need bodyguards?"

"Do you think they were the ones who killed Red?"

"Could have been. They're violent types."

"And they had the arrogance to show up at his funeral!" Mike shook his head. "It was bad enough that Chem-Tech sent flowers—a big old wreath crammed with gladiolas that the kitchen crew pronounced 'tacky.' Poppy pitched it."

"They didn't look so arrogant when they left," Freeman said, smiling. "They looked a few shades paler." He lifted Ruthie up and gazed at her. "You just remember what your Uncle Freeman tells you, little lady: the good guys always win."

Unless they die first, I added to myself.

In the interests of helping the good guys win, preferably before we got deep-sixed by the bad guys, I left the party a short time later to follow the Graysons home. Mamie and Wynn Grayson lived in a sprawling brick farmhouse about fifteen miles north of Cayter, between the river and Parkersville. We sat on a screened-in porch that overlooked a barn, some outbuildings, and a field of soybeans. They offered refreshments, but I couldn't have eaten or drunk another thing. Wynn had already removed his jacket, loosened his tie, and rolled up his shirt sleeves when I sat down. A soft rain now fell outside, and a cool breeze wandered through every now and then.

"Looks like you've got a nice farm here, Mr. Grayson," I said, indicating the field below, now glittering green in the rain.

"Yes, although my son-in-law does all the farming these days."

"His asthma is so bad, you see, Wynn can't work the farm like he used to," Mamie explained, settling into a chair with—I kid you not—knitting. Another one of those skills that women my age were supposed to have in their repertoire.

"Is that because of the incinerator?" I asked.

"We think it makes him worse," Mamie said, "but we can't prove it does."

"Tell me something about how you came to be involved with Healthwatch."

"Our families have lived in this county for generations," Mamie began, settling in to tell her story. "My family lived up near Kennessee—you know where that is? Close to Radlin?"

I was having trouble keeping all of these towns straight, but I nodded anyway.

"And then Wynn's family, of course, the Wynns and the Graysons both, they owned all of this land outside Parkersville. Wynn and me met at a church social, and we married and moved into a mobile home up the road on Grayson land. We didn't move here till Wynn's daddy died, and we came up here to look after his mother.

"Farming wasn't an easy life, but it was what we wanted to do. Anyway, we thought at the time that we could live off God's green earth and raise healthy children and go our way in peace.

"Well, the first thing that happened was that one of our grandchildren was diagnosed with leukemia. Ron and them were living up in New Union at the time, and Ron was working at one of the chemical plants. Ronnie and the other kids were attending school in New Union, not half a mile from that industrial park where all the chemical companies and the incinerator are. Well, we thought it was just one of those things, at first. But then another little class-mate of Ronnie's was diagnosed with the same thing.

"Next thing you know, why, the parents were talking to each other about their kids' health. And it turned out the kids were getting sick a lot. Well, kids do get sick, you know. But it didn't make sense for so many kids to be so unhealthy so much of the time.

"In those days, we'd never heard of Love Canal. We didn't know the first thing about toxic chemicals—nobody did. So most of it was talk at first—you know, rumors, and neighbors talking. It didn't occur to anybody to do any-thing. Why, every farmer in the county was spraying in-secticide on his crops, and nobody questioned it.

"Well, we spent a lot of time with Ronnie before he died," she continued quietly. "There was this new medical center in Dalton, and we used to take him for his treat-ments because the kids had to work. Then one day, a doc-tor said something to me. I don't think he thought much about it at the time. I'd said something about having that new clinic so close by, and he said something about going where the need is. I don't know even now what made me ask him what he meant, but that's when he said there was a high rate of cancer here in Millins County.

"I went home, and me and Wynn sat down at the kitchen table and made a list of everybody we knew who had cancer or had died of cancer. When we were done, we didn't quite know what we were looking at. We'd included everybody, from the past as well as the present. But we knew they didn't used to diagnose cancer the way they do now. It seemed like we knew an awful lot of people with cancer, and most of them in recent years, but like I say, maybe before that people never found out.

"The next week our youngest son, Kit, came to tell us that he'd just found out he was sterile. Him and Arlene had been trying and trying to have a baby, and now he knew he couldn't have one. He'd been driving a truck for Chem-Tech for three years."

"You mean, he'd been transporting hazardous chemicals? Was the incinerator operating then?" I asked.

"The incinerator was built in 1975," Wynn replied. "Before that, they had a landfill—still do, in fact. So to answer your question, yes, he was delivering hazardous chemicals to Chem-Tech. He didn't know what they were—just chemicals is all he knew. The way they write up those manifests, they don't give much away. They like to hire kids, because kids are hungry and don't ask too many questions. Hell, a lot of the drivers can't read and write much beyond a grade-school level, so they can't read the manifests anyway."

"But Kit could read," Mamie continued, "and once we started asking him questions about what he was hauling, he took to studying those manifests, and reading tank labels, and such. A month later, he quit. He said he thought some of what they were hauling was illegal, but he'd never cared about that before. He knew that some of the unmarried drivers worked a lot of overtime—driving at night. He'd heard stories about some of the tricks they pulled, but he'd never thought much about it."

"Like what?" I asked, curious.

"Oh, any number of things," Mamie said.

"They'll take something out in the middle of the night," Wynn said, "and dump it anyplace where they won't be seen."

"You mean, not in the landfill?" I gasped.

"Anyplace." Wynn shrugged. "In any farmer's field, any plot of open ground—usually where they don't expect anyone to notice until it's soaked in good. Or sometimes, especially on a wet night, they'll just open the valve on the truck and let it leak out on the highway."

I was dumbfounded.

"So, meanwhile," Mamie resumed placidly, "me and Wynn started reading up on those chemicals that the chemical plant produced and the ones that Chem-Tech was taking in. It wasn't like you could just drive up and take soil samples from the landfill, you know. There's only that one access road, and the whole place is fenced in and guarded like it was Fort Knox. Kit wrote down the names of some of the chemicals he'd been hauling, and we tried to find out about them. It wasn't easy. We weren't chemists, after all, so we didn't understand a lot of what we read, and we didn't know where to go to find somebody who would explain things to us. We contacted EPA regional office in Atlanta, and they sent us some brochures, but that wasn't much help."

"That's when we found Greenpeace," Wynn put in.

Mamie nodded. "Somebody—a friend of Ron's I think it was—suggested we call them. Well, they couldn't have been nicer. I didn't think anybody in Washington would take any notice of our problems out here in Tennessee, but they talked to us forever on the phone, didn't they, Wynn?"

"And sent us some literature on hazardous chemicals," Wynn added.

"That's right. And the more we read, the angrier and more frightened we got. So we called up that woman from Greenpeace, and asked her what to do, and she said to organize our neighbors. And she even sent a young man down to give us some advice and help us get started."

"Nice fella, he was," Wynn commented.

"And he found out some things we didn't know—all about how often Chem-Tech had been fined for violating regulations, and how they were applying for a permit to add another incinerator, but they hadn't filed the papers right. Oh, we learned a lot from him."

"And we went to some meetings."

"That's right. Well, to make a long story short, we called

a meeting, and Healthwatch was founded at that meeting. And we've been fighting that incinerator ever since."

"Has anybody ever threatened you?"

"Oh, sure. If you had all afternoon, we could tell you stories to make your hair curl. Like about how we used to keep rabbits and goats, but we don't anymore because too many of them got poisoned. But we're careful. And we keep the shotgun loaded."

Her knitting needles clicked in the silence that followed this declaration.

"Tell me about your association with Red McIntyre," I said.

"We didn't know about the insurance," Wynn said quickly.

"Oh, yes, Wynn's all hot and bothered about that insurance, he's so afraid somebody will think we put Red up to that. But we didn't know anything about it. All we knew was that Red started coming to our meetings, and helped out with some of the mailings and letter-writing campaigns. Dan Farley from Greenpeace said that there had been a special investigation of Chem-Tech last year, and that the EPA in Atlanta ought to have a copy of the report. Red was the one who tried to track down that report. But he never got anywhere with it. They just told him that the investigation hadn't led to any further action."

"You knew he'd worked at Chem-Tech?"

Mamie nodded. "Oh, yes, he told us that first thing. A couple of our other members worked there, too."

"Did he give you any additional information about possible violations at Chem-Tech?"

"Nothing we didn't already know about."

"So you knew about the overtime job he and Freeman and some of the others once did for Chem-Tech?" If they didn't know about it, I didn't think I should be the one to tell them.

She frowned. "I don't think so. Does that sound like anything he talked to you about, Wynn?"

"I don't remember hearing about a specific job, no," Wynn said.

"Did he ever give you anything to keep for him? You know, like an envelope to open in the event of his death?"

Mamie's eyes lit up.

"Now isn't that interesting! You know, I never thought of it till this very minute, but he did give me something. I clean forgot! I'll get it."

She left the room and returned with an envelope.

"I don't know how I came to forget I had it! It isn't every day that somebody gives me something to hold onto in case they die. I reckon I thought it was morbid at the time, so I put it away and put it right out of my mind. I wonder what it is." She turned the envelope over and broke the seal. She pulled out two pieces of paper.

"It says 'Do not show this to anyone except Greenpeace.' " She looked up at us with a puzzled expression.

"Well," she said, handling the pages gingerly, as if they were dipped in poison, "I don't reckon he means you, Mrs. Caliban."

She took a deep breath, and unfolded it.

"This first one looks like a list of Chem-Tech employees who have died of cancer."

She handed it to me, and I ran an eye down the page. She was right. It was a list of names and job titles, maybe thirty in all, and after each name was a type of cancer. In a third of the cases, this entry was followed by the word "deceased," and a date.

"What's the other page?" I asked, expecting it to be a copy of Red's notarized statement.

She shook her head and handed it to me.

I studied it curiously. It looked like some kind of read-out from a scientific instrument. It had one of those jumpy lines that made it look like it had been drawn by a schizophrenic. It reminded me of a seismograph.

"Damned if I know what this is," I said finally. "I just hope to hell it isn't what it looks like."

Twenty

"I don't know, Cat," Louella said, squinting at the graph. "Looks kind of like one of those heart things to me. You know—like when they strap you up to that machine that makes those little beeps? My cousin Nadine had one of those drawings that she'd saved from when she was in the hospital. Said the jumps on it came when they showed her the bill."

"Lord, honey, ain't that the truth!" Billie exclaimed. "That's when you really need the life support!"

We were sitting on Billie's patio, out back of her mobile home behind the motel. Louella and I were drinking gin, and Billie was drinking bourbon. Billie had found us a tow rope strong enough to keep Junior in the neighborhood but long enough to let him pretend he had escaped. He was lying in the shade of some bushes out behind Billie's garage. Louella, meanwhile, was painting her nails this godawful color that reminded me of moldy oranges. You'd think that what she was learning about toxic chemicals would have discouraged her from fooling around with them, but no. I voiced my suspicions about the graph which Billie was quick to confirm.

"I reckon the Graysons explained about the New Madrid fault," she said. "It runs all up through southeastern Missouri, just west of here. The big quakes was way back in the last century, but every now and then, why, we get a big earthquake scare. Somebody or other predicts that we're goin' to have another big one, and folks goes plumb crazy."

"So what you're saying is, that toxic landfill and that incinerator and all those chemical plants are next door to a fault," Louella said. "And if there's an earthquake, those chemicals will get picked up and thrown all over the place."

"That's right," I agreed.

"Well, Billie, I hate to say it, but I'm glad I don't live around here." She gave Billie a sympathetic look.

"At least Billie doesn't use carcinogens on her nails," I pointed out.

"It's beautiful here." Billie sighed. "It's a shame them bigwigs can't find an uglier place to dump their chemicals."

"They did," I observed. "It's called New Jersey. But they ran out of space."

"So they found a state greedy enough and dumb enough to let them come in and do whatever they wanted," she complained.

"I don't think Tennessee's the only state in that category. The Graysons told me Louisiana has the worst record. And there's plenty of competition, especially in the South."

"Well, shoot!" Louella expostulated. "Why'd Red have to be so secretive about it? Why couldn't he just write a note explaining what this stuff was for? Why'd he have to treat it like it was atomic secrets? I mean, it wasn't as if Mamie and Wynn were going to go blabbing anything to Chem-Tech, and he gave it to them directly, and told them not to show it to anybody but Greenpeace."

"Which they ignored when they showed it to me."

"But you're a good guy!"

"You know that, and I know that, but they don't know that, necessarily."

Junior got bored with his own company, and loped over. He sat abruptly on my foot, raised a hind leg to scratch, and knocked a few fleas off onto my ankles. Overjoyed to find so little barrier between them and their food supply, the fleas promptly bit me.

"So what do we do now?" Louella asked.

"First we find Junior a kennel," I groused. "Preferably one with a flea dip."

"You want me to cover him with toxic *chemicals*?" She frowned, blowing on her nail polish to dry it.

"Industrial strength," I affirmed. "Meanwhile, I think it's time we found out more about Isaiah Grubbs." I nudged Junior with one fleabitten foot, but he was not a dog to respond to subtlety. He laid one chop along my calf and gazed up at me like a saint looking at Baby Jesus.

"How we going to do that? Are we going to go see him?"

"I had in mind the library," I said. "But seeing him isn't a bad idea if we can swing it."

"Are we going undercover?" Louella wanted to know.

"That's right, Lou. No more orange nail polish."

She studied me to see if I was serious. "You get the appointment first," she said.

"I don't think it's such a danged good idea," Billie said. "Grubbs is surrounded by goons. It would be like walking in to see Marlon Brando, and he'd talk to you nice in that whispery voice when all the time his goons is outside the door screwing the silencers on their guns."

"Are we going to show this graph to that Greenpeace man?" Louella asked.

"The Graysons are going to call him tomorrow, and see what he says. They'll probably end up mailing him a copy of everything, including the notarized statement we have."

"Speaking of mail," Louella said, "are we going to show that videotape of the accident to Officer Danning when it gets here?"

"That all depends on what it's got on it," I said. "Danning already thinks we're nuts. I don't want to add to the impression by handing over a video that doesn't show enough to arouse his suspicions about Red's accident."

Louella said, "By the way, Cat, what am I going to tell that Owen guy when he calls about releasing Red's car?"

"Tell him to keep his goddam mitts off that car!" I replied. This roused Junior, who thumped his tail enthusiastically. "Tell him the insurance company hasn't finished its investigation. Hell, tell him you want to tow it home and put it on blocks in your front yard for sentimental reasons, I don't care. Just be assertive, and if he gives you a hard time, tell him your attorney will call him."

"My attorney?" She frowned. "Who's that?"

I raised my glass at her.

"Oh. *That* one."

Later on, I called home from a convenience store. I was beginning to appreciate what we were up against, and I was determined not to give anything away on a phone that could be tapped. Louella sat in the chair. As I talked, I scanned the parking lot nervously and fingered my Diane, which felt like a peashooter.

"Maybe it's just as well you're not here right now, Cat," Al said gloomily.

"What'd I miss?" I sighed.

"Well, Kevin broke down and cried when he went out to harvest some radicchio and discovered that the slugs had eaten holes in it. But don't worry—I washed the fur off the lettuce before he got to it. I guess we planted the catnip a little too close to the other stuff."

"Say, speaking of growing things, is my cousin still living with me?"

"Yep. In fact, he took the bus over to Xavier today to check out their computer lab, and they offered him a job helping out with the summer computer camp."

Why is it that when people come to visit me, they end up staying so long? First my daughter, now my cousin. I mean, I don't exactly put myself out as a hostess. I don't keep house. I don't cook worth beans. I don't even have an extra bathroom, or a quadraphonic stereo system. Hell, I don't even have a computer. I drink and I swear and I keep housemates to whom much of the world's population is allergic. So why do family visits turn into the Korean peace talks?

"How long does that last?"

"I think he said August some time."

"August?" I echoed faintly.

"Don't worry, Cat. He's really a good kid. And very low maintenance."

"Shit, he'd better be *no* maintenance if he's going to last till August," I grumbled. "Listen, is Moses around?"

"No, I think he's got a game tonight."

Moses played in the city softball league on a team of retired police officers called the Cop-Outs. Game nights were late nights for him. If they won, they'd be celebrating, and if they lost, they'd be drowning their sorrows. One way or another, they'd be over at Million's in Mt. Lookout until the wee hours (which come earlier when you're sixty-five, but still), deadening their arthritis pain with alcohol and reshaping the game into myth.

"Well, listen, I want to check something with Moses. I'm looking into the death of one of Red's friends in March. The medical examiner ruled it death by alcohol poisoning, but his friends don't believe he would've drunk that much. I haven't seen a copy of the coroner's report, but believe me, I'm beginning to suspect everybody around here."

A police cruiser had pulled into the parking lot, and parked next to Louella. My stomach clenched. They glanced at her, then went into the store.

"He had some other cuts and bruises on his arms, legs, stomach, and face. I hear the theory was that he was feeling sick and cold, and seeing double, and maybe lost his balance and fell. He couldn't call for help since he didn't have a phone at the house where he was living at the time. What I want to know is if Moses has heard of any way to kill somebody by inducing acute alcohol poisoning and how it would be done—aside from standing him drinks at the local bar, if there was one, which there isn't."

"Okay. Got it. You picked the damnedest place for your summer vacation, Cat."

"Oh, the place is beautiful, Al—a fucking mecca for us senior citizen types looking for outdoor recreation. Long's you don't drink the water, breathe the air, or eat anything that comes out of the ground or the rivers and lakes, it's a great place to spend your sunset years."

Twenty-one

The Millins County Public Library was a limestone building that looked to be WPA vintage. It was shaded by trees. It might have been the only public library in the county, but it was not what you'd call a research library. Still, I expected it to have more information on one of Millins County's leading luminaries than it did. Isaiah T. Grubbs did not warrant an entry in the card catalog, and the only entry for Chem-Tech WDI was a promotional brochure from the seventies that made me want to throw up. Its main message was that Chem-Tech was saving the planet with its pioneering waste-disposal technology, while acting as a good corporate citizen in its spare time. Generous gifts to pediatric cancer care featured prominently in its representation of the company as a model citizen.

I got my first squint at Grubbs, though, in a touching photograph of him handing a fake cardboard check to a kid in a wheelchair. I wondered if the kid in the wheelchair was fake, too. If he wasn't, I hoped he hadn't tried to use that check to buy himself a motorized wheelchair.

It was kind of hard to tell from such a small picture, but mostly Grubbs looked like a corporate executive, well-turned out but running to fat, shorter than you might expect considering the shadow he cast over Millins County. His height reassured me. If it came down to hand-to-hand combat, I felt confident I could take him. If my Diane had to go up against his .357 magnum or AK-47, I was in trouble. But Billie was probably right about him: he did all his killing by proxy.

I poked around in the reference section some more, and

eventually found a 1983 guide to Tennessee businesses. It didn't tell me much I didn't already know, except that George Packer, identified by Red as "operations manager" of Chem-Tech and by Billie as a county commissioner, was in fact the vice-president of Chem-Tech. The more I found out the higher the stakes seemed for him.

Out of paranoia, I'd initially broken my usual habit of shamelessly exploiting the librarians. I thought that if I went around Millins County asking questions about Isaiah T. Grubbs, I might as well draw a big red target across my chest and be done with it. But there might be a legitimate reason for someone to take an interest in the county commissioner, and I resolved to come up with one and throw myself on the mercy of the nearest librarian.

That turned out to be Melba Flatts. Now, most folks have the wrong idea about librarians. Most people think they are nearsighted antisocial creatures, overly sensitive to noise, who see themselves as the counterparts of museum guards, intent upon keeping the public away from the library's books. I've met a few like that. But most suffer unfairly from this stereotype. They see their job as public service, and wish the public would be more willing to be served. They spend a lot of time wistfully eyeing library patrons, hoping for a live one—a high-school research project on the Dakota Indians, say, or a question about the native bird species of all fifty states.

Melba perked right up when I told her I was writing a book on all the Tennessee county governments. She didn't even ask if I was going to finish before the next elections made my book obsolete. She didn't care. I told her that I would be interviewing all of the Millins County commissioners over the next few weeks, but that I wanted to start with Mr. Packer. That was good enough for Melba. She brought out the clippings file.

At the end of an hour, I didn't know a hell of a lot more

about Packer, Grubbs, and Chem-Tech than I had when I started out. Packer was divorced, and served on half the boards in Millins County; Grubbs presumably served on the other half. He liked to hunt and fish, and took frequent vacations to Florida for deep-sea fishing. I guessed he knew too much about what the Millins County fish were carrying around. He seemed to pal around a lot with a guy named Shelby Stubblefield, the Millins County assessor and a frequent adviser to the governor.

In fact, the most useful item I found was a news photo of Packer, Grubbs, Stubblefield, and the governor hanging out together on the lawn in front of the Governor's Mansion in Nashville.

This is instructive, I said to myself. These jerks obviously had friends in high places; otherwise, they might not have been getting away with all the things they were getting away with.

You don't know the governor, I reminded myself. You don't even know the governor's cat. You don't have the kind of money that would make it worth their while to sneeze, much less to cancel a contract on you. You'd best watch your back until you cross the Ohio River again, girl.

A little shiver ran along my shoulder blades, but when I turned around, Melba just beamed and waved.

Before I left, I looked up the names of some Park and Gainard County commissioners, and made up a few good stories about them to tell Melba. She was gratified, I could tell. I owed her that much.

For lunch Louella and I drove up to New Union, to the Riverview Cafe, because it had been mentioned in connection with Packer in one of the articles. You couldn't see the river anyplace, but maybe it was different when the trees dropped their leaves.

"Has Mr. Packer been in today?" I asked, just as if it were a natural question to ask.

The woman behind the counter shook her head.

"I ain't seen him lately. Must be out of town. Hey, Virgil!" she called to a man in back. "George out of town?"

Virgil shrugged. She turned back to me. "Time he spends in Florida, you'd think we was all fixin' to go into the orange-growing business."

I let that go, and we ate lunch. Afterward, I dropped Louella off at the bank in Cayter, and went looking for the library at Volunteer State in Dalton.

Here, the business collection was much more substantial. I read a lot, and took a lot of notes, but damned if I knew what it added up to. I'd copied down all the vital statistics for Chem-Tech from a business directory printed in 1984. On a whim, I asked the business librarian about the date.

"Well, the most recent information would come out of the state attorney general's office, of course. But we have a new database that will be more current than that directory. Would you like me to check it for you?"

I caught the gleam in his eye of a man eager to demonstrate the new technology, so I said yes. He didn't even bat an eye when I asked him to call up the records for Chem-Tech WDI.

I figured that I should take an interest in the technology for Cousin Delbert's sake, especially considering that I was likely to be living with him in close quarters until some as yet undefined time in the future. So I dutifully gazed at the screen over the librarian's shoulder.

"Which one do you want?" he asked.

On the screen was an alphabetical listing, followed by a date and something that looked like a reference number. I read:

Chem-Tech Waste Disposal, Inc. 3/17/74 (CT 35629)

Chem-Tech Real Estate, 4/13/83 (CT42083)

Chem-Tech Holding, Inc., 4/13/83 (CT42183)

Chem-Tech Development, Inc., 4/13/83 (CT42283)

Chem-Tech Investment Corporation, 7/16/83 (CT72383)

Chem-Tech Transit Company, 2/03/84 (CT66184)

Chem-Tech Management Group, Inc., 2/03/84 (CT66284)

Chem-Tech Incineration, Inc., 8/10/84 (CT93984)

Chem-Tech Landfill, Inc., 8/10/84 (CT94084)

Chem-Tech Waste Management Corporation, 1/08/85 (CT211185)

Chem-Tech Waste Services, Inc., 1/08/85 (CT211285)

Chem-Tech Resource Recovery Group, Inc., 1/08/85 (CT211385)

Chem-Tech Energy, Inc., 3/18/85 (CT409985)

I had to pick my jaw up off of his shoulder.

"What is all that?" I gasped.

"A list of companies called Chem-Tech. Which one are you interested in?"

"The one with a chief executive officer named Isaiah T. Grubbs," I said slowly. It should have been the first one, but I wanted to see.

He typed something that included *Grubbs, Isaiah T.* Five of the company names disappeared.

"That narrowed the field a bit," he said. "Now what?"

"Are you trying to tell me," I said, "that Isaiah T. Grubbs is CEO of every company on the screen?"

"At least," he said, nodding. He grinned up at me. "Isaiah has been a busy little boy."

I stared at the screen. "How can he do that?"

"Easy." He shrugged. "You can incorporate as many companies as you want to, as long as you file the papers and articles of incorporation with the state attorney general's office, and your tax forms with the IRS. There's nothing to prevent it. Most of these are probably subsidiaries of the parent company, with interlocking directors. They could exist mostly on paper, in the account books and in the tax records."

"What do the dates mean?" I pointed at the screen.

"That's the date the company was incorporated—the date the papers were filed."

"But some of these were incorporated on the same day!"

"Like I said, there's no law against it. Say a company decides to divide up its operations and assets among several subsidiaries—like Ma Bell did when she created the Baby Bells. It would make sense that all the paperwork would be filed on the same day. I don't even know how different the articles of incorporation have to be. Could be the same, for all I know. We could look it up."

"But why would somebody want to create all those companies? Sounds like a lot of work for them, and for their lawyers and accountants."

He grinned again, his glasses reflecting the list of Chem-Techs like a fun-house mirror.

"Well, there are tax advantages to doing it that way. I don't understand all the ins and outs of corporate tax law, though. Let me try something else."

He typed in Grubbs's name again, and the screen went blank. I panicked. I didn't know how these machines worked. Would I be able to get that list back again?

But now a new list suddenly leapt to the screen. It included many of the Chem-Techs which had appeared on the previous list, but also some other names, such as *Valcon, Inc.* and *GAP Land Development Company*. At the bottom, the screen said *(more)*. Again, several dates recurred.

"This time I searched the database for all companies in which Grubbs is named as an officer of the corporation. As you can see, he's not too proud to serve in a lesser position—vice-president, say, or member of the board."

"Okay, let me ask this. Are there any illegitimate reasons for setting up all these companies with interlocking directorates?"

"Sure. When you divide up a company's operations like this, you divide up assets and liability. So sometimes you see it in bankruptcy cases, where somebody's tried to protect assets that would be frozen if the company were forced to declare bankruptcy. Does that seem likely in this case?"

"Beats me," I admitted. "But I guess I'd be surprised. From the outside, anyway, this company looks fatter than a kennel tick."

He thought for a minute.

"Is it in danger of any other kind of prosecution or lawsuit?"

I caught my breath.

"Yes," I said. "It sure is."

I hooked a nearby chair with my foot, and sat down in it.

"What's your name?" I asked, studying him.

"Stan," he said cautiously, eyeing me with trepidation, as if I had a subpoena in my pocket that I was about to spring on him.

"Cat Caliban," I said, "private investigator." I shook his hand so that he could see I didn't have a gun in mine, or a subpoena, either. "Look, Stan, you know who we're talking about here, don't you? You know what this company owns?" University people don't always know much about the town around the campus. In this case, that could only work to my advantage.

"They own that incinerator up in New Union, don't they? And a landfill." He was still poised for retreat.

"Well, look. Suppose the EPA came in and closed the place down. Suppose they did tests and found out that the place was so contaminated that it couldn't continue operations. Suppose they declared it a Superfund site."

"Like Love Canal, you mean?" I could tell he was intrigued.

"Yeah, like Love Canal. Wouldn't the government sue the company for the cost of the clean-up? And wouldn't there be lots of other lawsuits against Chem-Tech on behalf of the residents of New Union? But if the company had transferred its assets to all these other companies, then couldn't it just declare bankruptcy?"

"I see what you're getting at. But I don't think it would work that way. See, I don't think a company can just transfer assets to a new company like that. Look, here's how it would probably work. Suppose Chem-Tech WDI *sold* the incinerator, the landfill, maybe even the land, to one of these new companies. The new company pays cash—their own cash, not the parent company's, strictly speaking—and now owns the incinerator or whatever. When the EPA comes after Chem-Tech, they say, 'Sorry. We don't own that anymore. You need to talk to Chem-Tech Waste Services.' But it turns out that the incinerator is Chem-Tech Waste Services' only asset. They obviously can't afford the clean-up, and they're not worth suing."

"But aren't they the same people who run Chem-Tech WDI?"

"Individually, yes. But they're not the same corporate

entity. You could probably try suing the individuals, but those guys know how to protect themselves, and you probably wouldn't win. You might find out that they've got no money, even though their children have trust funds that could underwrite the crown jewels. Hell, if we researched these companies one by one, we'd probably discover that they're not just subsidiaries, they're subsidiaries of subsidiaries of subsidiaries, just to complicate the issue of liability."

"God, is that depressing!"

"Yeah, isn't it just?"

"But look, Stan, you said that cash would change hands if Chem-Tech sold its assets. Where does the cash come from?"

"Investors."

"People who put money into the new company."

"That's right."

"Like the people on the board of the old company."

"Sure. Or the officers. If Chem-Tech WDI is as profitable as you say, they can afford to pay themselves huge salaries and bonuses, then invest in these new companies to keep the whole thing afloat and protect themselves. But the cash could also come from a bank loan, which would be made on the basis of a history of profitability on the part of the landfill or whatever."

I frowned and rubbed my forehead. A financial wizard I'm not, as practically anybody at my bank will tell you. Not to mention the fifty miscellaneous merchants a year who have reason to suspect I flunked addition and subtraction in grade school, and the junior-high class in how to write checks.

"There could even be outside investors involved."

"Outside investors? Who would invest in a scheme like this? I mean, wouldn't you do some research first? Chem-

Tech has a record of EPA violations that would choke a paper shredder."

"Either somebody very stupid, or"—he lowered his voice—"somebody very smart."

"I understand about the stupid people," I said. "Now tell me about the smart ones."

He crooked a finger at me. I hitched my chair closer, and leaned in.

"There's a lot of guys out there with cash income they can't explain," he whispered.

"Oh," I said. "*Oh!* You mean Italian guys, with names like Guido and Franco."

"You're getting the picture. Only they're not all Italian."

"But what do they get out of it? I mean, they put money in, right? And it's supposed to come out clean?"

"There are lots of possibilities. After all, if they invest, they become a shareholder, and shareholders receive dividends. They could be hired on, put on the payroll, even become a paid board member—either now, or later, when they decide to retire. On the other hand, if Chem-Tech is as close as you say to being closed down by the EPA, they probably want a more immediate return. In fact, now that you mention it—where was I reading just the other day about organized crime and garbage disposal?"

"The Mafia hauls garbage?"

"Yeah. It's the perfect business for them to be in. I mean, apart from the more lurid possibilities, it's an operation that involves a lot of cash transactions. That makes it ideal for hiding cash profits."

"Listen," I said, "suppose a certain party was rounding up these kinds of investments. Would he have reasons to visit Florida other than deep-sea fishing?"

He gave me a knowing smile. "There's a lot going on in Florida besides Mickey Mouse parades."

I stared at him. I realized that I had a death grip on my pen, and I was feeling a little lightheaded.

"Is this the kind of stuff they're teaching in library school these days?"

He had the grace to blush, but he grinned at the same time.

Twenty-two

I parked on the courthouse square downtown, in front of a sign proclaiming that the county had been named for Abraham Montgomery Millins, a former governor and senator who was described as a "champion of the people's interests." I wondered if Mr. Millins was still hanging around, fretting over his county. There were still a few champions to be had, but their life expectancy was declining, and they could use a little supernatural help.

I found Louella piling up her Visa debt at a place called Junk-Tique.

"Oh, good," she said when she saw me. "You can help me get this rocker in the car."

"You know I can't lift anything on my bad ankle," I groused.

"I don't want you to lift it with your ankle," she said. "Grab that end. Come on, Cat. It looks like it's fixin' to rain."

When I spoke of my arithmetical deficiencies a while back, did I mention that I am spatially handicapped as well? I stood clear and let Louella try to maneuver the chair into the back of her wagon.

"These things are in the way, Cat," she pouted, and thumped the runners.

I didn't offer any comment. I would have sawed them off, but I could see that my approach might have been considered impractical. I felt the first raindrop hit my cheek.

"Pardon me for asking," I said when she got the tailgate closed at last, "but is Junior going to sit in that chair all the way back to Cincinnati? I mean, he does take up some room, and you've just cut down on that room by half."

"Oh, we'll figure something out."

"As long as we've got one thing clear: he is *not*, I repeat, *not* riding in my lap."

The dog in question was lurking on the other side of the door when we arrived back at the B & J in a downpour. He burst through the door, sped to the nearest puddle like a mud turtle on a skateboard, and returned to shower us with water and spatter us with mud.

"Good going, chump," I told him. "You'll be happy to know there is no room in the car for you on the return trip to Cincy."

He barked happily, looking from me to Louella. For some reason, I seemed to crack him up.

We picked up our video at the front desk, and Billie let us watch it in her living room. She claimed we'd had no visitors all day, just a call from Owen at Owen's Towing.

Sitting in matching recliners in Billie's living room, our feet propped up in front of a screen the size of Cinemas I and II combined, it felt like we were in a sports bar. I fast forwarded through a birthday party and another family gathering, over Louella's protests.

"But Cat, you can't just cut to the climax! Where's the build-up? Where's the suspense?"

"You'd better hope we don't get any more of it than we've got already," I observed. Earlier, I'd told her about what I'd learned at the library, and about Stan's speculations concerning possible mob connections.

I glimpsed something familiar, and slowed the tape. No doubt about it: we were looking at the concrete and steel of the Volunteer Dam.

Brenda Perkins had been right about her father's cinematographic style. There were lots of pans and zooms, mostly unmotivated. We got a close look at the stains on the side wall of the lock. We got a close look at the warning sign on the side of the dam itself. We got a slow pan of the Chickawee River—first one direction, then the other. We got a close-up of a girl of maybe ten, presumably Brenda herself, wearing earphones and rolling her eyes.

And there were voices. I'd forgotten there would be sound. Lester Perkins was wondering aloud for the third time about the function of the large concrete structures which straddled the highway out on the dam, when he was drowned out by the sound of the explosion. The camera jumped, and then swung down to focus on the far side of the bridge. Amid the sounds of noise and confusion, the camera zoomed in on a cloud of smoke in the distance, and bounced around as if the photographer were running. But apparently the projection of the turnoff hid the actual accident from view. Then the camera slid to the right and caught a truck traveling east. It was a green tank truck, its logo reduced to a flash of silver. Then the camera shifted, and it was gone. The cloud of smoke had dwindled. You couldn't see anything else.

I glanced at Louella. She held a hand pressed to her mouth, and she was crying.

"I didn't think it would—" she whispered. "I didn't expect to hear the crash, and then that explosion. I don't think it would have bothered me so much otherwise. But—that's when he died, wasn't it? When we heard the crash."

"It was very quick, Lou," I said gently.

"I know," she said, so softly that I could barely hear her. "But that's not the point, is it? I mean, if they murdered him fast or they murdered him slow, it's still murder."

"Yes," I agreed. "It's still murder."

We ran the tape over and over again. I kept my finger on the pause button, and by the end of it we both had our noses pressed against the screen, and Louella had her bifocals on.

"Shoot, Cat," she said at last, discouraged, "I don't know what good this tape will do. Everything's so little and fuzzy. And we can't even see the accident."

"It's no evidence for Murder One," I agreed. "As for the tank truck, maybe somebody can blow it up—I mean, make it bigger."

"You reckon they can do that to where we can see the driver's face?"

"I don't know about that," I admitted. "Or even if we'll get a license number. But we might be able to prove the truck made impact if we could blow up that right front fender enough. And we might even confirm the logo on the side."

"How we gonna do that?"

"Beats me. But considering what we're up against, the first thing we're going to do is make more copies of this tape."

That turned out to be a job too technologically advanced for Cayter to handle.

"Rats!" I said to Billie. "You mean I have to drive all the way to Nashville?" To myself, I pictured a few hours in a bar while the tape was copied.

That just goes to show how technologically advanced I was. As it turned out, two copies were made in less time than it takes to mix a Mai Tai.

I stuck one in an envelope and mailed it to Moses. I would have mailed it to myself, but if we were really up against the Syndicate I supposed they had flunkies on contract to watch my mailbox if they decided it was worth their while. I don't read detective fiction for nothing, you know.

Even with rush-hour traffic, I was back in Cayter by six. So we were lounging around, drinking gin, waiting for

Louella's hair to dry, and debating our dinner options when Billie burst through the door, huffing and puffing like the Little Engine that Could.

"Turn on the news, y'all. They're talkin' about that dead man—the one they found in Mr. McIntyre's house. According to the police, it's not like you said—Mr. McIntyre's friend? They're a-sayin' that that dead man is Mr. George Packer, the Millins County commissioner! And he didn't die in that fire, he was shot!"

Damn! I thought. I guess that meant he was canceling our interview for *Face to Face with Tennessee County Government*.

Twenty-three

V. I. and me were lunching al fresco at some upscale Chicago cafe with an Italian name. We were eating some kind of pasta with tomato sauce, which I'd already dropped down the front of my white polyester pullover. Her white silk blouse was pristine, but when she moved a certain way, I could see a spot up near the shoulder where a bullet hole had been expertly mended. There was opera music playing softly in the background, and every now and then, Vic would hum along. I had refrained from asking her whether her Moglis were really that comfortable. This was a business lunch.

"So tell me again about insurance fraud," I was saying. "I'm not sure I understood what you were getting at."

I was suddenly interrupted by a commotion in the background. I turned around and there was Peppy, dragging Mr. Contreras by her leash, barking her head off and making for our table. Everybody was staring at us.

"Would you shut up?" I shouted at the dog. That's me all over: I can do a fair imitation of class until I open my mouth. "Me and Vic are trying to have a civilized conversation."

My own voice woke me up. My eyes popped open and registered darkness. But the dog was still barking its head off, and that noise was punctuated by dull thuds as he threw his body against the door.

I sat up in confusion, still tasting the tomato sauce of my dreams.

"Yo! Dog!" I yelled. "Christ, would you—"

As I spoke I heard a funny whoosh, like opening a door on a wind tunnel. Then a flash of light lit up the room. I dove for the floor, acting more on instinct than reason, just as the explosion rocked the room and shattered the window.

It even woke Louella up.

"What the hell was *that*?"

I peeked over the edge of the bed in time to see Junior leap from the floor to the table and out the window.

I watched the play of light in the room, and winced.

"How attached to that car were you, Lou?"

"The car! You mean—?"

She jammed her feet into a pair of pink satin scuffs with feathers, and was out the door before I could stop her. I groped around for my Adidas, stuffed my feet into them, grabbed my gun off the nightstand, and followed.

She stood just outside, hands pressed against her face, staring at what used to be her station wagon but was now a good-sized bonfire. I didn't blame her. I stared at it, too. And so did three truckers and a tourist family, all in various states of undress, all roused from sleep in what had appeared to be a perfectly respectable motel when they checked in.

"I had the 'Greatest Hits of Patsy Cline' in there," Louella whispered. "Willie Nelson and Waylon Jennings. The Statler Brothers. Elvis. Goddam it, Cat, I had every album Elvis ever made."

"That's what car insurance is for, Lou," I said gently, patting her shoulder.

I heard sirens in the distance. I heard Emery at my elbow.

"Anybody hurt?"

I shook my head. What I didn't hear was the barking of a dog.

Billie arrived wearing some kind of muumuu that gave the scene a festive air, as if we were attending a luau and

the Hawaiian dancers were about to appear. The shotgun she carried spoiled the effect, though.

"Anybody hurt?" she asked. We all shook our heads.
The curtains had absorbed most of the broken glass, and as
I surveyed the motel, I realized that all the windows were
shattered. The closest car to Louella's had belonged to the
tourist family, and they had moved it as soon as they took
in the situation.

"Here comes the firemen," Billie observed unnecessarily as the truck roared into the parking lot, lights flashing.
"Better put that thing away, Cat."

It was good advice, but where? Would the cops want to
search our rooms for any reason? Even an illegitimate
one? Luckily, the Diane was small. I stepped into the
room, emptied out the cartridges, and stashed it in the
pocket of my robe. I thought of flushing the cartridges
down the toilet, but I didn't want to add to the repair bills
we'd already run up for Billie. By the time I stepped outside again, the fire was almost out. One firefighter was explaining to Billie that the day's rain had probably helped
to contain the fire by wetting everything down.

The cops who showed up were Cayter city cops. One
looked old and jaded, his partner young and eager. They
took Louella off to the office before I got a chance to talk
to her.

Then it was my turn. No, I couldn't explain the fire.
Yes, I presumed it had been set, because I had heard the
dog barking just before the explosion. (Plus, as far as I
knew, no Ford wagons had been recalled for a tendency to
spontaneously combust, but I didn't point this out.) No, I
couldn't imagine why someone would want to do such a
spiteful, mean thing to Louella, who had only come to
town to bury her uncle and see to his estate. Yes, I was
aware that his house had burned down, but no, I wasn't

aware of any pyromaniacs among those in his inner circle. No, I didn't know where the dog was now.

That part worried me, to tell you the truth. I didn't want to see him end up in the Chickawee River with a block of concrete tied to his paw. If he didn't show up in the next forty-eight hours, I would demand that the cops start checking Grubbs's employees for flea bites.

"I didn't tell them a thing, Cat!" Louella assured me afterward. Trust a mother to know how to lie, I always say.

Billie had been questioned, too. It was possible, as far as the police were concerned, that the fire had been intended to hurt her business. So far, everybody had opted to stay in their rooms for what was left of the night. But now Louella and I were sitting in Billie's living room, having a nightcap to steady our nerves.

"I didn't give 'em nothin'!" Billie said. "I told 'em y'all was real sweet, quiet widow ladies, and I didn't think this fire had nothin' to do with y'all. Then I kind of hinted around that maybe the Holiday Inn was lookin' to take over the property."

"Good. Meanwhile, Louella, I think you should give Freeman a call so he won't worry if he hears something about the fire. And so he can be on his guard. And—so he can be on the lookout for Junior." We'd tried to call from the convenience store earlier to tell Freeman about the videotape, but there'd been no answer.

"He's not answering," Louella called from the kitchen.

"How can he not answer?" I asked, frowning. "It's, what, three A.M.? Are you sure you dialed it right?"

"Okay, I called twice," Louella said, returning. "Maybe he's asleep, and doesn't hear it. Or maybe he's got it turned off. Maybe he gets threatening phone calls in the middle of the night."

"That's what worries me," I said. "I hope he's okay."

"Well, the phone wouldn't ring if the house had burned down, would it?"

"You're asking me?"

"Well, there ain't nothin' you can do about it," Billie said, practically. "You best be worryin' about yourselves. What are y'all goin' to do now?"

"I've been thinking about it," I said. "The fire was just a warning. Somebody's trying to scare us off." I thought about all the people I'd talked to so far, and wondered if any of them had given information to the wrong person, either deliberately or inadvertently. The alternative was even creepier: we'd been followed or watched or bugged. "I think we need to make them think that it worked."

"You mean, leave?" Louella asked, aghast.

I nodded. "You ought to leave anyway, Lou. You've finished up your business with the lawyer and bank, haven't you? And you're worrying about your business.

"So here's my plan. Tomorrow, we go out and rent a car, so you can drive back to Cincinnati. We pack our bags and leave town. But first we drive to Nashville, where I rent a car and make a few changes in my appearance and my wardrobe. You go back to Cincinnati, and I stay here in Tennessee. Not here, though, Billie; I don't think that's such a good idea. I'm afraid I'll have to move to the Ramada in Dalton."

"Don't worry, darlin'. Them Ramadas has plenty of insurance." She stressed the "in" in "insurance."

"But I can't just go off and leave you alone with a pack of flame-throwing lunatics running around!" Louella protested.

"She ain't exactly alone, Louella," Billie noted.

"That's right. There's Shotgun Sal here, and Freeman, and the Graysons, and Poppy. I wouldn't want to count too much on Hunt Smith. But that's still a lot of players on my team."

"And Em'ry," Billie put in. "He's the strong, silent type. But I'll tell you what, that boy can shoot the whiskers off a groundhog fifty feet away."

"Yeah, but they've probably got contract killers with Uzis!" Louella protested.

"And they're stupid enough to think that lighting a match to a station wagon is going to scare a pair of little old ladies into beating it out of town. See, Lou, there's two big advantages we've got over them. One, we're smarter than they are."

"And two?"

"We know enough to be scared of them. I don't think they know enough to be scared of us yet."

Twenty-four

So we followed my plan, with minor changes.

First thing in the morning, I called Officer Boone Danning of the Tennessee Valley Authority Office of Public Safety and offered him a videotape of the accident. He seemed caught off guard, but agreed to take a look at it.

We tried Freeman again, and got no answer, which made me extremely nervous. Louella had to hang around and wait for Owen to show up and tow what was left of the station wagon. It crossed my mind to wonder if Owen himself had set the fire to drum up some more business and push Louella to release Red's car. But I left Louella to cross-examine him. I had Emery drop me off at a car rental office, and then drove out to Freeman's with my heart in my throat.

I saw the cop car in Freeman's driveway first, then the yellow crime-scene tapes through the trees behind Freeman's house. My favorite sheriff's deputy, Jasper Treat, was standing in the driveway, chewing the fat with another officer.

"What's happened here?" I asked.

"Are you a member of Mr. Quinn's family?" He didn't seem to recognize me.

"I'm a friend of his niece, Mrs. Simmons. We met the other day at the courthouse."

"Oh, yeah. Miz—"

"Caliban."

"Yeah, right." He hitched up his pants as if he believed it were physically possible to move his belt to his waist. It settled in again under his paunch. "Were you looking for Mr. Quinn?"

"Yes. Is he here?"

"Was he expecting you?"

I hate it when cops do that: answer a question with a question. For the record, I hate it when psychiatrists do it, too.

"No. Is he here?"

"Doesn't seem to be," Deputy Treat said, turning to gaze at the house as if he shared my puzzlement. "You know where he might be?"

I felt a wave of relief so strong I thought it might knock me down. I reached out and steadied myself with a hand on the police cruiser.

"No. What happened up there?" I nodded at the yellow tape.

"Man was shot last night. You know anything about that?"

"Dead?" I asked. Two could play at this game.

He shook his head. "Caught him low." He tapped a spot low on his chest, and studied me for a reaction.

"Anybody I know?"

He shrugged.

"And the gun?"

"Don't know yet. You got a gun, Miz Callahan?"

"No, but some of my best friends do."

"Would that include Mr. Quinn?"

"I wouldn't know, Deputy. What time did all this happen?"

" 'Bout three this morning. I reckon you was in bed."

I shook my head. "Not me. Somebody torched Mrs. Simmons' station wagon out in front of the motel, and it woke us up." I didn't think this came as a surprise.

"I see you got you another car." He ducked his head at the Nissan I was driving.

"I reckon it'll get us back to Cincinnati," I said evenly.

"I reckon it will," he said. "You drive careful."

As I drove away I considered how little he really wanted to know from me. Either he didn't want to find Freeman, or he didn't think I could help him. I preferred the second option; the first unnerved me. If he didn't want to find Freeman, that could mean he knew where Freeman was.

I turned on the radio, and got the commodities report, but no local news.

To my surprise, Officer Boone Danning turned out to be more forthcoming. He took the video from me and listened in silence to my explanation of how I'd gotten it. Then we went into another room and watched it a few times.

"What do you think?" I asked finally. "Can we blow up that right front fender?"

"We might could," he agreed. "Worth a try. I'll be honest with you, Mrs. Caliban. This accident has got me goin'."

"What do you mean?"

"Well, I've seen the autopsy report. No alcohol in his blood. No sign of a heart attack or stroke or any other serious medical condition. He died from the—uh, impact, no doubt about that. Medical examiner says he fell asleep at the wheel. Simple as that."

"You don't agree."

"Put it to you this way. When does a person fall asleep at the wheel? When he's tired, of course. Mr. McIntyre could have been tired, but the neighbors say he was always an early riser. And you're more likely to be tired like that at the end of the day, not first thing. So what else would make a person fall asleep? Well, boredom, usually. A long stretch of flat road without much scenery, and no reason to pay attention. But that's not what we've got here. Now, maybe he was used to the scenery, but heck, it's scenic. He'd just made that right turn at the junction of

225 and 79. He was just starting acrost the dam. You think you could fall asleep in a situation like that?"

He shook his head. "I don't mind telling you, I'm real interested in finding that tank truck."

"I think you should know that Mrs. Simmons' car was set on fire last night."

He frowned. "Where was this?"

"In the motel parking lot, where we're staying."

"Anybody see who did it?"

"No." Junior, I said to myself.

"I reckon I'd better talk to the Cayter police, then. It was the Cayter police that came, not the county?"

"Right."

He made himself a note.

I couldn't believe someone was going to take this case seriously. So I didn't. I wanted to trust him, but I couldn't.

"Mrs. Simmons and I will be going back to Cincinnati today. But I know she'll feel better if she knows that her uncle's death is being thoroughly investigated."

"Oh, it's being investigated, all right," he assured me. "We take any death on TVA grounds seriously. See, it's not just the death itself. We need to know, from a public safety angle, if we—well, if we need to make any changes."

"Negligence" was the word hovering in the air. They were afraid of a lawsuit. Lucky you, I thought, if that's all you're afraid of. Wait till you find out what's really going on.

I drove back to the B & J, where Louella was still emptying the drawers and folding her clothes with tissue paper. I found most of mine on the floor, and stuffed them in my suitcase in less time than it took Louella to wrap her shoes. We called the Reverend Poppy, but she hadn't seen Freeman, either, and didn't know where he was. There was no answer at Hunt Smith's.

"If they've gone off fishing together, I'll shoot them myself," I growled.

"I just hope they haven't gone hunting," Louella said.

"If they have, I hope they don't get caught."

We said an appropriately emotional farewell to Billie, standing out front by the Nissan so that anybody who was interested could see us.

Finally, we heard on the car radio that a man had been shot off Rymer Cemetery Road. Police were still investigating; no charges had been filed. We drove to Nashville, where Louella insisted on going along for my makeover.

I'll spare you the details. Suffice it to say that before the beautician started, she said, "Honey, are you *sure* you want to go through with this?"

Twenty-five

The knock on the door startled me awake. I had dozed off in the air-conditioned splendor of my new room at the Ramada. I glanced at the clock: four-thirty.

My heart banged against my rib cage like a kettle drum. The only people who knew where I was were either on the road to Cincinnati, or on duty at the B & J front desk.

"Who is it?" I croaked, fumbling to reload the Diane.

"Ding-dong, Avon calling."

I turned the bolt and threw the door open.

"Aw, damn!" said the voice. "Helena Rubenstein got to you first."

Moses Fogg was dressed in plaid Bermuda shorts, a red polo shirt, white socks, and high tops. He was wearing red-framed sunglasses and a camera around his neck. The reason I noticed was, he was taking my picture with it.

"Would you get your ass in here before you ruin my incognito?" I stage-whispered.

"That what it is?" He slipped inside. "I thought maybe it was these sunglasses. Hold on, let me take 'em off. Oooh-ee, girl. You got to get you a new beauty consultant."

"Moses, what are you doing here?" I demanded. Not that I wasn't glad to see him. Finally, a cop I knew I could trust.

"Nice to see you, too. What you think I'm doin' here? Damn, Cat, you opened the door to the first good-looking guy fed you a line! You don't get your head together, girl, you might lose it."

"I recognized your voice."

"Right. And you think the folks you're dealing with got no brothers on the payroll can imitate my voice?"

"I recognized your sense of humor."

I had him there.

"So how'd you talk Billie into telling you where I was?"

"With my sparkling sense of humor. And a driver's license that proved I lived at the same address as you."

"A driver's license! Shit, anybody can fake a driver's license!"

"And a Golden Buckeye card. Anyhow, looks like I got here just in time. So far, they only took out your car."

"Louella's car, actually. And a rocking chair she paid too much for, plus a Century Twenty-one jacket and her tape collection. Say, this little visit wouldn't have anything to do with the question I asked Al to ask you about Pat Kinneady's death, would it?"

He sat down on the edge of the bed and looked at me.

"Look, Cat. I know you're not going to like what I got to say. I know you're serious about being a detective, and I'm all for it. No point in sitting around all the time, thinking about your arthritis pain. But Cat, the killers you've been up against so far—they were amateurs. Dangerous, no doubt about it. But amateurs. From the looks of things, you're now dealing with professionals—men who make their living out of killing on contract, and they're damn good at it."

"Are you telling me I should give up?" I asked. I didn't say it defensively; I really wanted to know. After all, he wasn't telling me anything that hadn't crossed my mind in the last twenty-four hours.

"What I'm saying is that you don't have the resources to go after these guys. And it's not your job. There are people who get paid to do that. I know how you feel about finding the man who killed Louella's uncle. Believe me, I do. But even if you find him, and even if he gets convicted—which is a mighty big 'if'—he's not going to be the one you want, and you may never find the man who paid the bill."

"I don't have to find the bastard who paid the bill, Moses. I know who he is."

"Okay, fine. You think you can find the evidence that the prosecutor needs to take the case to trial, much less to get a conviction?"

"No," I said simply. "I've been thinking it over, Moses. I know what you're saying, and you're right. I'll never see Red's murderer convicted for that murder."

Moses visibly relaxed.

"I've adjusted my expectations. To tell you the truth, I could settle for convicting the bastard who drove the truck that forced Red off the road. I wish I could do better than that, but I'm resigned. Anyway, there's something I want more than any murder conviction now."

"What's that?"

"The same thing Red wanted—the thing he died for. I want to shut down Chem-Tech, permanently. I want to run Isaiah T. Grubbs and his cronies out of the county, and see the residents of Millins County get some peace and quiet for a change."

Moses began to chuckle, and shook his head. "That's what I love about you, Cat. You so practical. When you said you was adjustin' your expectations, I thought you meant you was lowerin' 'em. You got a plan, or you jus' playin' this thing by ear?"

"First tell me what you know about Pat Kinneady's death that made you come riding to the rescue."

He sighed, and fished a piece of paper and his bifocals out of his pocket. "Alcohol poisoning, right? Some abrasions and bruises, probably caused by a fall, right? There's a method used by some professionals which involves forcing alcohol down the victim's throat. Victim gets held down or tied down, resulting in some abrasions, but nothing that can't be explained by drunkenness. Sometimes they use a funnel—not a tube, 'cause that would cause swelling. You get a finding like the one in Kinneady's death: alcohol poisoning."

I felt sick.

"Now," he said gently, "you want to tell me the rest, or pack up and go home?"

So I told him. And he asked a lot of questions.

"You know, Cat, this Isaiah Grubbs makes a good villain. But how do you know he was involved with Red's death? Other people stood to gain, including this Healthwatch group."

"I thought you just got through telling me that Kinneady's death was a professional hit."

"Sure, or at least it could be. But that doesn't mean Red's was. Running somebody off the road is a hell of a lot chancier than shoving three bottles of whiskey down their throat."

"Well, if we're right about the tank truck, though, the driver had to be somebody who had access to a Chem-Tech truck."

"And you told me all these men worked for Chem-Tech at some point—Freeman Quinn, Hunt Smith, Kinneady, and McIntyre, even this Wade Oakley you thought got killed in the fire. Any one of them might still have ties to Chem-Tech. And Quinn got life insurance when Red died."

"You're leaving out the Graysons?"

"I ain't leavin' anybody out at this point," he said, a little irritably. "Anybody could have ties to Chem-Tech that you don't know about."

"That's true," I said. "But timing is a factor, too. Why

that day, of all days, when Red was on his way to Cincinnati to talk to somebody at the EPA about Chem-Tech?"

"Maybe because he was up and about earlier that day, before there was much traffic around."

"And somebody was just parked around the corner in a fucking tank truck, waiting for an auspicious occasion?"

"You got a point," he conceded. "But you said nobody knew he was going to Cincinnati, except Louella and Freeman. In your scenario, that means one of them tipped off Chem-Tech."

"Somebody at the EPA knew he was coming, and we're assuming they knew what he wanted to talk about. Maybe the two hits were different because the second one was rushed. Maybe Grubbs or Packer, or whoever, didn't have time to call in the professionals."

"Yeah, but even that EPA appointment doesn't make sense, Cat. The Cincinnati operation is a laboratory, not an enforcement branch."

"Are you sure?"

"Sure. I've been there. If somebody called up with a bee in his bonnet about a disposal site, my guess is he'd get referred to the regional office, wherever that is. It's not Cincinnati."

"So you don't believe that Red ever had an appointment to begin with?"

"Maybe he thought he did, but I'd be surprised. It's like if somebody called us up in Juvie, and told us they wanted to report a homicide, do you think we'd take the report?"

"You might if they threatened to hang up if you didn't handle it. Suppose they'd been given your name."

He shook his head. "Wouldn't matter. They'd have to go through channels. If they refused to do that, we'd probably write 'em off as a nut case anyway."

"I still want to shut down Chem-Tech," I insisted.

"I understand that. But what makes you think you can

do what this local group can't do, even with the help of a professional organization like Greenpeace?"

"I'm a detective, remember?" I grinned at him. "Maybe they don't have the right ammunition yet. That's where I come in. I think that's what Red was up to, right before he died."

I showed him my photocopy of the mysterious graphic.

"Looks like one of those earthquake readings."

"This whole area, including the chemical plants, the incinerator, and the landfill, is sitting alongside a fault line called the New Madrid fault."

"So you're thinking that a major earthquake could cause a major environmental disaster?"

I nodded. "Meanwhile, even if I caught Red's murderer, remember, there are still a few corpses unaccounted for."

"This Millins County commissioner, for one."

"Yeah. If that's who it is."

"You think the cops have misidentified him?"

"Or misinformed the public. Seriously, Moses, I don't know. I don't trust anybody in a position of authority around here. I just hope that the body in the woods behind Freeman's house wasn't Freeman."

"Maybe it was this Wade Oakley. Maybe he's finally shown up."

"God, I hope not. I'd like to think our side has won a few for a change."

"Trouble is, you don't know who's on our side."

"Right. Or at least—well, I'll admit I don't know for sure. But I'll be shocked if Freeman turns out to be one of them. And seriously upset if Freeman gets convicted for killing any of them."

We had a few drinks out of my private stash. Moses looked glum when I told him that Millins County was dry. The talk was winding down, and we were beginning to discuss dinner, when we were interrupted by a knock on the door.

Moses looked at me. I shrugged. He waved me into the bathroom, and pulled a gun out of his athletic bag. His side to the door, he called, "Who is it?"

I didn't hear the answer, but he glanced at me, rolled his eyes, and opened the door.

"Dad! Mom! Why did you run off and leave us like that? Why, little Sidney has been crying himself to sleep ever since you left!"

Kevin O'Neill was staring at us reproachfully. He was wearing white shorts, an electric-blue Hawaiian shirt, and neon sunglasses perched on his head. As I looked, two little black points appeared over his left shoulder. Two little yellow eyes followed like twin sunrises. I blinked, and there was Sidney, teetering triumphantly on Kevin's shoulder.

"*Mother!*" Kevin's voice dropped to a shocked exclamation. "What have you done to yourself!"

Twenty-six

"Christ! I can't believe you brought Sidney!" I exploded, plucking my youngest off of Kevin's Hawaiian shirt. "This is no fucking family picnic, Kevin! We're dealing with firebombings and contract killers, not to mention chemical warfare! How could you?"

"Now, now, Mrs. C., it wasn't my idea, it was his," Kevin said soothingly. "I didn't even know he was in the car until I turned off I75. He must have been sleeping on the beach towel on the floor in the back seat. I never saw him, honest!"

My little black stowaway snuggled happily into my arms, and purred contentedly.

"Well," I said, relenting, "I want you to take him back tomorrow. This is no place for him."

"Might be useful, Cat, having Kevin here," Moses suggested. "If they firebomb one car, we still got two left."

Kevin was circling me, studying my new hair color and style.

"How do they get that color of lavender, Mrs. C.? And how ever did they get your hair around those rollers?"

"I suppose you left Delbert in charge."

"Delbert's a great kid, Mrs. C., as long as you don't let him go shopping unsupervised."

"What's that supposed to mean?"

"Sidney loves Del, don't you, Sid? Say, did Moses tell you how Delbert set up this program on the computer that lets you figure out what to make by entering the ingredients you have on hand?"

"No, and he didn't tell me that Sidney had a lump on

his head the size of an artichoke, either." I glared at them both, fingering Sidney's head gingerly.

They exchanged guilty looks.

"See, Cat, we don't know how he got that—" Moses began.

"We have a theory, though, Mrs. C."

"*You* got a theory, you mean. I still say an eggplant wouldn't make that kind of a knot."

Kevin sighed. "Most eggplants wouldn't, but ours have kind of gotten out of hand since you left, Mrs. C."

"He seemed okay, though," Moses added.

"Yeah, we shined a flashlight in his eyes, and thumped his kneecaps, and he bit us, which seemed to indicate that his reflexes were normal. Really, Mrs. C., I hate to admit it, but he might be safer here with us."

"Christ, Kevin, this whole goddam county is contaminated, and we're not five miles downwind of the worst offender! The first person to die suspiciously in this whole business was a veterinarian who noticed high cancer rates in the animals she was seeing. I can give him bottled water and food out of a can, but I don't even want him breathing the air!"

For a few moments, nobody spoke.

Then Moses said, rubbing his hands together, "Then we best wrap this thing up as quick as we can, and get the hell out of town."

That's what I love about Moses: you have to put up with a lot of grumbling, but he's always there to grumble.

Dinner marked our debut as a family, minus Sidney, of course. Me and Moses played a matched set of older parents, salt and pepper, past our prime but attempting to recover it on a family vacation with our grown son, who was too tall and too Irish to look the least bit genetically connected to us. My plan to appear inconspicuous in my incognito was shot all to hell.

"Are we sure this restaurant is integrated?" Moses frowned, scanning the dining room.

"I hate to tell you this, Moses, but I haven't seen too many black people since I arrived," I admitted.

He dropped his voice to a whisper. "Are you trying to tell me that in addition to being nonalcoholic and carcinogenic, this county is all-white?"

I shrugged.

"At least all your people had the good sense to leave," Kevin offered, adding as an afterthought, "Dad."

"Yeah, and if I got any sense, I'll follow them."

Otherwise, we didn't talk about the case at dinner, since we'd agreed not to discuss it in public. Kevin whipped out some dopey tourist brochures he'd picked up at a rest stop, and started lobbying for the paddleboats. He was going overboard, if you ask me, but then, he usually did.

We held a war council in the motel room after dinner. In the car on the way back, I'd given Kevin an account of everything that had happened. He was now kneeling on the floor, peeling the coating off a piece of fried chicken, tearing it into little bits, and setting it on a paper plate for Sidney. To tell you the truth, I don't know why he bothered with the paper plate; Sidney caught every piece on the first bounce.

"Look, the main questions before us are these," I said, writing them down on a legal pad with tiny tooth indentations in its surface. "One: how do we prove that somebody driving a Chem-Tech truck deliberately forced Red off the road? Two: how do we prove that Chem-Tech is a contaminated site operating outside of all legal guidelines, and shut it down?"

"Well, shoot! That's only two questions," Kevin complained. "What am *I* supposed to do, sit out at the pool and work on my tan?"

"You and Sidney can work on tracking down Junior,

who is looking to be our best witness. I think I have a pair of shredded pantyhose Sidney can sniff; then you can take him over to the B & J and see if he can pick up a trail.

"But seriously, folks, we've got shit in terms of hard evidence of any kind. We've got the car Red died in, the piece of paper he died for, and a home video showing a cloud of smoke and a tank truck."

"Well, can't you blow up the image and tell whether the truck's got a dent in it on the right side?" Kevin asked.

"I don't know. I'm leaving that part up to the TVA officer in charge of the case. But it would probably take more than that to bring the truck driver to court." I glanced at Moses, who nodded.

"But if you identified the truck that was involved, couldn't they test it for a paint match with Red's car?" Kevin persisted.

"They could, but the question is whether they'd find anything. These trucks are hauling chemicals, and a lot of those chemicals are solvents. Hell, Chem-Tech is surrounded by chemical plants, and apparently a lot of their disposal business comes from paint manufacturers. If anybody knows how to get rid of unwanted paint, it's Chem-Tech and their cronies."

"Well, in that case, it sounds pretty impossible to me," Kevin said.

"Moses?" I asked hopefully.

He shook his head. "Beats me, Cat. Even if you could trace who it was knew Red was going to Cincinnati to talk, and even if you could prove the identity of the perps who searched Red's house and burned it down, you couldn't bring murder charges against them. The best you could do would be to get the perp who killed the commissioner—what's his name?"

"George Packer."

"Yeah, him."

"But what if that particular perp is one of the good guys—somebody on our team?" I sighed, and stared at my legal pad. The only things written there were questions. "Maybe we should go on to the second problem."

"You mean the easy one," Kevin said. "The one where we convince the EPA to do its job and shut down Chem-Tech."

"That's the one."

"So we go to the EPA office in—where is it?"

"Atlanta."

"Yeah, Atlanta. And we point out how many times they've cited Chem-Tech for violations in the past, of which they are well aware. Plus we throw in some cancer statistics from the county, and from Chem-Tech's own employees—of which they are probably also well aware. Then, as our *pièce de résistance*, we slap down Red's affidavit about the buried drums of chemicals, and suddenly, they are overcome with outrage and embarrassment, and announce that Chem-Tech has just violated its last regulation and broken its last law. And just like an avenging angel, they swoop down and declare Chem-Tech a Superfund site—"

"—at which point they award the clean-up contract to a wholly-owned subsidiary of Chem-Tech," I finished gloomily.

Kevin looked at me reproachfully. "Whose fantasy is this, anyway?"

"Just stick around a few days. The goddam acid rain will eat right through your smile umbrella," I warned him.

"Well, Kevin's right about one thing," Moses put in. "If—and I'm only saying if—Red was killed for that affidavit, somebody must have taken it seriously. That means maybe somebody thought the EPA would have taken it seriously enough to do what Kevin's predicting they'd do."

"Suppose we threatened to call a press conference, Mrs. C.," Kevin suggested.

"Wouldn't work," I said. "Healthwatch says none of the local press will touch this issue."

"Does it have to be local?"

"Well, I guess we could call the Washington Press Club, and see who's interested in flying out."

"No, but the *New York Times* must have a stringer in the area."

"You might be right," I conceded, "but from what the Graysons tell me, anybody who lives within striking distance of Chem-Tech will know to stay clear of them. Anyway, I know you think everybody reads the *Times*, Kevin, but around here people probably either wouldn't read it, wouldn't care if they did read it, or would resent Yankee intrusion into Tennessee politics."

"But it's not just Tennessee, Mrs. C. This place is within a hundred-mile radius of four states."

"It is?"

"I keep telling you to stop at those visitors' centers, Mrs. C. Look at a map. I'll bet Missouri, Illinois, Indiana, and Kentucky all get the benefit of Chem-Tech's smoke on a breezy day. And with a good wind, maybe Arkansas, Mississippi, Alabama, and Georgia, too."

"Shit! Maybe we should call *Sixty Minutes*!"

"That's the spirit, Mrs. C! Your daughter would be proud!" He meant my daughter the activist, not the accountant daughter, who would die of humiliation if she ever saw me interviewed on *Sixty Minutes*.

"I'll bet Healthwatch has tried it, though," I mused. "They seem to have tried everything to get some press coverage on this."

"Yeah, but they don't have your powers of persuasion," Kevin said enthusiastically.

"Best get you a bodyguard," Moses muttered.

"I don't need a bodyguard," I said. "I'm married to an ex-cop, remember?"

He just grunted. "You got a plan B?" he asked. "Let's say, just for the sake of argument, that the EPA thanks you politely, takes your piece of paper, and promises they'll look into it. Let's say you throw a press conference and nobody comes. What happens then? I mean, I hate to be a wet blanket, but Chem-Tech is not your problem, Cat. You live about seven hours away from here, in another state, in another city with plenty of problems of its own, not the least of which is that garbage incinerator they want to build. And I'm not even mentioning the aphids, the weeds, and the whitefly."

"We've got whitefly?" I said faintly.

"I see your point, Moses," Kevin said. By now he was stretched out flat on one of the beds, and Sidney was taking his postprandial bath on Kevin's stomach. "But now that we know what we do, how can we just walk away from it? These people aren't getting help from any of the agencies who are supposed to be helping them, from the local police on up to the Feds."

"The Feds," I repeated thoughtfully. "Moses, what would it take to get the Bureau involved?"

"Highly unlikely," he said. "Environmental law is the EPA's jurisdiction. They're not going to violate those boundaries."

"But racketeering—that's FBI turf. You're the one who thinks the mob is involved. What if we could prove it?"

"How? You can't use Kinneady's autopsy report—it's not enough to go on. Like I said, the Bureau's going to be real cautious about crossing the EPA. They're sure not going to make a decision like that on the basis of rumors from the local barbecue joint that a county commissioner takes lots of vacations in Florida."

"Maybe I'll put my friendly neighborhood business librarian on it," I said. "If he came up with a list of board members and officers for every company tied to Chem-Tech, would you be willing to show it to an agent who specializes in organized crime?"

Moses sighed. "Let's see what it looks like first, Cat. These kinda favors ain't like free suckers at the bank—you gotta hoard 'em. I hope we come up with something better than that."

"Yeah, and I hope it's not Cat's body in a box," Kevin offered.

"Well, we'll all have to put on our thinking caps, won't we?" I said.

"Yes, Mom," Kevin said.

"Anyway, we don't have any more time for that now."

"Where are we going?"

"To make contact with one of my agents."

"Ooh, neat! Should I put on dark clothes and carry a gun and a flashlight?"

"Only if you want to get arrested as a suspicious character at Dairy Queen."

Twenty-seven

"Laureen! How in the world are you, girl! I ain't seen you since the Elks spaghetti supper! Lord, I didn't hardly recognize you!"

Billie was playing her role to the hilt. If she was surprised to see me surrounded by family, she didn't show it.

"You remember my husband," I said, gesturing in Moses' direction in case she needed a prompt.

"I surely do," she said. "And this can't be—"

"Little Kevin," I finished for her. "It surely is."

"Hi!" Kevin said, slurping through his straw.

"Can you set?" I asked, getting into my role. Kevin moved over on the plastic bench. Billie sat down.

"You will never believe who called me today! This is just such a coincidence!"

"Who?"

Her voice dropped, even though we'd chosen the most isolated table we could find. "Freeman Quinn."

"No, not really!" I felt flooded with relief. "Where has that old rascal been keeping himself?"

Her voice dropped again. "He says he went fishin'. Says he couldn't get to sleep last night, so he got up and went fishin'. Didn't know anything about all the excitement until he got home around one this afternoon."

I looked at her in dismay. "Billie, nobody goes fishing in Millins County, do they?"

"Some still do, I reckon. He says he went up to Lake Collins and caught a largemouth bass and a couple of bluegill."

"Anybody go with him?"

She shook her head, and lit a cigarette, to Kevin's dismay. "Pass me that ashtray, honey," she told him.

"Was he calling from home?"

She shook her head. "Said he was at a friend's house."

"Does he know who got shot out behind his house?"

"It was a fella name of—wait while I get my glasses on, I wrote it down—Dylan McQuacken."

"You're kidding."

"That's his name. Used to work with Freeman at Chem-Tech, though he don't work there no more, Freeman says. Freeman says he's dumber'n a fence post."

"What's Freeman say about why this McQuacken was hanging out in his woods, and how he got shot?"

"Freeman says he figures McQuacken and maybe some other fellas was there to cause trouble—maybe even fire-bomb the car, like they did to Louella's, or the house."

"Is that what the cops say? I mean, you'd think they would have smelled kerosene or something."

"The cops didn't tell him nothing. They was a-talkin' like it was just some burglary that didn't come off."

"I guess if the house had burned down and nobody had been shot, they would have blamed kids playing with matches," I grumbled. "What about the questions I gave you? Did you ask him?"

"Yes, and he says he hasn't seen hide nor hair of Junior, but says not to worry. That dog is real smart, he says, and can look after hisself. But he reckons Junior will turn up, either at his place or at Red's, and he'll call Red's neighbors and let 'em know."

Real smart? Junior?

"About that Wade Oakley fella. Freeman says he did finally talk to him—says he's been out of town, visitin' an old army buddy. He was real sad to hear about Red's death."

"Did Freeman ask about the wedding ring?"

"He says that Wade says he give it to Red to give to Wade's daughter, who lives in Athens with her mama. I reckon it was just chance it come to be found near that dead body, way the house had fallen in and all."

"I reckon," I said, frowning.

"I told Freeman where you was stayin' and all, and told him to call you if he needed to. I told him you wouldn't call him in case his phone was tapped."

"Thanks, Billie. You're a real trooper."

"Don't you worry none about me," she said, giving me a wink. "This is the most excitement I've had since McKinley Fewks got drunk and tried to launch his Evinrude in the swimming pool up at the Night-O-Rest."

We set up another meeting at McDonald's the next night, so we could keep Billie posted and find out about any phone calls for me. Then we stopped at the counter to get some ice cream for our feline shut-in.

"Hey, Mom, look!" Kevin nudged me. "For just fifty cents extra we can get it in one of these cool karate cups that glow in the dark!"

"Goddam!" I exclaimed, startling the sweet young thing behind the counter and making her put a crook in the frozen dairy dessert she was dispensing.

"What?"

"I mean, golly, Kevin! That's it! You're a genius!"

"Come on, honey, we got to go." Moses gripped my elbow and steered me out the door.

"What is it, Mrs. C?" Kevin asked, trailing us with his souvenir cup full of chemicals got up to resemble ice cream. Sidney, being a child of the eighties, wouldn't know the difference.

"Glowing in the dark," I said softly. "Everybody's been warning me about getting too close to Chem-Tech if I don't want to 'glow in the dark.' What makes something glow in the dark?"

"Oh, shit!" Kevin said, regarding his souvenir cup with horror.

"What if that graph Red left with the Graysons wasn't a seismograph at all? What if he got it from Pat Kinneady, or somebody else who worked at Chem-Tech and could get close to that landfill without arousing suspicion? What if it's some kind of graph that measures radioactivity?"

Twenty-eight

"It's some kind of printout from a Geiger counter," Mamie Grayson confirmed. "You know those machines you see on television that make a noise when they get close to something radioactive? Well, it appears you can get them to print out a record. Wait while I get my notes.

"I'm so glad y'all stopped by. I was so disappointed when I called the motel and they said you'd gone home already. I'd just talked to Dan Farley, that nice young man from Greenpeace, and Wynn was out at an auction, and I was just dying for somebody to talk to!"

We were sitting in her living room this time, being plied with coffee and coffee cake. Kevin, who had eaten a four-course breakfast not an hour before, was scarfing down his cake like the growing boy he is.

"Not that it was news to me that Chem-Tech's radioactive, but still. We've been trying for years to get the EPA to test it, but they wouldn't. They just kept telling us that Chem-Tech wasn't certified to handle radioactive waste, as if that settled anything! Why, Chem-Tech wasn't certified to build and run a third incinerator, but they did it."

"So will the record Red left you do you any good?"

She shook her head. "I don't see how. It doesn't even say where it came from, or when the test was made. There's nothing official about it."

"Moses?"

"She's right, Cat. This graph could have come from anywhere, anytime. It could even be faked. It doesn't prove anything."

"Except that we've been right to keep pushing the EPA

on this," Mamie said. "I'll admit that it's gratifying from that angle."

"So what we need to do is to arrange the test again, only this time in the presence of witnesses," I proposed.

"Good luck," Kevin said morosely.

"That place is like an armed camp," Mamie agreed.

"Don't you have any contacts inside? Any plants?" I asked, thinking of Pat Kinneady.

"Not anymore," she admitted. "They run a real tight ship."

"But the landfill must be huge, right? Can't we sneak up on it in the dead of night?"

"We'd have to go over a barbed-wire fence, and then outrun the dogs."

I surveyed our human resources, which were heavy on senior citizens. Even as we spoke, Moses was massaging his right knee, sore from a day of driving. Kevin was the youngest on our team, and he wasn't as young as he was pretending. I supposed I could throw in Poppy MacDougal and her husband, Mike, but I didn't think Ruthie would appreciate it if I involved her parents in a nighttime mission impossible.

"I see your point," I conceded. "But there has to be some way in."

"We could climb on the back of a tank truck when it comes to a stoplight," Kevin ventured. "We could wear those suction cup things on our hands and feet, and put the testing equipment in a backpack."

I gave him a look. "I doubt if we could even run the equipment ourselves."

"We could parachute in," he said. He glanced at Moses' knee. "Well, maybe not."

"No, wait," I said eagerly. "You may have something."

"Now, Cat," Moses began, "I volunteered to help you out, but if you think I'm going to strap this tired old body into a parachute and jump out of a plane into a toxic land-fill protected by the mob, you even crazier'n I thought you were."

"No, don't you see? *We* don't have to go anywhere. It's the testing equipment that has to get close to the ground. Am I right?"

"Right," Moses admitted cautiously.

"So what if we could lower the equipment to the ground without getting close ourselves?"

"From a plane?" he asked skeptically.

"Uh-uh," I said, grinning. "Not a plane. A helicopter."

Suffice it to say my plan received mixed reviews, and I'll bet you can guess how it went: Kevin was all for it, while Moses was hanging back, thinking up all the "what-ifs."

But the biggest hurdle had to be cleared first. I could see how my plan would play in a Sylvester Stallone movie, but we had to find out if it was scientifically feasible. Like I said, my daughter Franny had never attempted a science major, and my own knowledge of physics was limited to how particles behaved in the presence of a vacuum cleaner.

"Can you get somebody from Volunteer State to help us?" Kevin asked.

"I'd rather not," I said. "It has to be somebody we know we can trust, as in somebody who doesn't owe their latest piece of equipment to a local corporation. We'd better ask Greenpeace for help. Shit, I don't even know what kind of help we need. What do you call somebody who runs a Geiger counter?"

So Mamie went to call Dan Farley, the Greenpeace guy. This made me more than a little nervous, but she explained that she had a nephew who was an electronics whiz and a part-time security consultant.

"He says they haven't yet invented a bug that he can't detect and de-bug. He spends a lot of time over here."

In a minute, she returned with a report. "Dan says we need a health physicist, and he'll try to get somebody from Nashville to drive over. Anything else y'all want to ask him?"

"Tell him I might want the physicist to conduct another test I have in mind."

Moses and Kevin raised their eyebrows at me, but I was used to that.

We left after arranging to call Mamie later for the scoop on the physicist. Kevin was brushing crumbs off his T-shirt and clutching a recipe card.

Twenty-nine

It was pretty uneventful there for a few hours. I say that because I had the sensation of standing in the eye of a hurricane, waiting for the next blast.

We stopped off at the Volunteer State library to talk to Stan the librarian, who agreed to produce the printouts I wanted. We warned him not to tell anybody what he was doing, and Moses flashed his police ID, and Stan looked impressed and said he understood.

We couldn't think of anything else to do, and Kevin was lobbying for a swim, so we went back to the motel. Freeman called just as I walked in the door. Just to play it safe, I took down his number, and called him back from the pay phone in the motel lobby. I told him what we were up to. I listened politely while he told me about his fishing trip. I didn't believe a word of it, but I wasn't sure I wanted to know what he didn't want to tell me. He asked me to keep him posted.

We went out by the pool and played cards while Kevin swam—over my objections about water quality, I might add—and Sidney sat hunched under Moses' chair, looking miserable in his new leash from the Piggly Wiggly. In no time we were arguing over who was going on the helicopter mission to hell. I maintained that Moses' police training made him an excellent candidate.

"Police training? I was trained as a cop, not a commando. I was in Juvie, not SWAT."

"Not even those rush-hour traffic reports from the sky? Didn't you ever do those?"

"Not me. Flying makes me sick."

Clearly, I was going to have to use my infamous persua-

sive powers on him. My ultimate goal was to make sure
that yours truly was not in that helicopter when it swooped
down over the landfill.

After a late lunch, I took them on a scouting trip around
New Union and the industrial park. Moses insisted on
driving because he said we'd look more like a typical family that way. I didn't think we could look any less like a
typical family, but didn't argue. We stopped in the parking
lot at Chem-Tech. I got out a map and studied it for cover.

"It doesn't look that imposing, does it?" Kevin observed, a trace of disappointment in his voice.

"You ever heard about the 'banality of evil'?" Moses rejoined. "There it is."

I understood Kevin's reaction. From its reputation, you
would have expected the place to be huge, like Dracula's
castle, or something. In reality, it was dwarfed by all the
chemical plants around it. The incinerator towers looked
like stovepipes.

"That's the road that leads back to the landfill," I
pointed out, nodding at the road that runs alongside the
parking lot. "There's a guardhouse just the other side of
the building."

"You count the guns?" Moses asked.

"Or the guards?" Kevin added.

"Or the dogs?"

"Well, they can hardly have a goddam army, now can
they?"

"If they got all the local PDs, they don't need one," Moses said.

Back at the motel, I checked in with Mamie and got the
name and number of our physicist in Nashville: Dr. Reiko
Fujimura. I called and got her on the first try. I admit I
was a little surprised by her voice. She sounded young,
and was soft-spoken, with a slight but noticeable Japanese
accent.

"You do understand," I said, "that there could be danger involved? I mean, shooting and all?"

She laughed. "When I work for Greenpeace, there is usually danger involved," she said, putting me in my place. "I do know how to shoot, but it's difficult to do that and operate the equipment at the same time. I assume you'll provide me with some cover."

I assumed so, too, although this part was a little hazy as yet.

She told me that Dan Farley of Greenpeace had made arrangements with a helicopter pilot for late Saturday afternoon. I'd supposed we'd have to go make our case with the pilot who ran the tourist helicopter, but Dan had vetoed that idea, saying that we needed someone we could trust not to give the game away to the opposition. Dan chose late Saturday afternoon because he figured that things would be relatively quiet at Chem-Tech, and because the guards might mistake us for a tourist helicopter long enough to give us some extra time before the shooting started. We were to meet Dr. Fujimura and our pilot at an airport across the county line in Gainard County, near a town called Lime. It had just worked out that the closest airport was across the county line, apparently, but Dan also wanted to cross jurisdictional boundaries just to confuse the issue in case we were chased.

Getting arrested was the least of our worries; if we were arrested, at least we would be alive.

"Dan also recommends that you videotape the whole operation," Dr. Fujimura was saying. "It may discourage violence, and it could be valuable in court."

Well, that pretty much left me out of the helicopter. I couldn't shoot a gun any better than a Keystone Kop, and my photography skills could be charitably described as dismal. It was easy to criticize old Lester Perkins for his

lack of polish on the accident scene footage; at least he re
membered to take the lens cap off.

I described the other test I wanted her to perform, and
she confirmed that it could be easily done. After checking
her calendar, she agreed to meet me the next afternoon,
Friday, at twelve.

When I talked things over with Moses and Kevin, we
realized that we needed more people involved in the operation.

"The Healthwatch people will help out on the ground,"
I said, "but I think we need Freeman in on this. I'm going
to call Billie and see if she can send somebody over to his
place with a message, or go herself."

"What you really need is one big meeting of everybody
who's going to be involved, Mrs. C.," Kevin put in. "Like
they do in the war movies."

"He's right, Cat," Moses said. "And the sooner, the better."

"Well," I said, looking at my watch, "we'd better go see
Mamie and Wynn. It's about dinnertime, so maybe they'll
both be home."

Kevin brightened. "Yeah! And maybe they'll ask us to
stay!"

Thirty

Kevin got his wish, and we got our meeting. It wasn't easy.

Wynn and Mamie again assured us that the latest tap had been removed from their phone by their nephew, the electronics whiz, or they would never have used it to call Dan Farley in the first place. I was beginning to realize how you never think about this security stuff until it becomes a part of your everyday life. When I thought about some of the movies I'd seen, what worried me was the possibility of guys in vans with remote microphones that can hear everything going on from across the street. I was beginning to feel like a member of the fucking French resistance, only the Gestapo had gone high-tech.

So Wynn and Mamie set up a meeting for the next night at somebody's barn on one of those numbered county roads I hoped to hell we could find. They talked in a pre-arranged code in case any other phones were tapped—something about a hailstorm and seeing folks at the seven o'clock service. We met Billie at McDonald's, and gave her the information to pass on to Freeman. She promised to send Emery with the message as soon as she got back to the B & J. She also promised to be at the meeting with her shotgun loaded.

"We don't want to shoot anybody at the meeting, for crissake," I told her.

"You can't never tell, darlin'," she said calmly. "You can't never tell."

And she was right, of course.

Back at the motel we called Delbert, who seemed at first to have forgotten who we were. I made Sidney go spend the night with the boys next door. He'd developed a fondness for jumping from one bed to the other, and he wasn't too particular what he landed on or at what hour.

"I'll take him tomorrow night," I promised grudgingly, "when you guys need to rest your trigger fingers."

On Friday morning, accompanied by Moses and Kevin, I went to a gun store for the first time in my life. To tell you the truth, it gave me the creeps. My .25 looked pretty damned innocuous next to most everything that was on display in the case.

"You think I should upgrade for this operation?" I asked Moses.

He shook his head. "If you're going to be on the ground, the only thing that would be any use would be a rifle." As the time grew nearer, we'd kind of tacitly agreed that it made more sense for Moses to ride in the chopper. "You don't have time between now and tomorrow to learn how to shoot a rifle."

"And if we took you out this afternoon to teach you, Mrs. C., you'd be too sore tomorrow to do any good."

So they both bought ammo, and we left it at that. I want to go on record, by the way, as having offered to pay for their bullets or cartridges or whatever you call them. But when I whipped out my credit card, they got this really funny look on their faces, and insisted on paying themselves.

We also stopped at any army-navy surplus store.

"You going to get sky-blue camouflage jackets?"

"Bulletproof vests, if they've got any," Moses said.

That made me nervous, and I was still arguing with them as we stood in line to pay.

"Look, are you absolutely sure that 'surplus' doesn't mean used or defective? If it's the cost you're worried about, I'll pay. These are probably seconds left over from Korea, when they didn't have bullets like they have now."

Then we went by the Volunteer State library, where Stan handed us a brown envelope with an air of great secrecy.

"When are you going to call the Bureau?" I asked Moses in the car.

"After tomorrow," he said. What he didn't say was that he wasn't even willing to trust the FBI.

At high noon we were staked out behind an abandoned roadside tavern across from Owen's Towing when a rust-spotted blue Ford pickup pulled into the parking lot behind us. The door opened and out hopped a young woman wearing jeans and a short-sleeved cotton shirt and boots. At least, I assumed she was a woman; she was less than five feet tall and looked about thirteen, with thick black hair that had been chopped off at her ears and left to its own devices, and freckles under dark sunglasses. She was shoving a gun under her waistband as she strode toward us.

Moses looked at me. "Well, at least she don't make much of a target."

I nodded. "Unlike some," I said, meaning Moses and me.

We all introduced ourselves.

"He still in there?" she asked, nodding at the salvage yard.

Kevin had the binoculars. We were watching for Owen to leave, figuring we'd have a better chance if he went away and left his son in charge. But we could be in for a long wait.

"Want a beer?" Reiko offered. "I have some in the truck."

So we stood around, drinking beer and swapping stories and wishing it was about 20 degrees cooler. You wouldn't think a health physicist would lead all that exciting a life, but you'd be surprised. Reiko showed us the monitor she wore on her belt to warn her if she was being exposed to dangerous levels of radiation.

Around one-fifteen, we got our chance.

"There he goes!" Kevin announced as a tow truck pulled out of the yard with Owen behind the wheel.

We'd already agreed that Kevin should accompany Reiko; he wouldn't be recognized, and he wouldn't be conspicuous.

"I sure hope Owen junior is in charge," I said to Moses, "and not some suspicious goon who can flatten a Caddy with his bare hands."

In twenty minutes they were back, grinning.

"No problem!" Kevin said gleefully. "The kid was up front. He looked a little confused when I told him that Reiko was Red's niece, but he took us out to see the car anyway. And Reiko, she's wearing this gigantic shoulder bag. And she walks all around, looking the car over, and stands up against that dent on the driver's side, asking him questions about insurance and salvage, her English all the time getting worse and worse—"

"It is a very difficult language to understand," Reiko said, nodding gravely.

"So then we thanked him and split."

"And here," said Reiko, calmly handing me a strip of paper, "is your evidence."

I gazed at it. Moses looked over my shoulder.

"What does it say?"

"It says that in the area of the dent, marked here and here"—she pointed—"you have clear signs of radioactive contamination. There are no signs of radioactive contamination anywhere else on the vehicle."

"Well, I'll be damned." Even Moses was grinning now.

"And you said on the phone that it would be hard to remove the contamination?"

"Yes, you can't just wash it off like paint, you know. It

will remain there for some time. Of course, I have to remind you that if this outfit routinely hauls radioactive wastes, every truck on the lot may be contaminated. If they do remove any traces of paint from Mr. McIntyre's car, there's no way you can prove which truck transferred the contamination to the car in the accident—or rather, in the non-accident."

"That's okay," I said cheerfully. "I'm counting on photographic evidence for that."

I hoped to hell Lester Perkins' videotape would come through.

Thirty-one

After our victory at Owen's, we celebrated by going out to a local firing range and practicing for our next operation. I practiced with the Diane, but Moses and Kevin had me fire their guns, too, so that I could get used to the feel of a bigger, more powerful gun.

"What's the point?" I groused. "I don't even think I'm hitting the target." But in my mind's eye I conjured up those war movies where the guy next to you in the trench dies, and you pry his gun from his hands because you're running out of guns and ammunition and the enemy is closing in.

"I keep telling you get your eyes checked, Cat," Moses said, looking at me through the tops of his bifocals.

"Just remember, Mrs. C., aim low," Kevin reminded me anxiously. "High is where the helicopter will be, with the good guys in it."

"Yeah, and if the sight is off on your gun, there's less chance you'll do any serious damage."

"I'll bear it in mind," I muttered, "but you can see how this thing kicks."

We spent the rest of the afternoon by the pool.

"My card game stinks," I complained to Moses.

"Yeah, but your detective skills is picking up. That was real good thinking to test Red's car like that."

I shrugged. "I got lucky. I counted on Chem-Tech to run true to form and be sloppy. They don't give a shit what they expose the workers to, and according to the Graysons, half the time the drivers don't know what they're hauling anyway. If Chem-Tech was legitimate, those trucks should be clean as a whistle. Then, too, I figured Owen had relaxed his guard. They'd cleaned out the car, and probably cleaned up the truck as well. Like I told Louella they would, they underestimated us, and we took advantage of the opportunity."

"When you learn to think like the enemy, Cat, you make your own luck," Moses said.

When the time for the meeting came, we found the barn without too much trouble. I was glad to see Freeman alive, and told him so.

To me, he said, "I almost didn't recognize you, Cat. Your new hairdo is real attractive."

"Liar, liar, pants on fire."

He grinned. "Guess who showed up at my place last night."

At first I thought he meant Emery, and then I knew he didn't.

"Not Junior?"

"His own self."

I was pretty damn relieved, I have to admit it.

"Did you ask him where he'd been all this time?"

"Didn't have to. He brought me a souvenir. A man's work glove like the ones they use up at Chem-Tech, only this one reeked of kerosene."

I sighed. I didn't see what we could make of it.

"Every little bit helps, I guess."

"That's what I told Junior."

Poppy and Mike MacDougal were there, despite my own reservations about involving new parents, and a few other people I recognized from the funeral, including Frank, the man who had talked so freely about murder. Emmet Cassidy and Garner and Clara Wells, Red's neighbors, were there. Hunt Smith, Red's old pal, was conspicuously absent. There were maybe eight people from Healthwatch—young and old, including some husband and wife teams. Freeman, Wynn, and Moses did most of the talking. Freeman had brought a map of the landfill area, and had already picked a spot for the ground troops. It was heavily wooded, he said, for camouflage, but there was enough space to maneuver in, and no houses close by. To one side there was an overgrown field, in case we needed additional cover.

"There's another consideration, too, Freeman," Wynn said gravely. "We don't know what's in this landfill, but some of the chemicals could be real flammable. If we want to use cherry bombs or Molotov cocktails, we best not aim 'em over the landfill itself, or the whole damn thing could blow."

"You got a point there, Wynn," Freeman said. "Tell you what—let's make us a second team, a diversionary team, and put 'em here." He pointed to a spot on the map on the adjoining side of the loosely constructed rectangle that constituted the landfill. "There's woods here, and a vacant field right alongside. That way, if anything catches fire, it won't burn up nobody's corn."

"Ray here is a volunteer fireman," somebody spoke up. "Why don't you put him in charge?"

Ray agreed, and we divided up the group.

"Now Mamie, she's going to run a second video camera on the ground," Wynn said. "She'll be here with the shooters."

"Sounds to me like we'll need walkie-talkies," somebody said.

"My nephew Jimmy here will take care of all that," Wynn said. "We'll have radio contact with the chopper, too."

My role was to fill them in on the test itself.

"Reiko's got two kinds of tests she wants to run. One involves a Geiger counter, which she'll operate from the helicopter," I said. "She's got a sensor, which looks kind of like a microphone, enclosed in a box open on the bottom. The box protects the sensor, and weights it down. She'll attach the box to several heavy cables, lower it over the side, and try to get it as close to ground level as possible."

"Is it bulletproof?" somebody asked.

"She thinks it can take a lot of abuse."

"How long does it have to stay put for her to get a reading?" Freeman asked.

"The reading will be instantaneous. But she's going to need to cover a lot of ground. She says some parts of the landfill may be hotter than others, so we need to cover as much as possible in what little time we have. She's got a friend working on a collection device that would allow her to do another kind of test as well."

"Collection device? You mean, she'd need to scoop up samples of soil or water?" someone asked. "Sounds risky."

"Yeah," Emmet Cassidy put in. "What would she need to do that for if the Geiger counter picks up the radioactivity?"

"I don't think I can repeat the explanation," I confessed. "It has something to do with alpha rays and beta rays and gamma rays, and some piece of equipment called a scintillation counter that I gather is more sensitive than a Geiger counter."

"I hope the pilot knows what he's doing," somebody said.

"I gather he's flown under fire before. He was a chopper pilot in Vietnam."

"And this Dr. Fujimura—has she been warned what we're up against?" Poppy asked in a worried voice.

"I gather she's been under fire before, too." I grinned, imagining what they'd say when they saw her.

"Okay, people," Wynn said at last, "see you tomorrow afternoon. You've all got an arrival time: don't be early, don't be late. We've got to stagger this so nobody gets suspicious. Remember, keep your heads down and your guns up. Our first priority is to come out of this thing alive. We've lost too many of us already."

His voice kind of broke when he said that. Somebody suggested that Poppy offer up a nondenominational prayer, so she did. It seemed kind of odd to me, standing there quietly in a barn, asking God to take our side in battle if it came to that. But I guess warriors have been praying like that for hundreds of years, and what were we in the midst of if not a war? I studied the people around me. Every one of them had lost somebody they loved in this war—everybody but Moses and Kevin and me. But we'd gotten mixed up in it, anyway, the way people and countries do, because you shouldn't have to know the individual victims to care about the fate of the people as a whole.

Poppy winked at me on the way out. "Love the hair," she said.

Thirty-two

At three o'clock on a hot, sultry Saturday, Moses and Kevin left for the airport in separate cars. They would stop at a field along the way, and drop off Moses' car. Wynn had made the arrangements, so that in case the cops were waiting at the airport later, they'd have nobody to arrest or interrogate except the pilot. Kevin was still mouthing something at me as they drove off. I thought it was "Break a leg!" But maybe it was "Aim low!"

At three-fifteen, I drove to the B & J with Sidney. Emery would keep an eye on him during what I was coming to think of as The Raid on Chem-Tech. If anything happened to me, Emery would look after him until Mel or Al or somebody came to get him. He squirmed with embarrassment as I kissed him goodbye.

At three-fifty, the Graysons arrived to pick up Billie and me. Billie stashed her shotgun in the trunk along with the rest of the arsenal, Mamie's video equipment, and enough electronic hardware to coordinate the Allied landing at Normandy. I had slipped my Diane into my pocket, don't ask me why.

We pulled off the main road twenty minutes later and onto a dirt road leading to what looked like an abandoned farmhouse. Other cars had arrived ahead of us. I helped Jimmy, the Graysons' nephew, haul electronic equipment to the site, less than a five-minute walk away. I hoped I could run it in two.

Today we had a pretty stiff breeze blowing, off and on, and I hoped it was blowing away from the guard shack. Then it occurred to me to look at the incinerator smokestacks. The good news was that the wind was carrying the

smoke, as well as any sound, away from the guard shack.
The bad news was that it was carrying the smoke, as well
as any toxins and carcinogens it contained, in our direction. I thought about riding in a helicopter on a windy day,
and hoped Moses had taken his Dramamine. At least the
breeze cooled the temperature down to tolerable.

I gazed out on the landfill, and felt sick. It looked like
a wasteland—a vast, flat expanse of dirt and chemicals,
cooking in the July heat. I could barely see the fence
marking its boundary on the opposite side. I could pick out
the road that ran down the middle of the landfill, and a
large pool on the opposite side of it. Freeman told us the
guards would probably avoid walking on the surface of the
landfill itself. I scanned the fence perimeter off to our left,
but I couldn't see any activity. This was a good sign, I told
myself; our diversionary team wouldn't be spotted. I
looked again through my binoculars. Still, I felt better
when Jimmy made radio contact.

The waiting was the hardest part. The helicopter pilot
checked in at a quarter of five, and everybody breathed a
sigh of relief.

"All systems are go!" the pilot announced enthusiastically, for all the world as if he were having the time of his
life. He told Jimmy that he would make one pass over the
landfill to scout the terrain before he dropped down to let
Reiko lower the equipment. Where they started would
have something to do with what she saw when they flew
over.

"I make it two guards hanging around the guardhouse,"
Freeman reported. "But there might be a third inside. They
seem to be talking to somebody. The dogs must be locked
up. Maybe they're only out at night."

Without the binoculars, I could barely make out some
brown blotches that looked like they had arms and legs.

Meanwhile, Billie and Mamie were blithely cutting a hole in the fence to give us an unobstructed view.

"We've got to do it so's we can put it back in a hurry," Billie said, her lips wrapped around a cigarette. "I surely would hate for a child or an animal to wander out onto that landfill and get hisself hurt."

At five o'clock, the pilot announced that he was taking off. At the same moment, if things were going as planned, a team of law enforcement distractors scattered over a six-county area were beginning to call the police from pay phones to report disturbances in progress.

"Here she comes," Freeman said, binoculars fixed on the western sky. A split-second later, I heard the distinctive sound of helicopter blades.

"Would you look at that!" Wynn said. "They've even painted a name on the side—Coglin's Copter Tours."

"So far, so good," somebody else reported. "The guards haven't even looked up."

The copter was too high up for me to see anyone clearly. It floated along slowly, taking its time, for all the world like a bumblebee on a sightseeing tour.

Then it turned in a wide arc to the east and headed down. Reiko would be on the other side. As it approached, sure enough, here came a small metal box, sliding down, gliding along, like a trawling line.

I winced as the chopper rounded the incinerator's smokestacks, lower now, and more vulnerable to whatever the stacks were putting out. Box and chopper dropped lower as they reached the western boundary of the landfill, and started along the perimeter. As they passed us, I could see Reiko crouched down, gloved hands holding onto the heavy cables that supported the instrument, Kevin crouched next to her with the video camera. A glint of metal behind them I took to be Moses holding a gun. The chopper turned again just past us and cut the rectangle.

"Here they come," Freeman announced succinctly.

Sure enough, two men—no, three, carrying rifles.

I could hear Jimmy's voice speaking low into the radio: "Three guards with rifles, one possibly an assault weapon."

Freeman turned his head and nodded grimly.

"We have a confirmation on that assault weapon," Jimmy said.

The chopper turned and headed back toward us across the landfill. The guards were running, but they had a lot of ground to cover. They looked madder than hell.

"Time for a little diversion," Wynn said.

"Team D, we are ready. Repeat, we are ready," Jimmy said.

The first sounds we heard were shots fired at the chopper. Luckily, they were frustration shots, fired at long range. The next blasts sounded like somebody had dropped a lit cigarette on the whole chemical complex. I turned to Mike MacDougal in alarm.

He grinned at me. "Every kid knows that firecrackers make a bigger boom if they're inside something." I could barely hear him.

"Make sure you get their faces, Mamie," Wynn was saying, close to my ear. Mamie stood next to me with the video camera.

"You should have seen their faces when the fireworks started," she said, grinning.

The guards had been thrown into confusion. Two of them had hit the ground when they heard the explosions in the west. The third, unfortunately the one carrying the assault rifle, had taken off in that direction. He was still thirty yards from the fence when he began firing.

The chopper had crossed diagonally again, and was racing back. I heard Moses get off a few shots. As far as I could tell, he wasn't aiming at anybody yet—just shooting at the road to turn Rambo around.

"Jimmy," Wynn shouted, "we're ready when you are."

Jimmy was holding a small device that looked like a remote control. When he pushed the button, a series of small explosions erupted in the tall grass on the opposite side of the landfill. I was beginning to understand why he had dark circles under his eyes, as if he'd been up all night.

The guards were frustrated and angry. They now had hostile activity on two sides, and overhead as well. There were only three of them, and they had a lot of ground to cover—ground the chopper could cover far more quickly.

The two who'd hit the ground conferred, and apparently agreed to go for reinforcements. Rambo decided to concentrate on the chopper. He took off after it again.

"Okay, folks, let's go," Wynn said. "We don't want those fellas to get back to the guardhouse and call for help. Fire at will, but remember the rules."

Wynn got the first shot off. We saw a small explosion around the boot heel of one of the men, who looked more surprised than hurt. Those were the rules: no injuries unless absolutely necessary. We were also supposed to be firing at the asphalt to avoid igniting anything in the landfill. Needless to say, nobody had handed me a gun and invited me to try my hand at it.

Through my binoculars I could see the shock as the man with the busted heel registered that he was pinned down in a crossfire. He shouted at his cohorts. The second rifleman had fired several shots at the helicopter, but I couldn't tell if he'd hit anything.

Billie sprayed them with buckshot to discourage any movement, and the two who were headed back to the guardhouse obligingly hit the ground again. But Rambo wasn't that easily discouraged. You could tell that two out of three of the guys we were dealing with did not want to

die defending a toxic landfill. Rambo didn't give a shit.
That made him dangerous.

"Team D is out of range," Jimmy reported. "No injuries."

The chopper turned again and headed to the opposite
corner of the landfill, as far from the guards as possible,
but now between them and the guardhouse. Rambo gave
up on the west end and headed for the guardhouse, stopping across from us to turn his rifle in our direction.

"Get down!" Freeman shouted.

But he didn't have to tell us. We knew a maniac when
we saw one.

"He'd better not bust this camera," I barely heard
Mamie mutter over the roar of Rambo's barrage. "I borrowed it off the Stowells."

I raised my face from the dirt to see him racing toward
the chopper, which had turned and started back across
again, its little silver anchor miraculously intact.

"We got comp'ny," Freeman said. From the direction of
the guardhouse came five men. I couldn't tell if they were
wearing uniforms or not, but I could see the glint of metal
across their chests. The first barrage confirmed my worst
fears: at least some of them were carrying assault rifles.
They piled into a Jeep and started up the road in our direction.

The chopper turned on a diagonal, apparently intent on
drawing fire away from our side of the field.

Suddenly, I heard a new sound beneath the gunfire and
the chopper blades—a rhythmic whir out of synch with
our chopper.

"Oh, shit!" I exclaimed, caught Freeman's eye and
pointed to the west.

A second chopper had just cleared the trees and was
headed right into the fray.

To my astonishment, Freeman smiled.

"Reinforcements," he said. "Ours."

While the first chopper moved away from the guard-house and the guys in the Jeep, the new one flew right toward them. When I found it in my binoculars, I counted three men: the pilot, who wore mirror sunglasses, a second man, whom I didn't recognize, and Hunt Smith, who held a rifle trained on the guardhouse.

Goddam, I thought, so he came to the party after all.

It was hard to tell what was happening, except that the second chopper seemed to be piloted by Son of Rambo. It buzzed the storm troopers on the ground, forced them to a standstill, and kept them occupied. From where I was standing, it looked like one or more of the Jeep's tires had blown.

When I next glanced up at the first chopper, the little metal box was gone. In its place was something that looked like a circular chain with smaller boxes attached. Reiko had told me that she didn't know whether her engineer friend would be able to rig something up in time to allow her to collect soil samples. Apparently, he had. The chopper dropped down for one last diagonal sweep of the landfill, while its counterpart kept the bad guys at bay.

Then the first chopper made its getaway; I watched it rise against the sun, now low in the sky, dragging its loop of chain.

I turned back to the commotion in the east. Most of the guards were sensibly staying down, though there was a lot of shooting going on. Suddenly, Rambo stood up and charged the helicopter, just like in the movies. But at that moment, the copter turned, its tail swung around, and Rambo fell off the road and into the pool of water alongside it. At first, I thought he'd been struck, and I felt sick. When I got the binoculars trained on him, though, he was getting up. He was soaked, and one arm and his rifle were covered with muck. I wasn't sorry about the rifle, but when I speculated on what the muck contained, I shuddered.

"Cops're on their way," somebody shouted behind us. I couldn't hear any sirens yet, so somebody must have picked it up on a police scanner.

Everybody scrambled, gathering up equipment, guns, ammo.

"What about—?" I started to ask, turning back to the battle.

But the second chopper had made its final sweep, and was already rising over the smokestacks, seemingly oblivious to the flak from the ground.

Mamie grabbed my wrist with a grip harder than I would have imagined, and yanked me down the path to the parking lot. Looking back, I saw Freeman and Wynn scan the ground for any evidence left behind. Then one of them threw a smoke bomb to cover our retreat.

I found myself shoved into a car with the engine running, and before I could catch my breath, we were moving. In the distance I could hear the first sirens. Something was digging into my hip. I hoped it wasn't a loaded gun. Every bump, and there were lots of them at the rate we were traveling, was agony.

We hit pavement for a while, and I sat up and pulled a walkie-talkie out from under me.

"I'll take that," said Jimmy, who was practically sitting in my lap.

"I think I've got the other one," Mamie said in a muffled voice to my left.

The car careened around a turn, and now it was Mike MacDougal on my lap. Then it was back to dirt road and joint-loosening jolts. You didn't want to open your mouth unless you had to, with the dust we were stirring up.

"Anybody see Wynn?" Mamie asked anxiously.

"He's about two cars back," somebody said.

The sirens got louder, then faded, then stopped. The car took another turn, and everybody in the back seat ended up in a heap on the floor as we screeched to a stop. When I had untangled myself and climbed out of the car, I was standing in a large barn. Two cars had pulled in behind us, and Mike and a woman in overalls were closing the barn door. In the dim light, I could hear Jimmy's voice calling Team D.

"Everybody present and accounted for," he reported, and we cheered. "Now I'll try the chopper."

We stood silently while he called.

"Everybody's okay, except for some minor injuries Melba's taking care of." We cheered again.

Melba? Melba Flatts? My public librarian? I knew I liked that woman.

Jimmy waved an arm to quiet us down.

"Hush up, y'all, I can't hear. She says what?" He grinned and looked up at us. "We've got our evidence. The damn landfill's radioactive."

Thirty-three

It was hard to know whether to laugh or cry after that. We felt the exhilaration of surgeons who had successfully completed the most intricate brain surgery, only to learn that a new infection had set in. We had expected it, but still. To be proved right was grim satisfaction to those who had lost loved ones. Like Wynn said, the war would go on, but maybe, just maybe, we had fought the decisive battle. Most importantly, we had fought and won it without significant casualties on either side. Except Rambo, I thought to myself. And what, I wondered, about Son of Rambo and the crew in the second chopper?

Freeman made a phone call, and reported that Hunt Smith had taken a bullet in the shoulder, and they were rushing him to a hospital in Nashville where they hoped fewer eyebrows would be raised. Everybody wanted to know about the other two men in the chopper, but Freeman kept his counsel, as he had at the funeral.

We held a small victory party in the barn that day before people straggled out, staggering their departures and leaving the arsenal behind, in case the police had set up roadblocks. Our police scanner told us they hadn't, but we wanted to err on the side of caution. Our police monitor also told us that all hell had broken loose on the police bands between five and five-fifteen, and that it had probably bought us the time we needed. We went home tired and satisfied.

Billie drove me back to the B & J to pick up Sidney, who had spent the afternoon terrorizing the potted plants in the lobby. Then I went back to the Ramada.

Did I say there were no casualties, except for Hunt?

Kevin was sporting a makeshift splint and bandage on his wrist, and a gauze bandage on his upper arm. He'd been grazed by a bullet, and he'd been so startled, he'd fallen backward, taking all his weight on his wrist. He couldn't have been happier.

"Just think, Mrs. C!" he enthused. "I might be scarred for life!"

"You should see the other guy," Moses muttered.

"Kevin! You shot somebody?"

"He means Reiko. I dropped the video camera on her when I fell."

"She's going to have a hell of a bruise tomorrow," Moses said with conviction.

"Say, who was in that second chopper, Mrs. C? They sure saved the day."

"The only one I recognized was Hunt Smith. I got my suspicions about one of the others, but Freeman's the one who knows, and he isn't saying."

Moses told me later that he had felt pretty queasy when the chopper first took off, but once the shooting started, he was too distracted to notice, and afterward, all he felt was relief. I asked him how it felt to be on the other side of the law for a change, and he just shrugged.

"The way I see it, Cat, all we did was steal a little dirt, set off some illegal fireworks, and shoot in self-defense when we were assaulted. We didn't even trespass, technically speaking."

On Sunday morning, I called Reiko from a nearby McDonald's. She had been up half the night, analyzing the soil samples, writing her report, and making multiple copies of everything. She had evidence of radioactivity from both instruments, the Geiger counter and the scintillation counter.

"We almost didn't go after the soil samples," she told me. "If that second helicopter hadn't shown up, we would never have gotten them. My friend Raj—who designed the collection device, by the way—will bring you copies of my report later this afternoon."

Unfortunately, everybody had decided that a big victory celebration was too dangerous. So on Sunday, instead of a victory party, we went to church. It was my last chance to say goodbye to Red's friends. On Monday, we would try to turn everything we had over to the TVA and the FBI. If they didn't follow up, we would then have to decide what our next move should be. Needless to say, we would have multiple copies of everything—videotapes, printouts from the two radiation tests, printouts from Stan's research into Chem-Tech's various subsidiaries and other connections, and the documents Red had left behind.

After the service, Freeman took me aside.

"Louella's got herself some good friends," he observed with a smile.

"So had Red," I said. "Amazing how people come through for you when the chips are down."

Freeman laughed. "Oh, I always reckoned Hunt would get involved, sooner or later. Can't blame a man for being cautious, though, when his family's involved."

"No," I agreed. Tomorrow I'd be gone. It was the people who stayed behind who would have to contend with the—what, the fallout? I had a better sense now of what that word meant, both literally and metaphorically.

"I'm worried about the other two men," I said. "One of them in particular. I don't think he killed George Packer, but he might have. Anyway, he was there that night, I think, and that puts him in serious danger."

Freeman glanced at me and shrugged. "If he was, he's managed to lay low so far."

"Until yesterday, when he flew that chopper in. See, I kept making a mistake about Wade Oakley. Not about him still being in Seattle—he could've been anywhere. And I think you were telling the truth about the wedding ring, about him wanting to give it to his daughter, I mean. Maybe he gave it to Red, or maybe he dropped it out of his pocket that night. But because he was a pal of yours and Red's and Hunt's, I kept imagining him your age, even though I'd been told he wasn't. I'd been told he was younger than Louella, and had served in Vietnam. Now, of course, I realize he was also a chopper pilot in Vietnam. And I suspect you're right—he probably can continue to lay low indefinitely. But if he was recognized yesterday, somebody has an even better reason to want to find him. Maybe they've even figured out about Red's funeral—that it was *his* voice we heard reading with you from the Book of Isaiah."

"He wanted to be there in the worst way," Freeman said quietly. "We figured there'd be spies, at least, and he wanted to scare the holy hell out of them bastards. We didn't reckon on the thunder and lightning, though," Freeman said modestly. "That was the Lord's contribution."

"What happened that night at Red's?"

"He didn't kill George," Freeman said quickly, then seemed to think better of it. "Oh, hell, I reckon he might've, in the end, if the Chem-Tech goons hadn't gotten to George first. It was Wade arranged to meet George that night—called him up like he was wantin' to blackmail George. Wanted to force him to say what had happened to Pat and Red. Knew George would come early and bring backup. So he got there even earlier and staked hisself out a place in the closet in the front room. Drilled a couple holes in the door so's he could see what was going on.

"It was a crazy plan—no real plan a-tall. I told him that afterwards, when he told me what he done. What was he thinkin'—that he could take on four or five men single-handed with a blamed rifle? See, George—he don't never travel with less'n three goons. That's the way cowards do.

"Come to find out, he didn't have to do anything. One of the goons, a big bastard name of Conroy, turns around and tells George his number is up, and shoots him. Then they wait around for Wade to show up. Wade figures they were either goin' to frame him somehow, or just take advantage of the bonfire to get rid of the two bodies at once. Well, sir, I reckon Wade had some time in that closet to think about how stupid he'd been. But by and by, they figure he's not going to show. Then they throw some kerosene around. Wade barely got out the back window before the whole place went up."

"But why did they kill George Packer?" I asked. "I thought he was one of the big cheeses."

"We don't know why. He'd been Isaiah Grubbs's right-hand man for years. Supervised all his dirty work. Knowed where all the bodies was buried, too. Maybe that was why. Maybe he'd outlived his usefulness. Maybe he'd got too greedy, or too talkative. We'd heard he'd been drinkin' more and more, so maybe he just got unreliable."

"And then Wade called you the next day while Louella and I were there."

"Yes'm, he did. Shook me up consider'ble—first to hear he was dead, and then hear his voice on the telephone askin' if I wanted to go fishin'—that's how I knew where to find him, in our old fishin' spot. But it wasn't my place to tell y'all what Wade didn't want nobody to know."

"And the guy who was shot out behind your house?"

"Wade and me, we was expectin' comp'ny. It's funny, when you think about it, how much these bastards get away with, stupid as they are. So after the shootin', we decided to make ourselves scarce. But, now, we didn't expect them to go after Louella, Cat. If I'da knowed they was goin' to do that, why, we'da camped outside your door all night."

"They were just trying to scare a couple of old ladies," I said.

He grinned. "See what I mean? They ain't that bright."

"What are the chances you'll get arrested for the shooting behind your house? I mean, your alibi is pretty thin."

He shrugged. "They got no weapon, how they goin' to arrest me?"

"Who was the other guy in the chopper?"

"Old army buddy of Wade's from Jackson. Wade just called him up, asked if he wanted in on the action, and he come along."

"I'm still concerned for Wade's safety," I said.

"Don't be, Cat," Freeman said softly. "His days is numbered anyway."

I closed my eyes. I didn't want to hear this.

"He's got cancer. Coulda got it from Vietnam, coulda got it at Chem-Tech. Don't hardly make no difference, now. Way he sees it, the gov'ment is partly responsible, either way."

The last thing Freeman said to me was, "You know how it is with friends, Cat. Sometimes they take a notion to do something, and you can't talk 'em out of it. Sometimes, maybe you don't even try too hard."

So when Isaiah T. Grubbs was shot leaving the Teamsters hall that night, I knew what he meant.

Thirty-four

Isaiah T. Grubbs didn't die. I don't know whether I expected him to. I thought that by now Wade should have figured out how to compensate for the sight on Red's rifle—the one Red had kidded him about in the will. I imagined that the sight had been off for years, and that they'd maintained a running argument about it, Wade admonishing Red to get the damn thing fixed, and Red insisting that he'd grown used to it, or that there wasn't anything wrong with it. If Wade had had any opportunity to practice after he'd picked the gun up the night he went to meet George Packer at Red's place, Dylan McQuacken would have been a goner when he sneaked up on Freeman's house in the dark. But by now Wade should've remembered to aim high. I didn't know for sure where Grubbs had been hit, of course, but I was guessing it was about the same place McQuacken had been hit—about three inches off the mark.

I can't say that I was happy about Grubbs; it muddied the waters, as far as I was concerned. I can't say I was sad, either. Let's just say I understood. And I wondered why somebody hadn't taken a shot at him long ago.

Anyway, on Monday we hung around the Ramada long enough to make some phone calls, then headed out. We dropped off my rental car, then drove to the Volunteer Dam. We put Junior in with Moses, whose car was already well-endowed with dog hair. Sidney, who had taken an instant dislike to Junior, got to ride with his uncle Kevin and me.

At the Volunteer Dam, I showed Kevin and Moses

where Red's car went over the side, then took them to the TVA Public Safety office, where Officer Boone Danning was waiting for us. He'd already told me on the phone that he'd managed to get a plate number for the tank truck off an enhancement of Lester Perkins' video. And something else—an unusual reflection off of something hanging from the rearview mirror. He didn't have any doubts that he could find the right truck in the Chem-Tech fleet, unless they'd switched plates or dumped the truck altogether. But we all doubted whether he'd identify the man who was driving that day, unless somebody panicked and snitched. Danning was grateful for the printout from Reiko Fujimura's test, though; it proved that Red's accident had been no accident. We were grateful to find a law officer who was on the side of the law.

To complete the picture, we went across the road to the lock and powerhouse, so Kevin and Moses could see the platform from which Lester Perkins captured the aftermath of the accident on video.

Both times we stopped, we left the animals in the cars and the windows down, mindful of how little time we could leave them in the hot cars. Junior's leash was wrapped around the rearview mirror in Moses' car, and Sidney's was tied to the stickshift in Kevin's. I was just turning back to show Moses the visitors book, when all hell broke loose in the parking lot.

Then Moses was running for the cars with his gun drawn. He shouted at me to stay back.

Everything happened so fast, I was never sure I could re-create it with any accuracy. What I saw was a large brown dog attacking a man near a rusty red Dodge. The wind carried a cacophony of snarls, barks, and growls, and even from where I was standing, I could see red.

A second man got out of the Dodge and entered the fray, apparently trying to throttle Junior and force him to loose his hold on the first man's neck. If I had blinked, I would have missed the little black streak that bounded from car to car (just as if it had been practicing, say, on side-by-side motel beds) and landed on the second man's shoulders, adding more frenzy to the tableau.

I saw Moses slow up as if he was winded, which didn't surprise me any, and as if he didn't quite know what to do. The first man, who resembled a water tank when he stood up straight, dragged Junior to the other side of the car, where they were obscured from my view. Kevin passed me, moving faster than I've ever seen him move. Then I saw Sidney go flying. Suddenly, the Dodge started up and roared off. The men were gone. The whole thing was over.

But Junior had missed the final bell. He'd been thrown against another car, and fallen to the ground. Just as I reached the scene, he staggered up, shook himself, and took off with a growl of indignation, trailing his leash and Moses' rearview mirror.

Moses brought him to a screeching halt with an ear-shattering whistle.

"Damn!" Moses muttered to himself, bending over Sidney. "I shoulda been payin' more attention!"

"Who were those guys?" Kevin said angrily.

"I don't know," I said, running my fingers gently over Sidney's body. "But Junior knew 'em."

Junior whined and nuzzled Sidney, who was coming around. Damned if he didn't start purring.

"That's one thing about Sidney," Kevin observed. "It doesn't take him long to figure out who the enemy is."

Moses was busy detaching his smashed mirror from Junior's leash, griping about seven years of bad luck. We found Sidney's leash and collar still attached to Kevin's gearshift.

An hour later, we were on the road again after an emergency side trip to the vet and the auto parts store. Sidney was snoozing in the back seat, his head growing a second bump to match the eggplant injury.

Thirty-five

We drove to the FBI office in Nashville, where it turned out Moses had a contact. This time, we took the animals in with us. By now, they were behaving like old rivals who had just been traded to the same team and made peace.

Moses' friend, Jerome Tillson, was a tall, muscular black man in his fifties with distinguished splashes of gray at his temples and a smile that was much too charming to be standard issue. He wore the requisite conservative suit, though, and so did his sidekick, a more conventionally nondescript agent named Vogel.

They heard us out, and showed some interest in the printout of Chem-Tech's subsidiaries and board overlaps.

"There are some names on this list that we might take an interest in," Tillson said, with characteristic Bureau understatement. Or at least, that's what I hoped it was. "But like you say, we need to proceed with caution, if we proceed at all. Unless Bureau policy changes, we can't really become involved in enforcing environmental policy. That's EPA territory."

"Even if we prove something as serious as radioactive contamination?" I asked.

"Even then. It's not really the seriousness of the offense, it's the nature of the offense," he said. "On the other hand, we have sometimes been called in to conduct surveillance on a suspected violator of environmental law, where ultimately the charges included racketeering, or conspiring to violate federal law. We may have something like that here. And, as I say, if we have some known organized crime figures involved, we might be able to proceed on that basis."

"What's the protocol for contacting the EPA and making a request for assistance?" Moses asked. "Is that possible?"

"Officially, it's highly unlikely. Of course, if we decide to conduct an investigation of Chem-Tech's corporate financial dealings, we would probably inform the EPA as a courtesy. Unofficially—well, as you know, Moses, a lot can be accomplished by working through contacts."

"If it couldn't, we wouldn't be here today," Moses said, grinning.

"You got that right, brother!" Tillson laughed. "You know what I'd say if anybody else called me up and tried to hand me a cockamamie story like the one you just told?"

"It's got some unlikely spots," Moses admitted. "But you aren't going to sit there and tell me that with all the Syndicate-watching you G-men do, this business about organized crime in Western Tennessee is news to you."

Tillson flashed his charming smile again. "Believe me, you don't want to know what I know about the connections between organized crime and the toxic waste disposal industry."

"No," Moses said gravely, "I don't guess I do."

We got a tour of the office, which didn't look like much to me, but Kevin and Moses were interested in all the state-of-the-art electronic equipment and computers.

"So you're thinking of turning pro, Cat," Tillson said to me at one point. "From what I've heard today, sounds like you'd be good at it."

"Yeah, but I don't have enough of what the State of Ohio regards as 'relevant experience' to get licensed," I told him.

"Well, Moses has," he said. "Why doesn't he get a license, and you can work off his? Y'all seem to make a pretty good team."

"That's a great idea, Mrs. C! Why didn't we think o that?" Kevin put in.

"I'm retired," Moses objected grumpily.

"Oh, hell, Moses, what you want to be retired for?" Tillson asked him. "Mind'll turn to mush, body'll turn to flab. Why don't you help Cat out here, and do yourself a favor, too? 'Less you're planning to buy a camper and move to Florida."

Well, I have to admit, I'd never had much respect for the FBI before, but now I was beginning to credit them with the intelligence they claimed.

On the road again, I said to Kevin with a sigh, "I jus hope that something comes of all this work we've put into the Chem-Tech business, and Red's murder, and all. No that I expect a murder trial, but I would like to see Chem-Tech shut down. Seems like it's out of our hands."

"It's not completely out of our hands as long as we've got the evidence we've got. Anyway, you're just feeling your customary letdown when a case is over."

"It's not over, Kevin," I said. "There's still a Cincinnat connection. If it's true that Freeman and Louella were the only people who knew that Red was going to Cincinnati to speak out, then somebody in Cincinnati tipped off Chem-Tech. I want to nail the bastard who set him up."

Cincinnati

Thirty-six

I walked into my office in the dark to lay the McIntyre file on the desk, tripped, and damn near broke my hip.

Al heard the crash and the profanity which accompanied it, and came running.

"That you, Cat? You home?"

"I was home. Now I'm deceased."

"Good lungs for a dead woman." That was Mel, behind her.

"I *told* Kevin y'all shoulda told her about her office." A cryptic contribution from Moses.

"I was working up to it," Kevin said defensively.

The room flooded with light.

"Holy shit, look at her hair!" Mel exclaimed. "Must be a live wire laying around somewhere."

I raised myself up painfully, and looked around. My jaw dropped. For once, I was speechless.

My office had turned into Mission Control. On every surface squatted a hulking piece of electronic equipment. My once-enormous desk, formerly covered with piles of paper sorted by relative importance, was now dwarfed by a television sitting on a metal pizza box. Where the papers had gone I didn't want to speculate. My bruised buns were resting on a nest of cables and wires that could have inspired an abstract painter. It did not inspire me.

I swiveled around to glare at my audience. On the far fringes of the crowd in the doorway, I glimpsed the perp.

"Maybe I went a little overboard," he said faintly.

"Maybe this wouldn't be a good time to tell her about the kitchen," Mel suggested.

The kitchen?!

I pulled myself to my feet and limped to the kitchen, parting the crowd like a gunfighter. At the door to the kitchen, I stopped and flipped the light switch.

Everywhere I looked, there were tomatoes and zucchinis—big tomatoes, little tomatoes, cherries and Romas and yellow pears, slender zucchini fingers in their prime and green excrescences the size of toaster ovens. Tomatoes in the dish drainer, and in the sink. Tomatoes marching across the windowsills and peeping out from behind the potted plants. Sophie was wrapped around a zuke on the kitchen table, snoozing. Sidney picked his way to her, and rubbed noses. Sadie sat on top of the refrigerator, flanked by two Beefsteaks, gazing down at us reproachfully.

"We kind of ran out of room, Cat," Al said.

"Don't open the refrigerator door," Mel added glumly.

"What's wrong with *your* apartments, for crissake?" I demanded.

"They look just as bad," Al said. "Worse, really, because Delbert won't let a tomato within five feet of the new computer equipment."

"Can't we invite a plague of locusts in here to restore the balance between Us and Them?" I asked.

As if that weren't enough, in the silence that followed I was suddenly aware that a distant baying was growing louder and closer.

"Jesus! Block the door! Don't let—"

Too late. Junior had pulled free again, and invited himself in to meet the rest of the family, dragging the heavy iron foot-scraper Moses had tied him to.

It had not been any part of my plan to spend Tuesday cleaning the kitchen. But when my aching hip and head woke me up that morning, the kitchen looked like the aftermath of a major food fight. Cousin Delbert, chastened by my reaction to being dragged kicking, screaming, and tripping into the Computer Age, helped with the clean-up. In fact, he scrubbed the floor out of deference to my injured hip, even though he pronounced it "optimally barfulous."

He took advantage of what he called our "face time" together to promote his investment, or rather, my investment, in a state-of-the-art computer setup.

"Don't be a zipperhead, Cat!" he urged. "I'll bet a year from now, you won't know how you ever got along without it."

"A year from now I'll probably still be looking for the on-off switch," I groused.

After putting a tank of tomato sauce on the stove to simmer, I took time out to call Louella to report.

"Hi," I said. "It's the dog sitter. Junior can't wait to go home with his Cousin Louella."

I invited Louella to dinner so that she could get a full report, complete with Kevin's embellishments, and so that she could be reunited with Junior. Meanwhile, I wanted the name she had passed on to Red as someone he could talk to at the local EPA.

"It's Dr. Howard," she said. "Dr. Leeanne Howard. But Cat, I already called her and she didn't know what I was talking about. She said she didn't know anybody named Walter McIntyre, and she wouldn't have given him an appointment anyway to talk about anything having to do with a toxic waste dump in Tennessee. She says she's a lab scientist, and wouldn't have anything to do with any clean-up decisions."

"Well, if she's the person we're looking for, she's not likely to admit she ever talked to him."

"She sounded real nice on the telephone, though," Louella said doubtfully. "I was all embarrassed when she came on the line. I thought she'd be a man, I don't know why. See, I didn't have her first name, just her initial. You'd think by now I'd learn not to jump to conclusions."

"Louella, did Red tell you he was going to see a *man* at the EPA?"

"Gosh, Cat, I thought he did, but like I say, I could've just assumed that."

I called up Dr. Howard anyway. She came across as friendly, but puzzled.

"I told Mrs. Simmons that this is a research facility, Mrs. Caliban, and it is," she said. "Calls from people wanting to report polluters or ask questions about environmental law are referred to the regional office by the switchboard operators. We just don't investigate claims like that."

"But don't some people call and ask you to run tests? You'd do that in the lab, wouldn't you?"

"We could, but we don't follow up on requests from the general public like that. The regional offices make the policy decisions about which sites will be tested."

"Doesn't anybody ever ask you to do it as a personal favor?" After all, she had been recommended by the Ohio Public Interest Research Group. There had to be a reason.

She hesitated. "They might, and depending on the circumstances, I might—just might—consent to work on something in my free time. But that would be highly unusual. And if Mr. McIntyre intended to make such a request, I never spoke to him about it."

"Do you have a secretary who keeps your calendar?"

She laughed. "No, I keep it myself. I'm an administrator, but I still spend a lot of time doing lab work, so it's hard for anyone else to schedule my time for me."

"Is there anybody else in your lab or your office who might answer your phone if you weren't there?"

"Yes, but as I say, they would probably take a message. They wouldn't schedule an appointment without my knowledge. Apparently, Mr. McIntyre said he had an appointment, didn't he? But I looked, just to make sure, and there was nothing about it on my calendar for that day."

"Can you suggest any other explanation?"

"No, I'm sorry, I can't. I'd like to help, but I just can't think of anything."

The only other explanation I could think of was that she was lying through her teeth.

That's what I told the others when we reviewed the case after dinner that night.

"I wish I could get a peek at that woman's goddam calendar," I said. "Then maybe I'd know for sure."

"Maybe you can, Cousin Cat," Delbert said, plying his pal Sidney with corn pudding.

"Oh, sure. I can break into a federal agency and rummage around in her office, but I'd never get my P.I. license, and I'd have a hard time practicing anyway from a federal prison."

"There's other ways to do it," Delbert said, unfazed. "Why do you think you got all that computer equipment?"

I stared at him. "What are you talking about?"

He shrugged. "It all depends on whether she kept her calendar on the computer or not. She might; lots of people do these days."

"But how do we get to her computer?" I persisted.

"Easy. We call it up on your computer."

"You mean like calling somebody up on the phone?"

"Sure. You've got a modem now. I'm not saying it will be easy, 'cause the first thing we have to do is find a back door and crack their security. I could maybe glark it, but

I'd probably do better to post my question on a couple of lists and see if anybody's done it before."

"Is that legal?"

A chorus of voices responded, "Don't ask!"

"Let me put it this way, Cat," Delbert said. "It's less conspicuous than breaking into a building."

Thirty-seven

So Delbert went to work about eight o'clock that night. He explained that it was better to work at night than during "prime time," when all the "suits" were crowding the system. He also said that most hackers worked at night for that reason, when all the "suits" were "gronked out."

I won't give you the keystroke-by-keystroke. To tell you the truth, I got bored after the first ten minutes. All I can tell you was that Delbert was doing a lot of "munching," which didn't seem to have anything to do with the bags of potato chips he consumed between eight and two A.M. Then around one o'clock, he started getting a "core dump" from a "cracker" in Minneapolis, and followed the instructions.

"Leeanne Howard, right? Director of the old Environmental Monitoring Systems Laboratory."

"Don't you need some kind of password or something?"

"Yeah, I'm just mousing around—you know, to see what they've got on the system. In a minute I'll kluge something to see if I can find the password. You better hope she's using her initials or her kids' initials and not Rumpelstiltskin or something."

Since this sounded like it would take all night, and since Delbert understood what I was looking for, I went to bed—or "gronked out." When I got up in the morning, there was a note on the kitchen table, weighted down with a tomato. When I translated his writing, the note read:

Cousin Cat: I checked Howard's calendar for Wednesday, July 10; also for Tuesday, Thursday, and Friday that week, and other Wednesdays. I even checked for

*stuff she might have deleted. No record of any appoint-
ments with McIntyre. Sorry. D.*

I sighed. Red had made an appointment with somebody,
but who was it and how would I ever find them?

At noon I met Louella for lunch and a quick turn around
Northgate Mall. I quickly discovered that my credit card
was overextended, so I wasn't paying that much attention
when Louella started talking about how her Tennessee accent had come back.

"Rosemary was kidding me about it the other day. She
said my return to my roots had really affected my speech."
She pronounced *root* to rhyme with *foot*. "She's right, too.
I used to have the worst accent!"

"I don't think about accents as good or bad, Lou," I
said. "People from different places talk differently, that's
all. How you talk says something about who you are and
where you're from. It would be boring as hell if everybody
talked the same way."

And then it hit me.

"Say, Lou, I'll bet your Uncle Red had a Tennessee accent, didn't he?"

"Lord, yes! If you think mine is bad, you should've
heard Red's. More like Freeman's, I'd say."

"Like Freeman's. Right." I fished a pen out of my purse
and wrote on the back of a deposit slip: *Howard.*

"Pronounce that name the way a Tennesseean would."

"Howard?" She looked puzzled.

I shook my head. "I don't think so."

Half an hour later I had Freeman on the phone. He'd
written the name down as I spelled it for him. When he
read it back to me, it sounded more like "Hard" or
"Hayard."

"Tell me something, Freeman. Do you know whether
Red's EPA contact was a man or a woman?"

"Seems like it was a man," he said slowly. "Leastways, that's how I recollect it. Seem like he told me he had an appointment with a feller from the EPA."

After dinner, Del sat down at the terminal again.

"We're looking for a man with a last name that starts with an 'H' and sounds something like *Hard*."

After a few minutes, he said, "Hyper-win, Cat. Here he is: Lloyd Buxton Hard. You are really wanky, you know that?"

"No shit?" I stared at the screen. There he was: Lloyd Buxton Hard, Deputy Director, Risk Reduction Engineering Laboratory. "What's that mean?" I pointed to a notation: *term. 7/20/85.*

"Might mean he's been terminated," Delbert said. "Let's hope he's still on the system."

"Are you going to have to clutch that password thing again?" I asked anxiously.

He grinned at me. "You're catching on, Cousin Cat, only it's 'kluge,' not 'clutch.' No, first let's just try his initials, since we've got 'em.

"Highly cretinous," he muttered, shaking his head. "Security through obscurity. Here's his menu. Let's take a look at his calendar."

He pulled up July 10th. We scanned the notations, but there was no reference to a McIntyre or a Chem-Tech or anything else familiar. We checked the days on either side, as well as other Wednesdays in the month, in case he'd written it down wrong. I was feeling frustrated, but nothing seemed to bother Delbert. He went back to July 10th.

"Let's see if we can restore anything."

"You mean, you can find things he might have erased? How can you do that?"

"Automagically," he said.

And just like magic, it appeared: *2:00-W. McIntyre.*

Now I knew who'd set up Red McIntyre. Now what?

But Delbert was off and running again.

"What are you doing now?"

"Taking a look at his personnel file."

"They've got that on the computer?"

Delbert nodded. "Some of it, anyway. Want his address and phone number? You might need it, since he's not at the EPA any more. Looks like he's at a place called Trans-Global Chemicals."

"What? Let me see that."

"You heard of it?" he asked, pointing to the name on the screen.

"Damn right I've heard of it! They've got a fucking plant in New Union, up the street from Chem-Tech."

"Well, there you are. The guy rats on Louella's uncle, and he gets a new job out of it."

Al and Mel wandered in, and I explained what was going on.

"I know who he is. Now how do I get to him?" I mused.

"Mel could take the Amazons over and break every bone in his body," Al offered. The Amazons were Mel's lesbian martial arts group.

"Why don't you let me handle it, Cat?" Delbert drawled.

"You're a little—uh, short, Del," I said. "Thanks, anyway."

"I don't mean that way. I mean this way." He gestured at the computer.

"What do you mean?"

"There are lots of things I could do. Like, I could screw up his credit."

Al's eyes lit up. "Yeah! That's a brilliant idea, Del!" I still looked skeptical, so she turned to me. "Don't you see, Cat? I've read about stuff like this. The phone company's beginning to get really nervous about the possibilities. See, Del could effectively erase this guy's assets."

"On paper," I said.

"No, on the computer. That's all it takes. He could screw up the guy's bank accounts, destroy his credit, who knows? What else could you do, Del?"

"I don't know. I'll need some time to consult people. This is going to be a moby hack."

"Yeah, the beauty of it is, he's not really stealing anything, really. He's just changing the guy's record," Mel said. "And once it gets changed, it'll take him years to get it all back to normal, if ever. It'll drive this jerk crazy!"

"Can Del get arrested for it?"

"I can get arrested for jaywalking," Delbert muttered.

So we left him to it.

As far as I could tell, Del didn't sleep much for the next few days. I delivered his meals to my office, where he sat mumbling "cruncha, cruncha, cruncha" to the machine. When he wasn't working at Xavier, he was sitting in front of the computer. Sidney took to sleeping on top of the monitor to keep him company.

At eight o'clock Friday night, he emerged with the gleam of victory in his eye. Curious as I was, I sent him to bed.

"You can tell us about it tomorrow."

So the next night everybody assembled except Kevin, who'd received a briefing from Delbert and gone off to work with a smile on his face. We ate—what else?—spaghetti with tomato sauce, salad with tomatoes, and zucchini bread.

"Are you sure you want to hear about all this illegal activity?" I asked Moses, who had Winnie stretched out by his feet.

"I'm retired, Cat," he said emphatically.

"So what I did," Delbert was explaining, "I took parts

of some of the worst credit records I could find, and moved them to the file of this Lloyd Hard guy. Then, I got into his back account, and transferred a lot of money into his ex-wife's account."

"All-*right*!" Mel enthused.

"Then I went after his company, Trans-Global Chemicals, and Chem-Tech. I kluged up this Trojan horse, see? So Monday, some suit's gonna be typing away and hit the right key and nuke whatever file he's working on. And he's gonna go to recover it, see, and when he does, he's gonna crash the whole system. And he won't get anything but this message, 'Compliments of Walter McIntyre.' "

Tears sprang to Louella's eyes. "Oh, Delbert, that's so sweet!"

"Yeah, but even sweeter will be the monetary contributions that will show up in the Greenpeace account on Monday morning—courtesy of Trans-Global Chemicals and Chem-Tech. Plus they're gonna get a highly generous individual donation from one Isaiah T. Grubbs."

Thirty-eight

"What is *this*?"

I held up a drawing of a woman in some kind of scanty futuristic space costume. She looked kind of like Wonder Woman, and was as well-endowed and poorly covered.

"And this?" I held up another in a similar vein. "And this?"

Delbert had the grace to appear slightly embarrassed.

"Sometimes information costs, Cat. Not always, but sometimes. I gotta have something to trade."

I felt like I was housing a computerized call girl service, like I was a modem madam or something.

"Whatever happened to the communal spirit of hackdom? The old nobody-owns-information motto? Share and share alike?"

He shrugged. "That's what I've got to share."

I started to say something. I started to point out the connection between demeaning pictures of women and demeaning attitudes toward women, which would have involved explaining why these pictures were demeaning. I started to suggest that it was only a small conceptual step between using pictures of women to buy information and using women's bodies in various other unethical ways. But in the end, I shut my trap.

Okay, call me a coward. But I have already survived three adolescences, one of them male, and have no wish to repeat the experience. In fact, if I ever volunteer to go through it again, I hope my friends will have me committed.

I wandered out to the kitchen to find cousin Raynell's phone number.

Buddy and Raynell Sweet had the longest answering machine tape on record, and it was just packed with Christian good cheer and platitudes about life. It ended with Raynell's assurance that she was praying for me.

I left a message letting her know that my prayers would be answered if she'd come collect her son some time before his eighteenth birthday.

I stood at the kitchen window, gazing out at the garden, where clouds of whitefly rose and fell in the summer heat. A faint breeze carried the scent of warm earth, clover, and newly mowed grass, and the distinctive odor of whatever soap Procter & Gamble manufactures the most of. Dark clouds were starting to gather in the western sky, promising rain. I picked up the nearest tomato and found myself nose-to-nose with a tiny green caterpillar. I studied him a minute as he folded and unfolded his threadlike green body, inching toward my thumb. I opened the kitchen window and flicked him out into the petunias.

Live and let live, I say.

EARLENE FOWLER

introduces Benni Harper, curator of San Celina's folk art museum and amateur sleuth

Each novel is named after a quilting pattern that is featured in the story.

"Benni's loose, friendly, and bright. Here's hoping we get to see more of her..." –*The Kirkus Reviews*

___FOOL'S PUZZLE   0-425-14545-X/$4.99

Ex-cowgirl Benni Harper moved from the family ranch to San Celina, California, to begin a new career as curator of the town's folk art museum. But one of the museum's first quilt exhibit artists is found dead. And Benni must piece together an intricate sequence of family secrets and small-town lies to catch the killer.
"Compelling...Keep a lookout for the next one."
                                            –*Booklist*

The latest Earlene Fowler mystery
A Berkley Prime Crime hardcover

___IRISH CHAIN   0-425-14619-7/$18.95

When Brady O'Hara and his former girlfriend are murdered at the San Celina Senior Citizen's Prom, Benni believes it's more than mere jealousy. She decides to risk everything–her exhibit, her romance with police chief Gabriel Ortiz, and ultimately her life –uncovering the conspiracy O'Hara had been hiding for fifty years.